DEAD DUCK

Mel Mckinney

ISBN: 0615878377
ISBN 13: 9780615878379
Library of Congress Control Number: 2013949404
Abalone Press, Little River, CA

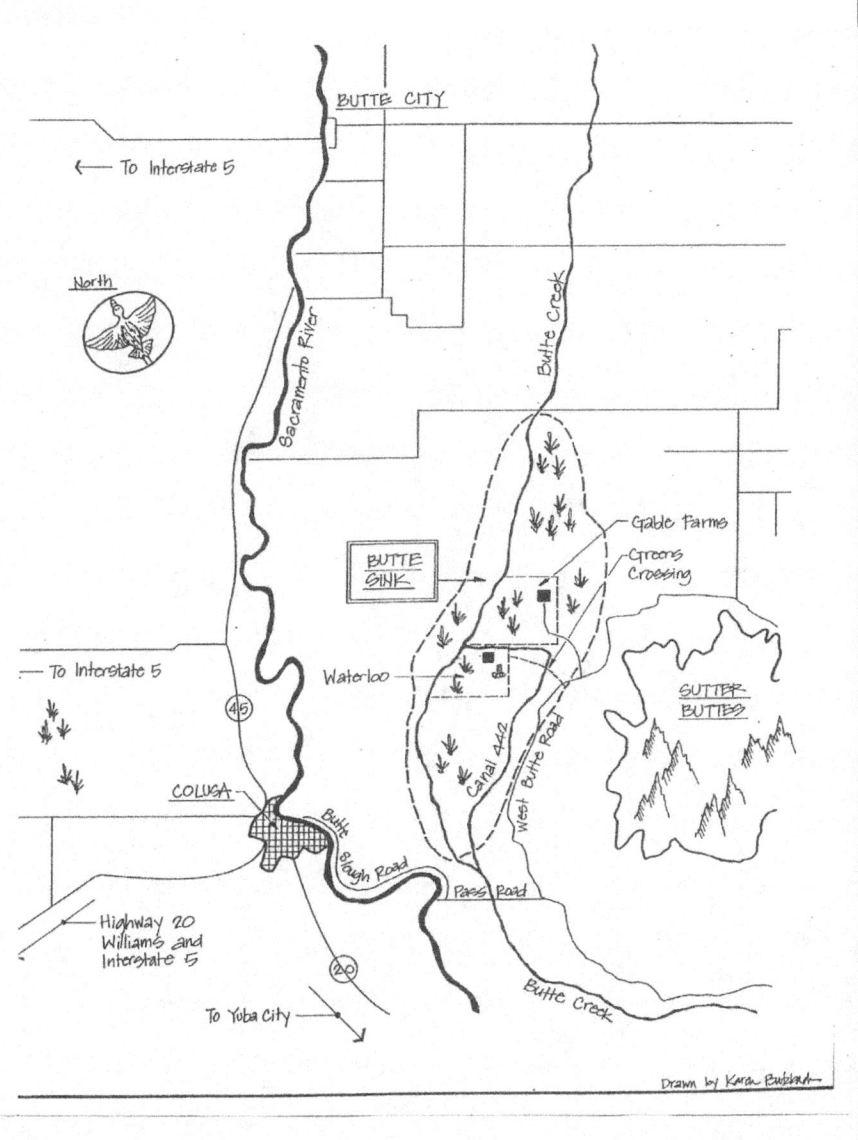

BUTTE CITY

← To Interstate 5

North

Sacramento River

Butte Creek

BUTTE SINK

Gable Farms

Greens Crossing

Waterloo

To Interstate 5

45

COLUSA

Canal 442

West Butte Road

SUTTER BUTTES

Butte Slough Road

Highway 20 Williams and Interstate 5

Pass Road

20

To Yuba City →

Butte Creek

Drawn by Karen Bubbard

Previously by Mel McKinney

WHERE THERE'S SMOKE, St. Martin's Press, 1999
THE FINN, THE TWIN & THE INN, Abalone Press, 1993

For Samantha,
who never met a duck she didn't like.

Midnight

The ducks that had made the trip before sensed the change...things below rising from wetlands habitat that had welcomed uncounted centuries of waterfowl. The metallic shine of pipes and valves caught the moonlight; bulky, new and threatening.

The first-timers missed them. Caution gave way to celebration, and they relished the stop. Their journey had been long and strange, the respite welcome. Restless, excited, they squandered their energy in gabble and exploration.

A trillion stars pricked the valley as the wary, tired veterans tucked their heads and rested. They had survived the dawn before and could do it again. The new ones would learn soon enough.

CHAPTER 1

Wednesday, September 8th, 1976 was an almost record hot day in San Francisco: 92°. It was also Marine Captain Drake Green's 33rd birthday. To honor that and his honorable discharge from the Corps he bought a tarnished 1956 Ford pickup that seemed to promise good years to come, signed his discharge papers at Treasure Island, crossed the east span of the Bay Bridge and headed north on I-80 to claim his inheritance. If it was this hot in San Francisco he knew the upper Sacramento Valley would be blistering.

Three hours later he stopped at the dirt road that led into Waterloo, his deceased father's five-hundred acre duck hunting property. A padlocked chain swagged between two pipes barred his way. A weathered sign hung from it:

POSTED
No Hunting. No trespassing.
Violators will be Prosecuted.
GABLE FARMS, INC.

Drake stared at the sign a full minute, then turned the pick-up around and headed for Colusa where he went directly to the local hardware store and bought a a set of bolt cutters. A half hour later, with the chain and sign lying in the late summer dust a half mile behind him, he stood at the edge of the charred wreckage that still scarred Waterloo's hilltop. The origin of the fire killing his father as it consumed the magnificent lodge that once graced the property had never been determined; the fire chief, a local tractor dealer, and his crew had all been volunteers. Now, twenty-three years and a far away war later Drake still clung to the knowledge that his father, Adam Green, had been a meticulous steward of the property. He would not have burned anything in the north wind of a hot valley summer.

As Drake surveyed the debris, a military-style jeep with side-mounted rifles in scabbards charged up the road. A pudgy driver with slicked hair swung out. He unsheathed the driver's side rifle and worked the lever as he stormed toward Drake. He stopped and planted his squat body two feet away.

"You're trespassing and destroyed private property to get in here."

Drake swiped the rifle away. Cartridges rained to the ground as he blurred the lever. He then grabbed the empty piece by the barrel and splintered the stock over the hood of the jeep. He turned and faced his stunned adversary.

"I'm Drake Green. I own this place. Whoever put up that chain doesn't know shit. Get the hell off before I drag you off."

So had gone Drake Green's introduction to Armand Styles Stilton III on that hot September day in 1976.

CHAPTER 2

7:48 a.m., Saturday, November 22, 2003

Armand Stilton III pressed the butt of his custom Parker Brothers AHE 12-gauge double-barreled shotgun against the stitched padding intended to further cushion his fleshy shoulder.

"Steady," said Jim Quesenberry, caretaker, hunting professional, and general factotum at Gable Farms. "One more pass ought to do it."

Jim cupped a wooden duck call to begin the soft quacks of contented feeding designed to lure the mallards closer next time around. He'd drawn the short straw before and knew the only way that Stilton might hit a duck was if the unfortunate creature tried to land on the shotgun.

Stilton rose and fired.

The ducks flared, their wings beating against a stall. Within seconds they gained speed, altitude, and life for at least another hour. Jim sighed and let the duck call drop from his hands. It clicked to rest against other calls tethered to the lanyard around his neck. He coughed. He'd try the lecture again. What the hell. Maybe the 565th time would do the trick.

"You see, Armand, callin' 'em in is what it's about. Wait till I tell you to take 'em, then shoot. You got to be patient. Takes a while, I know, but you'll see. Once you get the distance, you'll get the hang of it."

Stilton grunted and nodded toward the boat nestled in the camouflaged slot of the blind. "Put out the Roto Duck."

Jim cocked his head. His attempt to lose the hated device when they'd loaded the boat in the predawn darkness had already earned him a scorching rebuke. But his ethics demanded persistence.

"I'd rather not, Armand. Lots of ducks around this morning. I can call some in for you. You saw just now how those were beginning to work. That's the sport of it. Just give it a chance."

Stilton leveled his eyes on the caretaker. "I promised some important people a duck dinner tonight, and by God that's what's going to happen. Sport's got nothing to do with it. Now, put the goddamned thing out. I don't have all morning to freeze out here while you quack like an idiot. Sounds more like farting than a duck anyway."

The winner of two National Duck Calling competitions at Stuttgart, Arkansas, pursed his lips in contemplation. He decided in favor of continued employment and slid down into the boat.

Drake Green saw them first, distant specks rising above the jagged, dark outline of California's Sutter Buttes. "See those?"

Claire Wooley tracked his eyes and stared into the mist.

They'd met two months earlier when Drake had stopped at the Walmart in Willows to buy a digital camera. Her hip-length jet-black hair with eyes to match may have had something to do with it, but It was her smile and teasing laugh from the opposite side of the counter that had persuaded him he also needed a camcorder and tripod, both still boxed somewhere in the rubble that filled the camper shell of his truck.

This was their first real date, the relationship still platonic, stalled by two things: Drake's mixed feelings over seeing a woman who appeared half his age, and the opening of duck season. There was no ambiguity concerning Drake's responsibilities to the handful of members who paid for the privilege of shooting ducks at Waterloo—$10,000 each. Though they claimed to come for the sport, Drake knew better. They came to hunt with him.

He had taken Claire to dinner the night before in Colusa, then with bashful decorum had left her to get a good night's rest in the room he'd arranged at the only decent motel in town. When he had picked her up at four in the morning, she was ready, her enthusiasm apparent.

"East, just against the Buttes," said Drake. The sun crested the peaks, leaving them an ominous silhouette in sharp contrast with the pink and red streaks beginning to pierce the layers of fog and low clouds.

Claire shook her head. "I don't see them."

"Doesn't matter," said Drake. "Just stay down. They'll be over us soon. Then we'll turn them."

Seconds later, Drake heard the faint whistle of wings overhead. He paused, then raised his head slightly. "Seven mallards," he said. He waited a few more seconds before placing the call to his lips. Four loud hailing quacks jolted the post-dawn silence, then four more.

"I see them!" Claire said. "They're turning."

"Shhh, stay down," said Drake.

The ducks swung wide, descending and interested. Again they passed overhead. Once clear, Drake repeated his hailing call. "They're working," he said. "Just keep your eyes low. It's eyeballs that give us away."

Claire snickered.

"I'm not kidding," he whispered. "Though in your case it might be something else." The camo jacket he'd given her to wear failed to conceal the curves that, to some significant degree, may also have contributed to the camcorder purchase.

Three times the ducks circled, each time lower, each time slower. After the third pass, Drake began a series of low quacks that perfectly mimicked the close and busy sounds of the surrounding marsh. The birds cocked their wings in commitment.

"Get ready," he whispered.

Claire clutched the shotgun, her eyes down and her breath coming fast. It flashed through Drake's mind that he might be in more danger than the ducks. He shifted to the far edge of the blind and crouched lower.

"Not yet, not yet…I'll tell you when."

The ducks peeled away and Drake stood, his eyes wide with disbelief. "Damn!"

He watched the ducks sail low across the watergrass and tules. They rose slightly to crest the levee and canal that separated Waterloo from Gable Farms, then, still locked in a fatal attraction, they dropped from sight. Two shots came from Gable Farms' easternmost pond. Drake lifted his binoculars. All seven birds struggled to regain height, then beat away into the mist.

"Those were our ducks," he said. "I'll be right back. I want to check something out. Tar, come."

His black Labrador bounded from its hide next to the blind. Drake ejected the shells from his shotgun, pocketed them, and lowered the gun into the boat. He slid onto the stern seat and motioned to the dog. Tar stepped into the middle of the boat. Drake cranked the motor and pulled away. He steered around his decoy spread on the west edge of the pond and headed straight for the levee, ignoring several flocks of ducks to the east he could have called had he stayed in the blind.

Thirty yards from the levee he throttled back, then killed the motor and drifted up against the bank. "Stay," he ordered the dog. He picked up his shotgun, reloaded, and stepped carefully to the toe of the slope. He pulled the bow rope toward him and tied it off around a clump of tules. Cradling the shotgun against his chest, Drake lowered to all fours and, using his elbows and feet, inched military style up the muddy slope. When he reached the levee top, he crawled to the opposite edge, stopped, rolled to his side, and pulled out his binoculars.

"Sonofabitch, I knew it."

He turned back and watched another flock of ducks divert from his pond at Waterloo. They dropped as if hypnotized and headed straight for the whirring battery-powered wings attached to a pole thirty yards to his right. A lone figure rose from the blind ahead. Again, two shots. No ducks fell.

Gotta be Stilton, Drake thought. Not many hunters in the Butte Sink shot doubles, and no one else shot that bad.

A dog splashed into the water. Drake recognized Jim Quesenberry's voice commanding the disappointed dog's return. *Poor Jim,* thought

Drake. *A raw dog and a rotten hunter.* Drake waited until the dog was back in the blind and then uncradled his shotgun. He aimed and fired.

"My God!" Stilton's squeal rose tinny and hollow in the wet morning.

Quesenberry's dog again pounced from the blind, confused but driven by instinct. "Jethro, no!" called Quesenberry. "Back!"

The dog hesitated.

"Jethro, goddammit, get back here!"

The dog turned and started paddling toward the blind. Behind it, against a clump of marsh grass, pieces of the Roto-Duck fluttered and drifted, held aloft by the slight northerly breeze. The shattered spar that had anchored the contraption tilted and slowly began to sink, sputtering like a spent Roman candle. Seconds later, Quesenberry heard an outboard motor fire up. It settled into a buzz somewhere south, on Waterloo. *You've stepped in it now, Drake,* he thought. *Can't say I blame you though.* He turned to Stilton.

"Had enough for today, Armand? I pulled a limit of mallards from the freezer last night. Should be plenty for your dinner."

Quesenberry's lack of faith in Stilton's shooting was momentarily overshadowed by the spectacle of the mangled Roto-Duck as it disappeared beneath the pond's surface.

Stilton slammed a fist against a plank of the blind.

"That was Green, wasn't it?"

Quesenberry shrugged.

"That's it." Whitened teeth glistened through Stilton's sneer. "Get me out of here. It's time I took care of Mr. Drake Green once and for all."

Quesenberry looked toward the Buttes as ducks again began to drop into Waterloo. Though he'd heard the words before, he'd never seen that look.

CHAPTER 3

Claire watched Drake ease the boat into its slot under the blind as a wide Santa Claus grin creased his bearded face. The grin turned to a chuckle as he climbed from the boat back into to the blind. She stared in disbelief as he then rolled onto his back, a great bear of a man convulsed in open laughter. Finally he sat up.

"Oh, that was good…" More laughter. "It was wonderful, a moment of sheer beauty," he managed, wiping his eyes. "The damn thing just exploded, bits and pieces floating everywhere. Then it started to disappear, like the Duck God had grabbed it by the foot and was pulling it under."

Claire tried to question him about his mysterious mission that had culminated in a single shotgun blast and his jovial return with no duck. Each time he tried to answer, he fought back another burst of laughter. Finally he said, "Look, I've had enough fun this morning and it's getting colder. Let's go in. I'll make you a cup of the best hot chocolate you've ever had."

By this time Claire had begun to question how someone could consider duck hunting a sport. It seemed to consist of getting up in the middle of the night, a kamikaze-like ride through darkened passages in a dangerous-looking craft stuffed with fake ducks and a tail-thumping dog, just to sit for hours in a cramped shelter of brush and reeds that served as an insect resort and had no plumbing. Her host had demonstrated his skill at sounding like a duck, then had abruptly disappeared to wage war against his neighbor.

Later, comfortable and warm, sipping hot chocolate with her feet propped up on a worn leather hassock in front of Drake's wood-burning stove, she said, "So you went to all that trouble and had all that fun because of something called a Roto-Duck?"

Drake paused, studying her, as if composing his answer.

"Is that such a hard question?" she said.

"Well, it is and it isn't," he said. "Let me explain." He reached for the pan of hot chocolate and refilled her cup.

"You see," he said, "there's more to duck hunting than killing a duck. There's the dog, for instance. A good hunting dog doesn't just happen. It's trained from the day it's forty-nine days old. It has to learn discipline, patience, and to follow directions. The hunter and the dog are a team, more than an owner and a pet. A hunting dog is a limb, like an arm or a leg. Tar is almost part of me.

"Then there's the calling. Takes years to learn and is passed on from one caller to another. It's an art. Hell, I know guys who'd rather just call in ducks than shoot them. You can buy recordings and practice all you want, but there's no substitute for being in a blind with a good caller.

"So, when a guy like Armand Stilton comes along and sticks out a plastic battery powered robot that literally hypnotizes the ducks and sucks them in, the whole thing is reduced to killing for killing's sake. He should stay home and buy chicken for dinner."

Claire set her cup down on the table. She turned in her chair to face him.

"You are a very interesting man," she said, finally. "Tell me about yourself...who you are...what you are..." She looked around. "Do you do anything besides...this?"

Again, he studied her.

"Go on," she said. "I'm all ears."

"It'll take more than ears," he said. "How much time do you have?"

"As long as it takes," she said, settling back.

"It tells like a book."

"Well, maybe you should write it. Go on, tell it to me."

Drake exhaled, deciding, then began.

In 1882, when Drake's grandfather, Austin Green, opened his grocery store in downtown San Francisco, the young entrepreneur discovered that the gold flowing from the foothills to the city was easily mined again. Demand for everything precious and exotic far outpaced supply. Austin telegraphed his younger brother, Esmond, who had stayed on at their father's store in Portsmouth, Maine. "Spices," Austin urged in his telegram. "All you can send. Teas too."

Esmond emptied local warehouse stocks, carefully packed the condiments into crates, and watched them sail from Boston. Two months later rumors reached New England that the ship had gone down in a storm off Brazil. Esmond boarded a train and headed west.

After Esmond arrived, he and Austin decided to import spices on their own. They contracted with an owner-captain who was soon to sail for the Caribbean. Six months later they had their first shipment, and the firm of Green Bros. Teas & Spices was born.

By 1888 Green Bros. dominated the import of spices and teas to the western United States. By 1894 the firm was a thriving monopoly, and the brothers were rich men. Raised in Maine, they never shed their passion for the outdoors.

In 1896 the Southern Pacific Railroad sold most of its surplus right-of-way land along the Sacramento River. Austin and Esmond snapped up fifteen miles of forested river frontage, over ten thousand acres. Two wild streams that carried Mount Shasta's spring runoff tumbled through the property to join the untamed Sacramento River. The waters teemed with scrappy rainbow trout and each fall hosted a magnificent run of steelhead and salmon. The woods offered black-tail deer, bear, and mountain lions.

The Greens bought a string of packhorses, built a spacious log lodge they called Mountain Home, and started the tradition of packing into their mountain property from Redding for the fishing and hunting.

To get to Redding, they had to skirt the Sacramento Valley. Over months, then years, of grinding along primitive roads in unpredictable automobiles, Austin became enchanted with the valley's broad, fertile expanse—habitat for millions of ducks, geese, and other waterfowl. In

1920, he bought two thousand acres of woods and rice land at the foot of the Sutter Buttes. Two miles from the eastern boundary of the property the Sutter Buttes rose as sole testament to the volcanic forces that had once ruptured the earth's crust from northern California through the Cascades of Oregon and Washington.

A month after the deal closed, Austin stood on the only other hill within fifty miles of the Buttes. He surveyed the view that stretched south, west, and north and knew he had his building site. He paced off the building's footprint, then told his architect and builder to get started. His brother dubbed Austin's extravagant folly "Waterloo."

Austin Green's Waterloo Lodge was a two-story rock and log structure with a cavernous main room paneled in Sacramento Valley Oak. Green and his guests warmed themselves in front of a fifteen-foot, river-rock fireplace while they drank, swapped stories, and played cards or dominoes. Trophies from the Mountain Home forests stared down at them while the hides of bear and large mountain cats softened the madrone-planked floor. A fifty-point antler chandelier lit the adjoining walnut-paneled dining room, cheered by another imposing rock fireplace and served by a king's kitchen. Miniatures of the two ground-floor fireplaces warmed the twelve upstairs bedrooms.

Austin's entourage soon sparkled with Hollywood's elite and bristled with the powerful from D.C. and Sacramento. The ancestral wintering area for waterfowl, offered by the water-collecting depression dubbed the Butte Sink, was favored by many of the high and mighty, who bought their own properties and followed Austin's lavish example. By the mid-thirties, Austin's neighbors and guests included Clark Gable, Robert Stack Sr., Earl Warren, Wallace Berry, Ernest Hemingway, and Carole Lombard. The sport, privacy, and quiet beauty of the bird-filled marshes became their haven from the unsettled glitz of a troubled Europe.

On a crisp January day in 1940, at age eighty-nine, Austin Green fell asleep in his favorite duck blind and never woke up. Though he had enjoyed wild success as a businessman and sportsman, he never mastered marriage. Four broken unions had produced eleven sons and eight daughters. Esmond, who died five years earlier, had remarried after his first wife's death. He was survived by three sons and a daughter.

All of Austin's and Esmond's sons, except one, were more interested in expanding the family fortune than hunting and fishing. Adam Green, Austin's first son by his second marriage, couldn't tell coriander from cumin but knew every species of duck and goose, carved his own decoys, and tied his own flies.

The week after Austin's funeral, Adam quietly moved from San Francisco to Waterloo, which he declared in a letter to his brothers, sisters, and cousins would be his principal home. He took his two-year-old son, Drake, with him. Their summers, he announced, would be spent at Mountain Home. Adam's wife, already a widow to duck and trout seasons, opted for a generous settlement and the refinements of San Francisco.

Adam's decision simmered while the heads of the family occupied themselves making money and keeping the United States out of Europe's spreading quagmire. Whoever and whatever Hitler was, he was a long way from San Francisco. Money siphoned off to curb his bellicose ways would be money taxed from consumers, who, in a Spartan wartime economy, would scarcely be able to afford luxury provisions.

Within a year, Adam's grasp on the family hunting and fishing preserves triggered internecine warfare. Adam had quit counting his cousins when their number passed fifty. Many of his relatives staked claims on Mountain Home and Waterloo. They weren't alone.

Armand Styles Stilton Jr. was the sole son and heir of Armand Stilton Sr., who died in 1932, leaving Armand Jr. responsible for the family's vast Hawaiian sugar holdings as well as a large copper pit in eastern Montana. Armand Jr., a passionate blue-water sailor, managed to navigate the Depression's shoals and by 1938 had expanded Stilton Industries to include steel and aluminum production. Unlike his San Francisco neighbors, the Greens, he saw the war clouds as an opportunity. By war's end, thousands of ship hulls and plane fuselages had tripled the Stilton fortune. Armand Jr. sought new horizons.

As a diversion, he invested in a motion picture production company. He soon collected Hollywood celebrities as one would collect art or books. Clark Gable introduced him to duck hunting, and after two seasons Armand shed his blue commodore's blazer for a tan-and-black hunting parka. He kept his seat at the head of the boardroom table but yielded daily management of Stilton Industries to qualified underlings in order to focus on two things: duck hunting and the acquisition of Butte Sink property.

No longer satisfied with his guest status at Gable's place, Stilton decided to buy it. He named a price Gable could not decline, particularly when Stilton stipulated the actor was to retain lifetime hunting privileges. Stilton then launched phase two of his invasion. He formed a land company and, capitalizing on the cachet of Gable's name, called it Gable Farms. Stilton saw Gable Farms as the head and neck of a sleeping giant. The body sprawled all around him, and he began to buy it up, paying premium prices for adjacent properties. In the center of the giant pulsed its heart, the land Stilton planned to convert to rice production that would ensure prime hunting at Gable Farms for all time: Waterloo.

Stilton stalked his prey with methodical precision and soon sensed its weakness. The Green family, once centralized and powerful, was fragmented and quarrelsome. There was one pie and not enough pieces for all who claimed seats at the table. It seemed that all the Greens, save one, wanted to keep their lives of privilege, but none knew how to run the ship. Stilton made it easy for them. In 1955 he offered to buy Green Bros. Teas & Spices for $60 million. The sale was to include Waterloo.

A Green family meeting was hastily arranged. Waterloo was not viewed as a deal-breaker by anyone but Adam. He stunned the group by stating he would waive any participation in the $60 million in exchange for title to Waterloo and Mountain Home. He told his eager relatives that Stilton already owned too much of the Butte Sink and that was a damned shame. No one understood what Adam meant, and no one cared.

The counteroffer was relayed to Stilton, who fumed. He'd already planned to sell off the tea-and-spice company, as he had no use for it. He responded by threatening to withdraw his offer altogether if the Green family didn't accept his terms within forty-eight hours.

A delegation of Green brothers went to Adam's hotel room. They told him there was no way the rest of the family would sign off on Waterloo or Mountain Home if the deal soured because of Adam's intransigence. In fact, they threatened, both properties would have to be partitioned and sold anyway. Why not just go along and become a multi-millionaire with the rest of them? Then go buy another place to kill ducks.

"I was fifteen years old when Dad told me all this," said Drake. "It seems like yesterday. Dad was bitter…but proud."

Claire's mug sat, untouched. Drake looked past her, his eyes and mind still many years back.

"I remember his exact words. 'I was down but not out,' he said. 'That bastard Stilton wanted the place so bad I knew he'd go for some then and count on snatching up the rest later. I also knew I'd never let that happen.'"

Drake blinked, returning to the present. He stared directly at Claire.

"Then Dad said, 'Neither will you.'" He paused. "You asked me who I am…what I am. Those three words from Dad sum it up."

"Really? How?" she said.

"Dad told his brothers to tell Stilton he could have fifteen hundred acres and Dad would keep the lodge and the five hundred acres around it. The family had to sign off to Dad on Waterloo and Mountain Home. They went for it. So did Stilton. But he, and now his jerkwater son, never stopped trying to get the rest of Waterloo. He's on me constantly about it. It's an occupation."

Claire sat quietly, digesting what she had heard.

"There's more?" she said, finally.

"Oh yeah, there's more," Drake said. "Think I'll have something a little stronger." He stood up and went to the side-board that served as a bar. He reached for a bottle and two glasses. "Whiskey?" he said, turning towards her.

"Too early for me," she said. "But go ahead. I'm still all ears."

Drake poured himself a double shot, added some water, and sat down. "It picks up two weeks after Dad told me the family history I just told you." Caressing his drink, he again leaned back and closed his eyes.

"It was August twenty-second, nineteen fifty-eight. Hot. Strong north winds. A day Dad never would have picked for burning. I was up at Mountain Home with Dad's girlfriend and her family. Dad was down here supervising work on the levee between our property and Gable Farms. A fire broke out in Waterloo Lodge, that pile of burnt wreckage you see up the hill." He gestured toward the slope that rose from the concrete block building they were in.

"A worker on the levee said Dad ran in to save a litter of pups and their mother. He never came out."

Drake reached down and stroked Tar's head.

"We were keeping the sire, Coho, in an outside kennel until the pups were weaned. Tar is a fourth generation descendant." He sipped his drink.

"The rest goes pretty fast. They shipped me off to San Francisco to live with Aunts and Uncles. I finished high school down there, joined the Marines and ended up in Vietnam. I took to the life pretty well. It was…well, let's just call it 'hunting,' which I was already damn good at."

He stopped.

"You don't want to talk about Vietnam, do you…" said Claire.

"No reason to," he said. "Fast forward to September, nineteen seventy-six. I left the Marine Corps and moved back up here. I built this place," he said, sweeping his arm to take in the two story concrete structure. "My members, the five guys who hunt here, call it 'The Palace,' which you see it clearly isn't. It's a place to sleep, eat, have some drinks and tell stories. Also, it'll never burn down."

And, probably no place for a woman, thought Claire, though she wondered.

CHAPTER 4

Armand Stilton III took the sack of plucked and wrapped birds from Jim Quesenberry and moved toward the tank-like bulk of his Hummer. He grabbed the custom hoist bar and strained his 260 pounds up and onto a donut pillow in the driver's seat. Not only did he require a height boost, the Hummer's rock-rough ride inflamed his hemorrhoids.

"I'll be back Friday," said Stilton. "Ladies Day weekend, remember?"

Jim nodded. The annual event was circled in red on his calendar.

Stilton continued. "Watch the ducks this week. Next weekend put me where they want to go."

When Armand's father, who had topped the scales at 305, died fifteen years earlier, all pretext at an open, honest, and democratic blind rotation among the members ended. Though memberships in Gable Farms, when available, currently sold for $1 million, with a yearly assessment of $40,000, an unwritten and unchallenged rule of the club held that Armand had first choice of blinds whenever he showed up to shoot.

"Yessir," said Jim, who raised his hand in an ambiguous gesture that turned into a single raised digit seconds later when the Hummer was out of sight.

As Stilton commandeered the narrow county road to Colusa, forcing oncoming vehicles to cling to the precarious rim of the levee bank, he planned his evening. By the time he reached I-5 and headed south toward Marin County and his Greek Revival mansion on four acres in Ross, he was smiling.

For years, the notion of gas wells on Gable Farms had been rejected out of hand. "This is a duck club, not a pipe farm," the old commodore had declared to his son, who was searching for a way to transform his image from that of the ne'er-do-well heir to that of financial genius. Gas wells, Armand told his father, were the future of the Sacramento Valley. Rice farmers all around them were making more money while they slept than they were from farming. Revered for its waterfowl habitat, the valley had become downright sacred for the fortunes piped from its bowels.

"No, and that's the end of it," his father had declared. "This is prime hunting land. We're not going to defile it with pipes and valves. You want to make your mark, then do it the right way." The old man raised his arm toward Waterloo. "Get me that."

Following Armand Jr.'s death, Armand III found himself shut out from meaningful participation in management of Stilton Industries by the protective sheath his father had constructed. His link to Gable Farms grew from hobby to obsession. The eight paying members didn't much care who ran the place, so long as it ran well. And it did—until Texas energy companies brought California to its knees and Armand III once again began to dream of making his mark as a gas baron.

Before California's energy crisis, the Gable Farms members agreed that Armand's restraint from signing gas well contracts had demonstrated an admirable and previously unseen sentimentality. In truth, gas prices had been down and Armand was biding his time. When the state's botched energy program and two major utility failures sent natural gas prices soaring, his true colors emerged. He contracted with a group of Texans to sink exploratory wells and perform geological studies. The "Christmas trees" of valves, pipes, and lights had angered the members, but Armand saw only their potential for augmenting the Stilton fortune. A dinner of wild ducks for the Texans who sunk the wells and whose boots were crammed with money for the rights to more struck him as the perfect merger of business and sport.

"Oh, these here are mighty fine ducks, Ar–mand, mighty fine. Don't y'all agree?" Braxton "Dink" Deerlink's two associates nodded vigorous assent. A froth of duck blood and wine dribbled from their chins as they tore the intentionally undercooked dark meat from bones. Dink's attention returned to the partially destroyed mallard before him, and he licked his fingers before plunging once more into the fray.

An elaborate sterling duck press dominated the center of the long table. Pink streaks riddled its white marble base as if someone had drawn varicose veins on a lush Botticelli nude. Blood-tinted grease dripped from its spout into a small silver bowl.

"Glad you're enjoying them," Armand said. "There's plenty more, so don't be bashful."

From a corner, his butler discreetly raised two fingers. Armand had always thought stories about Texans were exaggerated. Now he began to wonder how to stretch the remaining two mallards into second servings for three crazed oilmen in the middle of a feeding frenzy. He motioned to the butler, who stepped up to the table and bent down. Armand whispered in his ear, "Tell Harold to be creative. Loaves and fishes." The butler nodded and faded away. Armand's chef was accomplished at turning his employer's meager results from the field into dishes that were more "essence of duck" than the real thing.

Dink mopped up juice with a hunk of bread and downed a fresh glass of '76 Bordeaux in one gulp.

"Ar–mand," the Texan began. Armand bristled at the pronunciation of his name. "Clive, Homer, and me have poured over the geological survey and test results. Things look pretty good. There's gas all around you out there." Armand forgot his irritation and smiled.

"And that's the problem," said Dink.

Armand's smile froze. "How is that a problem?"

"It's around you. Not under you," said Dink. "Why, that Waterloo property just south of yours is probably one of the richest gas fields we've seen in the whole Sacramento Valley. Now, we'd really like to move forward, but gas prices are dipping again with all these government witch-hunters snooping around. That don't matter. We sink wells all the time and cap 'em off till we get the price up again. Fact is…" He leaned forward and gave a conspiratorial wink. "Hell, more than half the wells of your neighbors are either capped or running at half production. Those rice farmers are bellyaching now, but they always go quiet when we get the price jacked up and turn on the flow again."

Armand had tuned out most of the Texan's speech after *Waterloo.*

Gas. Under Waterloo. Acres of it. He'd been right that morning when he'd told Quesenberry that Drake Green had to go. The Roto Duck was nothing compared to the millions of reasons he now had. His annoyance eased. The Texan could call him anything he wanted.

"To our venture then." He raised his glass. "Have your lawyers contact mine. The sooner the better, don't you think?"

Dink placed a leg bone between his teeth and made a sucking sound as he skimmed off the meat. He dropped the bone to his plate, now a charnel platter of shredded duck parts. "Not that easy, Armand," he said.

Armand blinked.

"What? We sign papers, you dig wells, we all make money. What could be simpler?"

Dink shook his head, obviously amused at his host's naïve take on the natural gas business.

"Well, Ar–mand, far as we can make out, you don't own that property. Mr. Drake Green does. Then there's the question of a pipeline. Pipes, Ar–mand. The gas has got to get from the wells to market."

What is with these hicks? thought Armand. *Must have left their brains in their saddlebags.*

"Gentlemen," Armand said, lowering his tone, "the property is as good as mine. Don't worry about it. As they say, I'll be making Mr. Green an offer he can't refuse. With your help, I'll turn that place into a pipe farm. We, you three and me, will own that property. We'll put together our own syndicate and pump it dry."

Dink looked at his associates, then shrugged. "Well, Ar–mand, yuh see, we took the liberty of talkin' to Mr. Green."

Armand stiffened.

"Now, we didn't tell him about all that gas he's sittin' on. After all, we've been dealin' with y'all, and we have our ethics. Right, boys?" Clive and Homer nodded, obviously well-schooled in business ethics.

"We just suggested to him that there might be some gas on your property and that we might want to run a li'l ol' pipeline across his to get it out. That's really the only way to go, it being the most direct route and all. Well, to make a long story short, he ain't willin'. Fact, he had a pretty strong suggestion concerning your backside and where we could shove that pipeline."

"Green? He said that?"

"Oh, and lots more. Said you and your daddy had been itchin' to get his property for years, and that it ain't going to happen. Right, fellas?"

Clive and Homer nodded again. Homer held up his plate and looked toward the butler. His plate was whisked away and replaced immediately with a fresh one bearing a jelled mound that Armand recognized as one of Harold's alternatives to a whole duck. "Duck mousse," he said darkly. "I think you'll like it."

Dink brightened. "Looks good. Mind if I try some?" His plate disappeared and a serving of the mousse took its place.

"So, Ar–mand," Dink continued between bites and slurps, "long as your neighbor resists sellin' and refusin' to a pipeline, we just got to look elsewhere. There's plenty a' people out there who want wells and pipes and are willin' to wait till we get gas prices up again."

Armand scowled. Though he rarely considered input from the Gable Farms members, their complaints about the three test wells had escalated to near revolution.

"What about those ugly messes of pipes you've already put on my place?" he said. "My members think they're scaring away ducks."

Dink shrugged.

"Oh, they're all closed down, Ar–mand. Ain't doin' anyone any good without a pipeline. What little gas they might produce wouldn't justify a pipeline. When you get Green to sell and gas prices come up, then we'll open the valves again. Till then, far as we're concerned, they're yours. Read the contract."

Armand forced a smile to conceal his seething boil. He'd signed the ten-page document in a flourish of confident bravado, looking forward to the day he'd show it to his lawyers as a sign of what he could get done without their expensive meddling. Now he was stuck with three eyesores of pipes and valves in the middle of what had been pristine hunting land.

The three Texans polished off all the mousse, another bottle of the Bordeaux, two crème brûleés each, six Cuban cigars, and a vintage port. All while they commiserated with Armand and assured him that when and if he acquired Waterloo or made a deal with Drake Green, they'd be happy to do business with him. Until then, they'd explore other opportunities in the valley and Butte Sink. After all, with gas prices down, there was no real hurry.

CHAPTER 5

Drake stepped onto the deck. From out of the dark came the chatter of thousands of resting waterfowl and the gentle lowing of cattle. He traced the Big Dipper, then Orion, as he relieved himself through an opening specially cut in the railing for that purpose. His gaze settled on the overgrown ruins of Waterloo Lodge, still marked by the rise of the river-rock fireplace. When Drake had reclaimed the property twenty-six years earlier, he hadn't had the stomach to bulldoze the charred remnants away. New-growth trees and brush had all but covered the site.

After his 1976 homecoming with Armand Stilton III, Drake had begun to plan his resurrection of Waterloo as a prime place to hunt ducks. He'd towed in an old fourteen-foot house trailer. Then he'd scrounged a rusted Caterpillar D-6 bulldozer from a farm equipment supplier. The Green name went a long way in the Butte Sink, and Drake's project was welcomed by many as long overdue. But within days of moving back to the property, Drake realized something was missing—something he needed to take care of before anything else.

When Austin Green had built Waterloo, he had established a herd of cattle to ensure a fresh supply of diary products. Refrigeration then was a hit-or-miss thing, particularly in remote stretches of the Sacramento Valley.

Waterloo's cows became a fixture, maintained by Drake's father, even though their presence was no longer necessary. Adam Green went so far as to hold that the cows improved the duck hunting, a concept Drake came to regard as an honored superstition rather than proven logic. Within days of reestablishing himself on Waterloo, Drake had a fresh herd trucked to the property. When he woke to a mixed symphony of cackling waterfowl and bawling cows, he knew he was ready to go to work.

Drake spent the first duck season of his return hiding out in tules and skulking along the berms that formed the maze of old ponds once yielding sport to his father, grandfather, and their guests. Week after week, he studied the flight patterns of ducks and geese that dropped into Waterloo and the adjoining sprawl of Gable Farms. He counted, charted, and calculated. When the season ended, he holed up in his trailer and drew plans while the rains of February and March drenched everything outside. When spring began to tease the Sacramento Valley, he was ready.

With Michelangelo's perfection, he used the old bulldozer to sculpt six new duck ponds. It took him four months. Always he took into account Waterloo's cows; as he designed his ponds, he left patches of high pasture and wild grasses where the cattle sauntered and grazed in their constant movement along the banks of Butte Creek and Canal 442. That September Drake opened the weirs that flooded his ponds.

Another duck season came and went as Drake monitored what he had done. Every day he set out decoys, watched them, moved them, and moved them again. When the season ended, he started building blinds.

The following season Drake hunted, moving from blind to blind, perfecting decoy placement and honing his skills as a caller and dog handler. That spring he recruited paying members and built a place for them to stay. There was only one spot to put it, really—on the hill, just down from the ruins of the old Waterloo Lodge. The hill not only commanded a sweeping view of the Butte Sink, but also stood high above winter floods, was cooled by summer breezes, and shaded by a mix of oak and pines that had survived Waterloo's fire.

An early member took one look at what Drake had built and cracked, "Christ, what a palace!" And the name had stuck. Far from palatial, the Palace was a two-story, concrete-block bunker. It might catch on fire someday, but it would never burn down. The first floor served as a dormitory-style room with bunk beds and a bathroom with a shower. Stairs led to the second floor: one large room where members cooked, ate, drank, and socialized. The east end was walled off as a room for Drake. Sliding doors opened to a deck that spanned the north and east sides.

During the three years it took Drake to bring Waterloo back to life, he was barraged with calls, overtures, and threats from the Stiltons. When the old man died, Armand III, who had never forgotten his unceremonious eviction the day he and Drake met, picked up the sword. Drake's rebuffs grew in tone and language. Even without Adam Green's admonition, he swore he would leave Waterloo only one way, and when that time came, he would be beyond caring.

The night, the sounds, and the strange mix of feelings from a day in which he'd bested Armand Stilton and enjoyed Claire Wooley's company left Drake shaking his head. Had he just been showing off, trying to impress her?

He knew the Roto-Duck interlude, satisfying as it was, would only bring trouble. Listening to the cackle that pulsed through the valley, he regretted his indulgence. Stilton's inevitable revenge was certain to cost Drake money and grief. For years, lawyers—squads of them—had assaulted him when and where he least expected. Quiet title actions, trespass suits, water diversion claims, nuisance allegations, zoning violations—the record of litigation captioned *Stilton v. Green* already occupied volumes in the Sutter County Clerk's office, and the end was not in sight.

Drake had managed to fend off each wave, but now all ten fingers were plugging holes in the dike as more were being bored. Three's cash resources were unlimited, whereas Drake's were almost exhausted. His lawyer, Todd Millar, had been on a hunting-for-services retainer. Millar had even considered it sport to take down the three-piece-suited drones from San Francisco who'd ventured onto his home turf. It hadn't hurt that Sutter County's only judge had been Drake's frequent guest at Waterloo and had enjoyed the fine shooting, followed by long, lazy meals. Neither the judge nor Millar had seen a reason to inform the Stilton forces of the arrangement.

But, as all good things end, so had Drake's unique and practical access to the courts. Millar's gout had become disabling, and he'd retired. The judge, the Honorable Stanley Bell, had the misfortune to have his spinster clerk—who'd always fantasized he'd sweep her away into retirement with him—storm into his chambers while Stanley, his pants around his ankles, stood behind his comely court reporter, who was bent over his desk, her panties on the floor with his shorts and her dress around her shoulders.

Judge Bell's abrupt retirement was felt by most to be long overdue. His replacement, a former rice farmer turned lawyer who'd gone into the grain elevator business and who had the governor's ear, didn't care much about hunting or hunters. Besides, he was of the nobler mind-set that litigants and their judges should not socialize, much less share a duck blind.

Drake stepped back inside and poured another shot of the unla-beled corn liquor the three Texans had left behind. Jovial outdoors-men, the men from Dallas hadn't fooled Drake with their down-home ways. *These boys are sharp as cat's teeth,* he'd thought while they'd swapped stories and sipped the potent amber brew. Armed with advance intel-ligence from Jim Quesenberry, Drake had been prepared for their proposition.

"Boys," he said when Dink had finished, "step out here with me a minute."

He led them onto the deck. "What do you see?"

"A whole bunch of gorgeous hunting land," Dink said. The other two nodded. They'd done a lot of that.

"Correct, my friend," said Drake. "And that's just the way it's going to stay." He had amused his guests with a comment concerning the proposed pipeline and Armand III's anatomy. Then he'd told them there was plenty of gas in the west valley and lots of rice farmers who thought gas wells and pipelines as pretty as sunsets in Hawaii.

Now, in the dark, the gabbling wetlands seemed to scream at him, and he wondered if he'd made an enormous mistake.

CHAPTER 6

Donna Stilton peered down from her first-class seat and saw that San Francisco and Marin County were covered with the same fog that had chased her off to Maui. Were it not for the annual Ladies Day weekend at Gable Farms, she'd still be sipping Mai Tais at the Four Seasons.

The 737 banked, and Donna strained to pick out landmarks. Only the distinctive spires of the Golden Gate Bridge pierced the fog. *That's me,* she thought. *Rising above it all.*

She'd been warned—not only by her circle of confidants at the Metropolitan Club, but also by the former Mrs. Armand Stilton III herself.

"Honey," Francis Stilton had told her, "he has a mistress and he's obsessed with her. Her name is Gable Farms. If you can live as number two to that duck club, you'll get along just fine. If not, well then you can just join my table. There are three of us there already, and we all get along very well. Armand may love his ducks, but he pays his wives."

Armand's age—fifty-eight—when they'd married four years earlier, the same age as her father, had not presented itself as a problem. At thirty-two, Donna considered all men her age idiots. She'd yearned for sage wisdom and a more relaxed pace. Armand III's incalculable wealth had seemed a solid platform on which to build. Now, after four years, the idiots were looking better.

The hang-up was lifestyle. As Donna Stilton, she enjoyed unlimited and unquestioned spending. Not that she abused the privilege. It was just nice to have it. Donna was the daughter of a man who'd stretched a neighborhood delicatessen into a comfortable catering business, and she figured she had paid her dues. She respected money and the effort required to make it. With a prenuptial agreement that shielded Armand's fortune from his propensity to marry women he promptly abandoned to chase ducks or other game, Donna would receive a comfortable settlement. Comfortable was one thing. The glow on life cast by the heat of real wealth was something else entirely.

As they had with Donna's predecessors, Armand III's lawyers had presented a carefully drafted document that endowed Donna with all a woman could desire, so long as she and Armand were married. After that, the radiance fizzled, and she'd be expected to live on $500,000 a year, with modest cost-of-living increases. Oh, there would be a house thrown in—nothing comparable to the estate they shared in Ross, of course. And that was it. An allowance and a house.

There was one more thing, a moot issue really, something the lawyer her father had hired came up with. So long as she and Armand III remained married, Armand had to maintain a life insurance policy in her favor. Not much, really, considering Armand's wealth. Just twenty million.

The aircraft leveled on final approach for San Francisco International. Donna buckled her seatbelt and stiffened at the thought of resuming her empty life. The alternative, a taxable $500,000 a year in spousal support might not be so bad, she thought. As the landing gear greased the runway and a slight shudder pulsed her seat, another thought struck her: a nontaxable lump sum of twenty million would be a lot nicer. Invested in tax-free municipal bonds, it would generate a million a year, and the government would not be her partner.

The valet parking attendant drove up in her new Mercedes SL500 Roadster, and Donna slid in. She left the airport pondering the worrisome risks presented by the fact that Armand III spent most of his time with loaded guns, trying to kill things. The poor man could have an accident.

Whereas most would consider visiting their lawyer a cut below a trip to a dentist who'd foresworn the use of anesthesia, Armand III relished it. Next to killing ducks, or at least shooting at them, it was his favorite thing. Nowhere else was he greeted with such hushed reverence and made to feel so powerful.

From their offices in the holy of holies, the imposing granite and marble structure that had once been the Pacific Stock Exchange, the tentacles of Orland, Mulvaney & Merck curled themselves around all aspects of finance and commerce, elements that had defined Armand's family for three generations. Every fifteen years or so, a retiring senior partner would ceremoniously pass the baton on to the next "biller," the lawyer whose function was to oversee statements generated from the firm's many departments and to stroke the client into grateful obligation.

Louis DuBois, the current biller for Stilton Industries and Armand Stilton III, had never found stroking Armand to be the problem. DuBois viewed him as a lion with a thorn in its paw. The thorn had a name: Waterloo. DuBois, whose ethics and sense of propriety were pure old school, spent a great deal of his time counseling restraint and caution as he took in Armand's bombastic plans.

"Oh, we could file this lawsuit, for you, Armand," DuBois would say, or "Yes, Armand, you could take that position, but..." Inevitably the sessions ended with DuBois explaining the cost of Armand's proposed course of action and Armand saying, "The money doesn't matter; just see it's done." On it had gone, year after year, lawsuit after lawsuit.

With Stilton's global industrial and financial presence, it amazed DuBois that 75 percent of the office time he spent with Armand dealt with his neighbor in the Butte Sink, a place DuBois had never been but thought of as a swamp without alligators. Each time one of the firm's litigation partners or associates returned from Sutter County claiming "home-towned again," DuBois's image of a money-sucking quagmire at the base of some barren peaks bearing the strange name "Sutter Buttes" became more cemented.

"The bastard's contributing to the energy crisis, for Christ sake," Armand said. "He's sitting on a gas gold mine and not sharing it with the people of the State of California."

DuBois peaked his hands in the classic prayerful pose he resorted to when he needed to mask the fact he didn't have a clue what to do next. The state's so-called energy crisis actually was history, leaving Californians paying extortion-level utility rates and the Texas energy company executives who'd pocketed millions from their insider manipulations ducking for cover behind an army of eastern lawyers, including a well-fed contingent from the New York City office of Orland, Mulvaney & Merck.

"Now, Armand," DuBois said, "it's hardly a crisis anymore. Besides, that's his right." As always, DuBois was at a loss as to how to contain his litigious client's enthusiasm for leaping into court. He wondered why the man couldn't be content to simply clip bond coupons and enjoy his wealth like the firm's other high-net-worth clients.

"Bullshit," said Stilton. "No one has the right to come between the public and scarce natural resources."

Louis DuBois was too tactful to remind his client that several companies under the Stilton Industries umbrella did just that. One whole team within the law firm engineered new and ingenious ways to circumvent federal price fixing and antitrust laws. He continued to ponder and let Armand lead him to where they always wound up.

"I want to sue the bastard," Armand announced in a tone of new discovery.

"Because he shot your Moto-Duck thing?" said DuBois, already calculating the fees generated by sending a junior associate to Sutter County to file a small claims action.

Three scowled.

"How'd you hear about that?" he asked. "It was a *Roto Duck.*"

"The newspaper, Armand. Our library has a clipping service that catches items pertaining to our clients. The, uh, incident was mentioned in yesterday's Hank Cline column."

Hank Cline, the popular *bon vivant* who kept tabs on all the local movers, shakers, and socialites, was the reason 40 percent of all San Franciscans bought the *San Francisco Telegraph.* Usually the subjects mentioned in his column welcomed their spot of notoriety as an acknowledgment of arrival. Armand Stilton III needed no such confirmation, and his dark expression conveyed his displeasure.

"That bastard," Stilton said. DuBois couldn't tell if his client meant Green or the columnist.

Armand stood and walked to the window of DuBois's office, which framed a panoramic view of the Embarcadero and the bay. He turned and faced the lawyer, his voice now a grating hiss. "I meant a lawsuit that will force him to sell me his property."

DuBois had never heard this tone from his troublesome client. It was something he did not want to explore. "I'll have someone get right on it, Armand," he said, reviewing which of his lieutenants would lead the charge.

Armand walked to the door, then stopped. "Your library would have a copy of yesterday's *Telegraph*, right?"

DuBois nodded.

"Have them send it to the reception desk. I'll pick it up on the way out."

CHAPTER 7

A final check in her mirror told Claire Wooley she was ready. She hurried down the stairs from her apartment, unlocked her car, and set off for Waterloo. The map Drake had drawn for her lay face up on the passenger seat.

As she headed south on I-5, Claire reflected on the events of the day before, and where they were taking her.

By the time he had driven her back to her apartment on the outskirts of the small town of Willows, Claire had decided to give the ducks and Drake Green a second chance. She guessed he was at least twenty years older, but he was a hell of a lot more interesting than the guy at the Jiffy Lube, who had been pestering her ever since she'd had her oil changed.

She had accepted Drake's invitation to come out to Waterloo the next night for a duck dinner and then took his hand. "Thanks for a wonderful day," she had told him. "And for sharing your story." Seized with an impulse, she had then drawn him close, leaned up and gave him a short but full kiss on the lips. "Till tomorrow evening," she said, then turned, unlocked her door and entered her apartment. She closed the door and stood with her back against it, her eyes closed.

Drake spent the day cleaning the Palace in preparation for his dinner with Claire. It wasn't that he was messy or unorganized. As a confirmed bachelor who had spent twenty years in the military, he took pride in neatness and order. The challenge was the Palace and its location—a living diorama of waterfowl and waterfowl habitat. Not just ducks and geese, but sandhill cranes, blue heron, coots, muskrat, river otter, pheasant, quail, and various owls surrounded the Palace with the sights and sounds of another world. With the beauty came the beasts, in the form of mice, rats, snakes, spiders, and bugs that defied description. Drake worked to shove aside these latter features of duck club life for at least the few hours of Claire's visit.

Webs and dust gave way to cleanser and disinfectant as Drake prepared the Palace for a white-glove inspection. At afternoon's end, he was satisfied he'd done his best, but wondered why.

Drake had hosted other women at the Palace, but never had he undertaken such an overhaul, not even when the connection had shown signs of progressing toward the dreaded word *relationship*. He even trapped and relocated Clyde, the wood rat that for three years had occupied the firewood bin next to the wood stove. As he watched Clyde scurry into the brush pile behind the dog kennel, Drake said, "Hey, it's just for tonight. You'll be back soon." As he spoke, he wondered whether the same could be said of Claire.

Drake climbed the stairs and shoved another piece of firewood into the stove. He looked at his watch: 4:45. Claire was due at 5:30. He had just enough time to trim his beard and have a shower.

At six, Drake went out on the deck and searched for headlights on the dirt road connecting Waterloo to the county road one mile away. The day before, when he'd picked Claire up and brought her out to Waterloo, he hadn't thought to show her landmarks, their predawn conversation mulled by the morning quiet and their mutual guarded outlook toward their first day together.

The post-dusk curtain was dropping fast, and Waterloo would soon be lost in the black of a moonless valley night. He'd drawn Claire a map and described the wrought-iron mallard mailbox at the turnoff, but now he feared that in the darkness she'd miss it. At 6:20, Drake said, "Tar, come."

The Labrador followed Drake down the stairs and jumped up alongside him in the pickup. They set off down the hill toward Green's Crossing, the old concrete bridge spanning 442, the dirt-banked canal that bisected Waterloo and angled to form the boundary between Waterloo and Gable Farms.

It was still early in the season, but all signs pointed toward heavier-than-usual rains. Already the road into Waterloo was a rutted mess, and Drake had warned Claire not to drive outside the deep depressions carved into the clay-like mud by the comings and goings of his weekend members.

Earlier he'd come out to Green's Crossing and unlocked the heavy pipe-bar gate that was Waterloo's final barrier to overland intruders. He'd considered giving Claire a key when he'd left her the day before but then decided that would be pushing it. Besides, picking out the right ruts to track along the rim of the dark canal would be daunting enough. He wanted to spare her the added burden of stopping, unlocking the gate, and swinging the heavy bar aside.

He crossed the bridge and turned, then headed east toward the county road. He drove with his window down, a habit of his father. "If you ever wind up in that canal," Adam had warned, "you won't have the time or sense to crank down a window."

He hoped to see Claire's headlights turning in and coming toward him. Instead, the impenetrable darkness of the vast valley night swallowed the sparse efforts of the pickup's beams. Forced to concentrate on tracking the deep grooves, he cursed himself for not arranging to meet Claire at Waterloo's entrance. Relieved she was not in sight, he decided to drive out to the road and wait.

Tar suddenly bristled. The dog placed its front paws on the dash and began to whine. Drake tried to shake off a sense of foreboding and brought the creeping truck to a stop. Tar broke into barks and scratched at the passenger door. Drake grabbed the flashlight he kept behind the seat and stepped out into the night.

He quickly played the light in all directions, reluctant to let the dog out until he had some handle on what was out there. Tar had led Drake down Skunk Road one too many times.

As Drake began to swing the light away from the canal, something caught it, like a magnet from the dark. He stopped the beam and slowly played it back. It merged with another light, a faint glow. Then he saw the fresh tracks that veered away from the main ruts to become a smear that spread down the canal bank.

"Oh, Christ," he said, and ran toward the glow. Tar leapt from the open driver's door and followed.

"Claire!" he called, suddenly hating the silence and blackness that usually brought him so much pleasure. He reached the top of the bank and saw the dark expanse of an automobile roof inches above the canal's murky surface. Weak fans of light from the car's front probed the watery gloom.

Drake kicked off his tall rubber boots and plunged in, vaguely aware of Tar hitting the water at the same time. He dove and groped, unable to see more than the dark shape of the partially submerged car. He found the driver's side handle and strained to open the door against the slow but relentless current. Once he had the door open beyond halfway, the current took over and pinned it open for him.

Claire lay in the driver's seat, her head barely above water. Drake reached in, clutched her waist, and lifted. He met resistance and grappled to find the seatbelt buckle. Waves of another darkness began to claim him. He gasped air from the scant space above.

The seatbelt parted and Claire's limp form began to drift free. Drake strong-armed himself backward against the current, grabbing Claire by one arm and looping it around his neck. He kicked, forcing himself out and up. When he broke the surface, he gulped more air and clawed the slippery canal edge for a handhold. Tar surfaced next to him, Claire's other hand loose and soft in the dog's mouth, like a downed duck.

Drake squirmed to a half-sit at the base of the canal bank and pulled Claire from the water onto the muddy shelf. She moaned for several seconds, then blinked her eyes open. She gently pulled her hand from Tar's mouth and looked down, her pants and top a mud cocoon. She started to speak, then stopped and began to spit her lips free of murk. Finally, after a rash of choking, she looked Drake full in the face.

"If we're going to see any more of each other, you're really going to have to fix that road."

Suddenly, her eyes widened. "What's *that?*" she screamed, staring over his shoulder.

He turned and found himself nose to nose with one of his cows.

Jim Quesenberry walked in the dark, the edge of the walnut orchard the only guide he needed. Row after row of the thick-trunked trees butted against the gravel road that led from the Gable Farms clubhouse to the boat dock. Up since four that morning, Jim was bushed, yet he needed the short, cold walk to decompress in order to fall asleep and do it all again the next day.

On shooting mornings, the members gathered in the clubhouse dining room for Jim's lumberjack breakfast. While they wolfed down stacks of hotcakes and platters of sausage and eggs, Jim would hustle down to the dock. When the convoy of members' trucks arrived, the hunters simply stepped into their respective boats and shoved off, outboards already purring and boats pointed toward the channel they would follow that day.

When they returned, Jim was there to tie up boats, tag ducks, and cheerfully send the hunters back to the clubhouse, where hot soup and a buffet lunch waited. Then he'd toil at the dock, cleaning the boats, checking fuel tanks, and rearranging hastily retrieved decoys. Jim and his work were some of the perks of a million-dollar duck club, and part of the price Jim paid for the privilege of living there.

Like his father, Armand III held membership in Gable Farms to eight hunters. The members' guest privileges were limited and scheduled on a rotation basis. Armand hosted a guest whenever he wanted, usually someone he was trying to impress or whose company he wanted to buy. His guests rarely returned.

When he came alone, which was happening with distressing frequency, he expected someone to share a blind with him—an honor the members took pains to avoid. The excited quacking from ducks fleeing Armand's calling had caused one Gable Farms member to wonder quietly to the others if ducks could laugh. Armand also had the nasty habit of shooting at anything, anywhere, a practice that had left several members nearly deaf, and, in one case, almost scalped by the rush of number four shot Armand had discharged in the direction of a passing mud hen.

Jim, always tuned to the dynamics of the membership, had tactfully begun to shoulder the burden, and the members gratefully acknowledged his sacrifice by contributing to what they termed the Guide's Fund. At the end of each season an envelope discreetly appeared in Jim's hunting jacket, balm for the pain he suffered while undertaking the dreary and dangerous task of hunting with Armand. Of course, on those awful days, Jim also had all his other chores— breakfast, lunch, boats, bartending, dinner…

Whether or not he'd spent a morning ducking for cover in Three's blind, Jim's days were consumed with the details and frills of a duck club for millionaires. His night-time walks became his sole escape from the heady discussions of finance, politics, and, invariably, sex, that dominated the Gable Farms cocktail hour, usually a good three hours, and the dinner that followed. He'd often thought he should write a book based on the things he'd learned from the captains of industry and commerce who shared the clubhouse at Gable Farms. Not only would a reader gain financial insight, the medical profession would marvel at the sexual exploits claimed by a small group of men whose median age Jim guessed to be seventy.

Jim stopped at the dock. Everything appeared to be in good order. All eight boats bobbed in the gentle breeze, their dark shapes reflecting little from the mass of stars above. Mud hens chattered from across the channel, and somewhere nearby an owl hooted.

As Jim turned to start back, he glanced south toward Waterloo, taking in the stationary headlights on the road that ran along the canal. "Probably stuck in all that goddamned mud," he said to himself. "Stubborn bastard should put in a proper road."

But Jim knew why the road into Waterloo was so terrible. Drake had said it himself. "Your boss and his passel of lawyers," Drake had told him over a beer in Butte City. "Hell, what I paid in court costs last year would have paved that road ten times over."

Well, Drake, Jim thought, *you've got your problems, and I've got mine. Right now I'm looking at Ladies Day.*

CHAPTER 8

"**M**mmm." Claire snuggled her spine into the hairy burrs of Drake's chest. "Weren't those shots I just heard? Shouldn't you be out hunting?"

Drake buried his face into the sweet smell of her long hair. "I am hunting."

She rolled over, faced him, and toyed with his beard. "Drake Green, Drake Green…You've told me your family's story but I'm still wondering. Just who are you, Mr. Drake Green? Who is this hairy ape who showed up at my counter, took me hunting, saved me but drowned my car, wrapped me in blankets, and plied me with strong drink, fed me an amazing dinner, and then shamelessly ravished me? Who are you? *What* are you?"

Drake stared into Claire's eyes, now wide and teasing. Two hours earlier, when the first streaks of dawn lay siege to the night, he'd decided that this woman with golden skin and a long, black ponytail, which she'd loosed to flow and shake as their excitement woke his dogs in their kennel outside, was the most beautiful he'd ever seen.

"Oh, the strong, silent type," she said. "Well, let's start with some basics. Where does the name Drake come from? How old are you?" Her eyes now blazed and her mouth settled into a curious, thoughtful expression. Drake decided that shaving off two years was acceptable and that the best way to stay in her game was to go on the offense.

"Sixty," he said. "I'm named for a trout fly. My father's favorite, the Green Drake. Now, how about you? I need to know whether I'm going to jail or not."

Claire cocked her head and laughed. "That's sweet. Thirty-three, darling. Going on thirty-four in two weeks, December seventh, Pearl Harbor Day. Easy to remember."

She stretched and wrapped up in a sheet, then swung her legs from the bed. "Seriously, aren't you supposed to be out there killing things? Someone is. I just heard more shots. And cows. Don't I hear cows? I remember now. There was one last night, at the scene of the crime. I didn't know that duck clubs had cows."

Drake smiled. "The shooting's from Gable Farms. The cows are mine. Gable Farms members shoot on Wednesdays as well as weekends. My guys only shoot weekends. I keep the place to myself the rest of the week." He stood up, then sat down, suddenly modest. "Unless I have a guest."

Her eyebrows peaked. "Oh, you have many of those, do you?"

Drake said, "Let's have breakfast." She was enjoying this too much.

"Wait," she said. "I still want to know about the cows. It's been a long time since they woke me up in the morning."

"Ahh, the cows," said Drake. "My grandfather had cows, my father had cows, and now I have cows. When my grandfather had this place, he ran a small diary operation that provided him and his guests with milk, butter, and cheese. He didn't believe in hardship and could afford just about anything he wanted. The cows were simply part of the whole picture. When my dad took over, he kept cows, mostly out of sentiment. He'd grown up with them. I guess that's why I keep them. They've always been a part of the place. Dad used to tell me they helped attract ducks. Who knows? The hunting's so good here, I'm not about to change things."

Drake paused and sipped his coffee.

"So, now you know about the cows. Let's have breakfast."

They spent the morning lingering over coffee and Drake's special version of sourdough French toast. Finally they settled into a drowsy silence.

Claire reached across the table and stroked his beard with the back of her hand. "So, named after a trout fly," she said. "But it's the what you are that fascinates me. I've been giving it a lot of thought. Want to hear my conclusion?"

Drake 's eyebrows arched. "Run it by me and I'll tell you." She laughed.

"I think you were destined to live the life of your father and grand-father. That's what you're doing, isn't it?"

He began to clear away dishes as he digested the simple truth of what she'd said.

"You mean," he said, "here's a man who spends his time living at a duck club in the middle of the Butte Sink and an old fishing lodge up in the mountains—every man's dream, right?"

She shrugged. "Am I wrong?"

He turned and laughed.

"There are dreams and there are dreams," he said. "The guys who pay me to shoot ducks here all say they'd trade places with me any time. The thing is, they don't have a clue."

"About what?"

Drake set down a plate and leaned back against the sink. His eyes rested on her a few seconds and then lifted to the wetlands outside.

"About the loneliness. About living on the fringe. Don't get me wrong. I wouldn't trade with any of them. Hell, I'm so much a loner now, I couldn't. I drive into Colusa for groceries and almost break out in hives. Colusa! Population seventy-five hundred. I went down to San Francisco four years ago for my uncle's funeral and damn near passed out."

"But you choose to live this way. No one is forcing you. So there's more that bothers you, isn't there," she said. "More than your life as a modern-day hermit."

He sighed. *Where is she going with this?* But he continued. "Yeah, a bunch. Like the fact I have to watch my backside twenty-four seven because of my land-hungry rich neighbor. Hell, I can handle the soli-tude and I don't care much about money, so long as I have enough to take decent care of this place and provide a quality experience for my members. It's the feeling I'm a spot of grease on a hot skillet that gets to me. One thing about my neighbor, he's predictable. That fun I had the other day is sure to cost me."

Drake dried the last dish and looked up at the big clock mounted beneath a stuffed pheasant. "Time to call for a tow and get that fish tank of yours out of my canal. Then I'll drive you to Redding and buy you a new one. Whatever your insurance doesn't cover, I'll pick up."

"You don't have to do that," she said.

"Of course I don't," he said. "But I will. Read the fine print at the beginning of the road: 'All cars dunked in the canal replaced free of charge.'"

She laughed and let the robe slip away. "That tow truck will take an hour to get out here, won't it?"

He smiled. "At least. And on the ride in you can tell me all about Claire Wooley. I'm off-limits the rest of the day."

Armand III pushed the button on his telephone console and cut off Louis DuBois before the lawyer could say good-bye. Stilton had heard all he needed to hear.

Condemnation. A harsh word and an elegant solution. All Armand needed to do was find a proper condemning authority. Any public entity would do. A utility company would be even better. He picked up his leather folio of unlisted telephone numbers and rifled to the Ds.

Chester Durant was CEO of Gas-En, the country's largest energy conglomerate and the holding company for Nor-Cal Gas and Electric Company. Nor-Cal was in Chapter 11, and the front pages frequently featured Durant as he shuttled between hearings of a Senate committee and the California Public Utilities Commission. Nor-Cal's principal assets and most of its cash had been funneled into Gas-En partnerships owned by Durant and his fellow board members before Gas-En imploded, leaving thousands of employee-shareholders holding empty retirement plans, the Teapot Dome of the new millennium. The investigating politicians, most of them beneficiaries of generous campaign contributions from Gas-En, missed no opportunity to skewer their benefactor as they decried the manipulations of Durant and his pack of thieves.

Ah, Chet, thought Armand as he dialed, *you're my kind of guy. Sure glad you like to hunt ducks.*

The call was forwarded to Durant's assistant, who informed Armand that Durant was tied up in Washington for the week. "Fine, I'll call him when he's back in Houston," said Armand. *Perfect,* he thought, after he'd hung up. *Poor bastard could use a break from all those hypocrites looking for scapegoats. Get him out to Gable Farms. Kill some ducks. Talk some condemnation. What could be better?*

It didn't take Drake long to convince the insurance adjuster that Claire's Corolla was totaled. One night in 442 would do in a Sherman tank. The car would smell like marsh forever, and there was no way to get the muck out of its innards. Claire tucked the check in her purse, and they set off for Redding, where one of Drake's shooting members owned a car dealership.

"OK," said Drake, "your turn." The blur of I-5's winter-barren orchards hung lush with the promise of fruit to come.

Claire sighed, apparently dreading the moment.

"Come on," Drake said. "I opened up to you and it wasn't so bad. Hell, may even have done me some good."

"All right," she said. "Be kind."

Drake soon learned that Claire was half Klamath Indian. He had followed the antics of her father, Pete Wooley, in the newspapers. Wooley was a notorious Indian activist who had spearheaded a movement to curb water diversion in the Klamath Basin, the huge volcanic bowl 250 miles northeast of Waterloo. Tule Lake and the Klamath Basin formed a natural breeding ground and resting place for millions of migrating waterfowl. Months earlier, rice and potato farmers had literally gone to war against the Indians and the federal government, the farmers steadfast in their claim that crops took precedence over the Indians' right to harvest salmon from the Klamath River. Shots had been fired, and government-installed padlocks on water weirs had been blasted away.

Just a week earlier, Drake had picked up a *New York Times* and chuckled over a full-page spread featuring a photo of Wooley cradling a suckerfish, considered by most whites to be a trash fish, best left to die on the bank. The accompanying article dealt with irrigation cutbacks mandated by the Endangered Species Act to ensure adequate water for the endangered suckerfish of Upper Klamath Lake, revered as sacred by the Klamath Indians. Behind Wooley stood two boys, irreverently holding their noses.

"My nephews," Claire said, wincing. "Twins. They're terrors." She went on to tell Drake about the Indian casino at Riverbend and how her father and most of her relatives lived in comfortable suburban-style homes with RVs and expensive boats parked in the driveway.

"And you work at Walmart?" Drake said.

She looked out the passenger window. "I moved away too soon. To receive income from the casino, I had to be a member of the tribe in 1991. I left in 1988 because there was no work, and I was tired of watching my relatives drink themselves to death on welfare money. Now they're all rich, including my father, and have no interest in sharing the spoils. It's happened all over the country. Once an Indian casino gets established, tribal loyalty means just one thing: Who can we cut out in order to keep more for ourselves?"

Drake had no response, and they drove on in silence. Finally Claire drew her legs up beneath her and turned in her seat toward him. "Well?"

"Well, what?"

"What do you think of your new girlfriend?"

Drake let one hand drift from the steering wheel to her knee and laughed. "I'm with your nephews. Suckerfish stink. If your daddy wants to save something sacred, he should knock off the bullshit and concentrate on getting the water turned back on in the Klamath Basin. Ducks, now there's something sacred. And ducks need water."

An hour later Drake presented Claire the keys to a new, cranberry SUV and kissed her good-bye.

"Nice young woman," Henry Neeley said to Drake as Claire pulled out of Neeley Motors. "Niece or something?"

Drake's eyes tracked Claire's new car until it turned at the corner and disappeared.

"Or something," he said. "See you this weekend?"

Neeley looked up at the sky. "You bet. Paper says this new system will bring lots of rain. Should drive down a bunch of new birds. Flood warnings, even."

Drake looked north, up the valley. Dark, as far as he could see. How had he missed that?

Every five years or so, the Sacramento Valley was deluged by torrential rains. Floodwaters spilled over riverbanks, overwhelmed levees and left the maze of canals and creeks that laced the valley under anywhere from five to ten feet of water. On those occasions, Drake's hunting took on an added dimension of sport, taught to him by his father: joining a number of valley outlaws who adhered to the maxim that they had the right to hunt anywhere they could go on "navigable waters."

For Adam Green, and then Drake, the navigable waters most accessible to them were those that covered Gable Farms and their ancestral heritage, the 1,500 acres of Waterloo sold by the Greens to Armand Stilton Jr. in 1955.

Of course, the Stiltons objected to penetrations of their privileged sanctuary by riffraff. In flood years Drake's pushing of the high-water envelope kept game wardens and the county sheriff busy responding to angry calls from the Stiltons, followed by chases over wind-driven floodwaters, rarely resulting in apprehension. Drake knew the waters and shifting channels better than his pursuers. The two times law enforcement had cornered him were when he'd been looking for downed ducks and had cut his margin of escape too close. Each time, Judge Bell had agreed there were technical flaws in the prosecution's cases and Drake had avoided the standard $1,000 trespassing fine.

"Gotta go, Henry," Drake said to Neeley. "Thanks for the deal on the SUV."

"My pleasure, Drake. Watch out though. Those 'or somethings' can ruin a duck hunter."

On the drive back to Waterloo, Neeley's crack gnawed at Drake. He'd just granted Neeley five years of duck hunting in payment for Claire's new rig—the cash equivalent of $50,000. *What* am *I doing*, he wondered. *Just what in hell am I doing?*

CHAPTER 9

Ladies Day. Many duck clubs have one. Hunting historians may disagree on many things, but on the concept of Ladies Day, there is unanimity.

Duck season, because it spans Thanksgiving, Christmas, and New Year's, imposes on many domestic pairings a level of stress over and above that already inherent in the holidays. The husband and father is gone for days on end. No shopping, no cooking, no holding a ladder while his mate strings decorations or tops the tree, no driving her around as she braves the crowds and markets. When he does surface, he smells bad, sleeps all day, and often can't remember his children's names.

Oh, there are some wives who have come to view duck season as a welcome respite, particularly as the Old Boy lapses more and more into Geezerdom. But, on the whole, the entire quadrant of a year consumed by duck season is viewed by the non-hunter as an expensive time-wasting frolic that deprives her of a second pair of hands and legs during that time of year she'd rather escape to Hawaii. Like Donna Stilton.

So, for generations, the accumulated guilt of duck hunters has resulted in one weekend a season when wives are wined and dined at the duck club. Many of the beneficiaries of this largesse would just as soon skip the honor, as duck clubs are notorious for their marginal toilet and shower facilities with posters of women in anatomically impossible positions.

Of course, this was not the case at Gable Farms. In fact, the members' wives had come to view the weekend as a welcome break from the holiday frenzy. Not only were the accommodations five-star, the service and attention to detail were unmatched. For that, they had Jim Quesenberry to thank.

Early in his twenty-five-year stint at Gable Farms, Jim had learned that a successful Ladies Day went a long way. It smoothed troubled waters at home, helped allay suspicions about orgies, mistresses, and the like, and, in rare instances, made hunting converts of his once-a-year guests. Not that they would have much opportunity to pursue their newfound passion. An unwritten and unquestioned rule forbid their presence at any other time during the season.

Donna Stilton was Jim's prize student. She had taken to duck hunting like a Labrador pup. She had attended every Ladies Day since her marriage to Three, and she always insisted on Jim guiding her during her stay. In the off season she practiced calling and attended a trap and skeet range where she honed her shooting skills. Her calling lacked something, probably because she treated the duck call more as a phallic symbol than an instrument of quasi-musical potential. But her shooting made up for it. Nearly every time she fired, something fell. Jim considered her to be one of the finest shots he'd ever seen. He took pride in the fact he had taught her to hunt and that she bested most of the paying members.

In spite of the added burden, Jim looked forward to the weekend. The two mornings each year he shared a duck blind with Donna were worth it. Not only was she a great shot, her wit and intelligence distinguished her from the others, all of whom were impressed beyond words with themselves, their husband's wealth, and their high grip on society's ladder. Donna reminded Jim of his old Arkansas sweetheart, not that he ever crossed the line, or even came close. Jim loved his job at Gable Farms and would tolerate almost anything to keep it—even sharing a duck blind twice a year with a lovely slice of lush forbidden fruit.

There was another reason Jim Quesenberry looked forward to his hunting sessions with Donna. After each Ladies Day, she sent him a Stilton Foundation check for $5,000, payable to Cedar Hills, the rehabilitation home in Little Rock that housed his crippled sister, a victim of cerebral palsy from trauma at birth.

"I know what a terrible strain that puts on a family," Donna had told him in the duck blind on the Saturday morning of their second Ladies Day weekend. "I have a brother who was in a terrible car accident. He's a paraplegic." The first check had followed.

With the money from Donna Jim had funded concerts at Cedar Hills, a small patient library, trips to local events, campouts, and even an appearance by champion duck callers from all over the country. Of all he had done to entertain Cedar Hills residents, the duck callers had been the biggest hit. For five hours they had quacked, chuckled, grunted, hooted, and cried until tears of delight and laughter rained from the wheelchair and gurney-bound audience.

"You know, Jim," the Cedar Hills director had said to him after the duck callers, "I think these entertainments you provide are the best thing that happens here. It's too bad we don't have a small theatre and stage. Then we could *really* put on some shows." And that became Jim Quesenberry's dream.

Early Friday afternoon Jim set off in an ATV for a last quick tour of the Gable Farms clubhouse and Members Quarters, his laminated checklist on the seat beside him.

For their initial million-dollar payment, each Gable Farms member received a lease on a three-bedroom, octagonal structure set five feet above ground on concrete piers designed to ensure that no floodwater would ever soak the Oriental carpets or custom furnishings.

The eight homes formed their own octagon around an octagonal main structure, the Clubhouse. In it was an elaborately carved mahogany bar from a turn-of-the-century San Francisco hotel, a paneled game room with two billiard tables, side tables for dominoes and cards, a dining room with panoramic views south toward the hunting grounds, and a modern kitchen that any restaurateur would envy. A circular staircase led to a smaller, octagonal cupola and an observatory, complete with a state-of-the-art, electronically guided telescope. The whole complex had been featured in *Architectural Digest*.

Jim's Ladies Day checklist called for once-a-year linens in each residence, toiletries from Fortnum and Mason, fresh-cut flowers in crystal vases, a decorative selection of imported waters, and an array of aperitifs. Gone from sight were the hunting and fishing magazines along with copies of *Playboy* and *Penthouse.* Instead, end tables and coffee tables displayed copies of *Vogue, Cosmopolitan,* and *Women's World.* None of the women were fooled, but they appreciated the gesture.

Jim completed his rounds at three in the afternoon, just as Three's Hummer turned into the gravel parking area. The forecasted rain was just beginning to fall.

"Mrs. Stilton, greetings again," Jim said, extending an arm as an assist from the oversized vehicle. It always reminded him of one of the arctic all-terrain transports from *The Empire Strikes Back.*

Donna smiled down and said in a voice loud enough for Armand to hear, "We go through this every year, Jim. It's Donna."

Jim offered a weak, self-conscious smile and helped her down.

At 6:58 a.m. on Saturday morning twenty-three minutes of legal shooting time had passed and no ducks had shown. To the south, over on Waterloo, the shooting was furious and steady.

"Sounds like a war zone," Jim said.

It had rained all night, and a steady shower continued to drench the Butte Sink.

Donna Stilton cupped her hands and blew into them.

"Here," Jim said, reaching into his pack on the floor of the blind. He drew out a pair of Gore-Tex gloves.

She shook her head and smiled. "No thanks, I shoot better bare."

Jim let that image warm him as he scanned for birds.

"Jim," she asked, "why are there so many ducks over Waterloo and none here?"

He shrugged. "That's the way of it. Sometimes it's the other way around."

Every member's boat that Jim had seen pull away from the Gable Farms dock that morning was carrying a Roto Duck. Drake Green had banned them on Waterloo and, this morning at least, Waterloo's members were out-gunning their Gable Farms neighbors ten to one.

The morning wore on, as only a duckless morning can. Low rain clouds scudded overhead, and slowly the optimism that sends duck hunters into the cold darkness gave way to reality. Jim twitched as he confronted the fact that it was to be one of those days when the only sport would be scenery and conversation. The scenery took care of itself as the cloud-blotted sun and the Buttes to the east formed a kaleidoscope of changing color and shapes. The conversation, he knew, would be a problem.

In the past, when he'd taken Donna hunting, and they'd been favored by the Duck God, her excitement and Jim's sense of accomplishment had spanned the gulf between them. When the ducks were not flying, like today, Jim felt a prickly discomfort at his inability to fill the gaps. Though Donna had little in common with the other wives and always went out of her way in her attempts to put him at ease, Jim could not shake the fact she was the wife of the man who signed his paychecks and made possible his life on one of the country's premier duck clubs.

With the exception of those awful times he had to share a blind with Three himself, Jim usually was an excellent source of duck-blind humor and banter. Much of that art he'd learned from Drake Green, considered by all the pros in the valley and the Butte Sink to be the consummate gab master. From politics, the economy, religion, and sex to hunting and fishing anecdotes—fact, fiction, and everything in between—Drake was known for his ability to make a duck-blind partner forget they had gone to all that trouble to shoot ducks.

By ten, it was clear the morning was going to be a dud. Donna didn't seem to mind as she filled the time keeping as dry as possible while she hummed to herself, commented on the sky or the Buttes, or launched into chatter about things she had recently seen or done. As Jim spent virtually all his time tending to Gable Farms and hadn't seen a movie since *Raiders of the Lost Ark*, he simply listened and nodded, tormented as he groped to come up with something, anything, but never finding the hook.

"So, how are things at Cedar Hills?" Donna asked, finally.

Jim brightened. Here, at last, was something he could talk about, endlessly, if need be.

He told her about the September campout, when he'd hired five vans, loaded up all the Cedar Hill residents who could make the trip, and caravanned them deep into the Ozarks to a private campground equipped to handle their needs. For five days his charges had fished from the bank of a pine-studded lake, rolled their wheelchairs along paved, forested paths, and enjoyed sing-alongs and ghost stories around a blazing campfire. Then he told her what a hit the duck callers had been. As he finished, he cut himself short, aware that telling her of the director's comment about a theatre at Cedar Hills would sound like he was rattling the beggar's cup for more.

"You started to say something about the director, Jim. What was it?"

Jim scanned the clouds. *God, what I'd give for some ducks to fly in right now.*

"Jim?"

"A theatre," he blurted. "The director said what a world of difference a small theatre would make. The residents could do plays, have more concerts..." He stopped, reluctant to reveal the obsessive grip the idea had on him.

He felt the sweep of her eyes—wide, full, and somehow thoughtful.

The next morning Donna was the first in for breakfast.

"Well, you're eager this morning," Jim said, as he filled her coffee cup.

She smiled. "Eager. Well, that's one word for it."

Jim blinked and then dismissed her strange comment as just another quirk of the rich. While he preferred the company of Three's pretty wife to any of the rest of them, even she could be a bit eccentric.

"There's a nice north wind this morning," he said. "Should be ducks all over the place. Not like yesterday. I guarantee we'll have a great shoot."

Others began to trickle in, and the hush of hangovers interrupted by the necessity of a 4:30 wake-up call settled over the dining room. Only two of the remaining five wives made it, the other three sending word that they'd had enough and would be sleeping in. Finally, at five, Three appeared, looking haggard. Jim judged he'd stayed up late drinking and playing dominoes with the die-hards. Three poured himself a cup of coffee and took his seat at the head of the table.

"Think I'll join you and Jim today," he said to Donna, seated half-way down one side of the long table. Jim, twenty feet away in the kitchen, saw the momentary clutch in her expression and hoped that Three had missed it. Thirty seconds went by, filled by the clink of silver and the increased tempo of conversation as the caffeine kicked in.

Donna quietly withdrew and carried her plate to the kitchen. She returned to the dining room with a fresh cup of coffee and pulled up a chair alongside her husband. She nuzzled his ear and whispered something. A minute later Three announced, "Well, boys, I'm giving lessons today. Who's my lucky student? Come on now, don't all raise your hands at once."

Laughter percolated from the group, recognized by Jim as the forced bonhomie of their dilemma. With Jim committed to Donna, one of the hapless seven was stuck.

Finally Nick Pappas said, "I'd be honored, Armand." Pappas owned the California Grizzlies, the state's new NFL franchise. He'd made his millions in the wholesale produce business and, as the newest Gable Farms member, shouldered the burden as heads nodded approval.

Relief settled over the room. Donna stood to go put on her hunting clothes. As she passed the kitchen, she winked at Jim.

The rain slowed to a steady drizzle, though heavy clouds to the west and south promised more to come. True to Jim's prediction, the north wind had scattered ducks all over the Butte Sink. Darting, jinking teal whizzed by, birds that challenged the best of shots.

By eight thirty, Donna, shooting with machine-like precision, had her limit and was working on Jim's. She remained cool and detached, as if in another time and place. Absent were the delighted shouts that usually accompanied each kill, and the vibrant praise she'd laud on Jethro when the stocky Lab swam back to the blind with its prize.

Finally, the bonanza ended. The barrage of shooting that had filled the Sink quit, replaced by the quiet fall of a steady rain.

"Well," Jim said, "that was about as good as it gets."

Donna propped her shotgun against the corner of the blind but kept her silence. Jim frowned. The best morning of the season and it was like she had missed the whole thing.

"Is something wrong?" he ventured, at last.

She bit her lip and stared at him.

Oh, Christ, he thought. *Whatever's coming, I don't want it.*

But then she smiled and her eyes widened.

"Jim," she said, "this is a very dangerous sport, isn't it? Two people in a cramped area with weapons capable of blowing them apart."

Jesus, he thought. *Where'd this come from?*

"Uh, you bet it is," he said. "Last year a guy in a club just north of here shot off his partner's hand. Horrible."

She appeared to ponder this and then said, "I suppose other things could happen. I mean, besides one person shooting another. The shotguns themselves. You could hurt yourself without someone else being responsible, couldn't you?"

Jim hesitated. "Well, yes. That's why we always clean our guns after hunting and check them carefully before we shoot again. About the worst thing that could happen is if something plugged the barrel. When that happens, the whole receiver body of the gun explodes. Takes the top half of the shooter with it. Not a pretty sight."

Jim concentrated on the sound of each raindrop as he watched her process this.

"The reason I ask," she said, finally, "is that I worry so about Armand. I mean, he's so preoccupied with business most of the time and not very attentive to details like getting the oil in his car changed, getting a haircut, things like that. I don't see him taking time to clean his shotgun or tending to all the fine points of gun safety, like you and the rest."

"I always clean Three's gun," Jim said, biting his tongue. "I mean Armand. Sorry."

She chuckled and leaned near him. "I've called him worse," she said in a mock whisper. Then she straightened. "I'm so relieved to hear that you take care of that for him, Jim. Armand trusts you implicitly. I know that. I can't see him ever checking his gun before setting off and using it. He probably has come to rely on you completely."

She gazed upward, her face slack and her eyes now those of someone witnessing tears of blood from a holy shrine. This brief halo of beatitude crumbled in the grit of her voice. "If Armand were to have some terrible accident it would leave me a devastated but very wealthy widow. I'd have to find ways to ease my grief and fill my time. You know, projects." Her eyes lowered. She looked up seconds later and a wide smile brightened her face.

"Did I ever tell you that Armand made me chairperson of the Stilton Foundation? I suppose he thought it would be a good way to keep me busy. Oh, we have a board, but they're all my friends and do what I say. I give away millions each year to charities and worthy causes. I'm always on the lookout."

Her smile disappeared as she stepped closer and looked him full in the face. "Like funding a state-of-the-art performing arts theatre at Cedar Hills."

CHAPTER 10

Drake waved from the deck as the last of his members' SUVs began the slow trek down his road, which was a churned channel of mud. All ten members had limited on both Saturday and Sunday morning, reassuring Drake that no matter how the hunting was the rest of the season, they'd had at least one memorable weekend.

He stepped back into the Palace, glad to have it to himself again. His member weekends, full of camaraderie and the boisterous vitality of men shedding their workweek woes, left him drained. Like his friend Jim Quesenberry, Drake saw to the details that made the duck club a place of refuge and cheer. Drake's Waterloo, while not the grand enterprise his grandfather had maintained or the lavish spread of Gable Farms, satisfied ten serious hunters, none of whom could afford a club like Gable Farms and would have opted for Waterloo even if they could.

Drake pulled a bottle of beer from the refrigerator and settled into the overstuffed chair he'd found at the Goodwill store in Redding. He turned on the television and found Sunday afternoon's football game. He didn't know who was playing and didn't care. Within ten minutes he began to nod off, his body reclaiming the output expended providing the best he could for his members. As sleep claimed him, he thought of the rain and the rising water. Soon it would be time to go hunting again—his way.

"Chet, glad you're back from the wars," Armand quipped into the telephone. From what he'd read in the newspapers, he thought it lucky that Gas-En's CEO wasn't on his way to prison.

"Armand," said Durant, his voice heavy, "you have no idea. These sonsabitches, including my very good friend, the president, and his henchman the attorney general, want my head. It's like I raped and ax-murdered their grandchildren."

"Well, take heart, Chet. These things blow over. Hell, within a couple months the witch hunters will be onto some congressman's tryst or some senator's lie about what he did or didn't do in some war. Listen, here's why I called. Right now the duck hunting out here is fantastic. I want you to get in that jet of yours and come out here. It'll help take your mind off all this crap."

Armand heard a sigh, then silence.

"Sure sounds tempting," Durant said. "In fact, I'm due in Sacramento next week. Might as well come out a few days early. Only thing is, all my stuff is over in Louisiana. I hunted there a month ago and was hoping to get back before the season ended."

"No trouble," Armand said. "I've got everything you need at Gable Farms. Just bring yourself and enough cash for a few domino hands. You've got some left, haven't you?" Armand laughed at his own joke, but cut his amusement short when Durant remained silent. "It's settled, then. I'll have someone pick you up Friday at the Colusa Airport. Just let me know the time. Oh, and Chet?"

"Yes?"

"You're still in charge at Nor-Cal Gas and Electric, aren't you?"

"Yes, for now. Probably not for too much longer, though. The bankruptcy judge is making noises. I may have to resign before next spring."

"Not until then? Perfect. See you Friday."

Armand hung up, tilted back in his desk chair, and closed his eyes. *OK, Mr. Drake Green, you thought blowing away my roto-duck was pretty cute. Let's see you blow away a condemnation lawsuit.*

Two days had passed since Donna Stilton's eyes had bored into Jim Quesenberry's soul and she'd delivered what Jim had no doubt was her husband's proposed death sentence. It had been two days without sleep, buffered only by long walks on the property that had fused day and night into a gray blur of turmoil.

Of all people to depart planet Earth before their natural time, Three was probably Jim's first choice. The man had never earned a dollar and projected the magisterial arrogance of Henry VIII. Were it not for the fact that Three had inherited Gable Farms, he would not be shooting there. The members stomached him simply because he was their key to great hunting at a legendary site. Jim had no doubt that if Three were to die during duck season, the seats at his funeral reserved for Gable Farms' members would be vacant.

But murder? It was hardly in Jim's vocabulary, much less his emotional arsenal.

Would it be murder? Donna had described an accident, an event that tragically visited hunters as an infrequent reminder that their lives were as fragile as the lives of the creatures they killed.

As Jim walked and pondered, he caressed an envelope he'd just received from Cedar Hills. The director had enclosed a scrawled letter from his sister, along with a photograph that displayed her askew in her wheelchair, an ever-present glisten at the corner of her mouth. Jim's eyes teared from the frustration that he couldn't do more for her. He remembered his mother's pain as she lay dying, shattered from years of caring and toil.

Jim looked toward the sky and was surprised to see that day had reclaimed itself. There was a break in the clouds, and the rain had stopped. To the east a rainbow arched, touching down near the base of the Buttes. His mother had adored rainbows. Near the end she'd whispered to him, "Jimmie, whenever you see a rainbow, it will be me smiling down at you."

Jim shook his head and smiled. "Thanks, Mom. I know what I have to do and just how to do it." He started back toward the Gable Farms clubhouse. It was Wednesday, and Three was arriving Friday, along with some fly-in guest. Jim would see that he had the hunt of a lifetime. As for Three's guest, well, it would give him something to talk about for a long, long time. Of that, Jim was certain.

CHAPTER 11

Wednesday, December 7.

This time Drake met Claire at the entrance. Even her new SUV would not have handled the deep muck. A week of solid rain had transformed much of the Butte Sink into a giant lake. Fences, roads, levees, and canals had been swallowed by the slowly rising water. Were it not for the foresight of some long-forgotten county engineer, vehicle access to the handful of duck clubs nestled against the Buttes' western toe would have disappeared. West Side Road, a paved, narrow cow track, had been intentionally carved into the slope of the Buttes, twenty feet above the Sink's floor. It remained high and dry in all but catastrophic conditions.

Claire parked in the widened area at Waterloo's gate and ran through the rain to Drake's waiting ATV.

"I don't know why I ran," she panted. "I'll be soaked by the time we get in."

Drake smiled. "We'll have to get you out of those wet clothes soon as possible. Happy birthday."

Claire climbed onto the machine and clung to Drake's waist. As they drove down what remained of his road, the water in the canal on their right was scarcely a foot from the top.

"What happens when the water comes over the edge?" she shouted in his ear.

"You'll be my prisoner," he called back. "Want to talk terms?"

As Drake steered the clawing vehicle in toward the slope that led up to the Palace, he couldn't remember when he'd been happier.

Later, her feet propped next to his on a bench in front of the wood stove, Claire shifted against Drake's chest in the hug of his huge chair.

"Guess what?" she said.

"I'd never."

She smiled. "No, you wouldn't. My mother and father sent me a letter. They want me to come up and visit. It's the first I've heard from them in two years."

Drake grinned and dropped his voice. "Him wantum smoke peace pipe?"

Claire pulled away and drilled him with her dark eyes. Then she covered her mouth and laughed.

"More like Big Chief wants to climb back in his squaw's tepee, I think. My mother hates what that casino did to our family. She put him up to it."

She again drew close. "So, want to come?"

Drake did a quick mental calculation. If the rain continued as forecasted, ideal "navigable water" conditions should be reached in three or four days. After the flood peaked, it would take several days for the water to recede. As soon as his weekend hunters pulled out, he'd be ready to forage among the forbidden fruit of Gable Farms. After that, a prudent retreat would be in order. Why not the Klamath Basin? He had some connections up there and had heard the goose hunting was at its prime.

"Middle of next week work for you?" he asked.

"You'll come?" she said, excited. "I never thought I'd get you out of here during duck season."

Drake shrugged. "There's life beyond ducks," he said, not meaning a word of it.

Jim made the fourth pass of the cleaning rod through each barrel of Three's prized Parker AHE 12-gauge side-by-side. He held the gun up, letting light from the shop's overhead fluorescent tubes infiltrate and reflect the sparkling results of his work.

"Like new," he said. "Wish I could think of something else."

He laid the gun on the workbench and stood in front of his MEC reloader. Jim couldn't remember when he'd last laid out cash for store-bought shotgun shells, preferring the consistency and reliability of the ones he loaded himself. Most of the Gable Farms members, including Three, had taken to buying their shells from Jim, providing him with extra cash and something do to on off-season nights.

He remained still a full minute, the consequences of what he was contemplating tumbling his mind like a spinning Bingo cage. His sister's number came up, and he set to work.

First, he pulled a spent 20-gauge shell from a wooden crate and ran it through the resizing cycle of the reloader, popping out the old primer. He went to the next cycle, loading in a new primer and then, rather than progress to the powder-loading cycle, withdrew the shell from the reloader.

He reached onto the shelf over the bench and pulled down a container of Bullseye Pistol Powder. Carefully, he weighed out forty grains. He poured the powder into the casing, returned the shell to the reloader, and packed in the wad. Next, he cycled to the shot dispenser where he dropped in one and a half ounces of shot. Two stages of crimping followed. He held the completed shell up to the light and turned it slowly. A shotgun Molotov cocktail.

He picked up the Parker, stroked it, and said, "Hate to do this to you, pal."

He slid the shell into the left barrel, then picked up a pencil. Using the eraser end, he pushed against the brass cap of the shell, slowly moving it forward until the rim of the cap caught on the ridge at the end of the shell chamber forming the beginning of the barrel. He closed the breach of the gun and immediately reopened it. The shell was undetectable unless someone held the gun up and visibly inspected the barrel, something he knew Three would never do. *Damned shame,* he thought. *It is truly a lovely gun.*

When he finished, he walked over to Three's residence and slipped the gun into its place inside Three's gun cabinet. Then he looked at his watch. It was time to drive to the airport and collect Chester Durant, aka Mr. Gas.

Jim busied himself serving drinks and appetizers, and preparing dinner. Through it all he reflected on Three's true talents—scheming and manipulation. He also noted that Three seemed oblivious to the reaction of the Gable Farms members, who sat in silence while Three spun his web.

By the end of cocktail hour, Three had convinced Chester Durant that the gas under Waterloo would play a significant role in bailing out Nor-Cal Gas & Electric. Durant, an old Texas oilman himself, was impressed that "Dink" Deerlink had expressed interest.

"So, Deerlink's group is on-board?" Durant asked.

Three smiled, radiating confidence. "Well, not right now, but it's just a matter of time. As soon as Nor-Cal condemns a pipeline right of way across Green's property, he'll sell. I'm sure of it. He's a purist who won't like pipes. He'll probably run away to his place in the mountains. And once he sells to me..." Three turned to the glum circle of Gable Farms members. "I'm saving the first shares in Stilton Gas for you guys. Think of it. While you're out here shooting ducks, you can look next door to all that money you'll be making. My guess is that it'll be enough each year to pay your annual dues."

Jim paused in clearing glasses to take in the group's reaction. Nick Pappas set down his drink and stood. "That's one investment I'll pass on, Armand. I joined this club to hunt, not to tear up good duck habitat for more money. I suggest you give this whole thing more thought." His eyes swept the group. "You could lose members over it."

There was a "Here, here" and others nodded in silent agreement.

Uncomfortable seconds passed before Jim reached for the clapper of the dinner bell, a splendid bronze casting from the deck of Commodore Stilton's yacht. "Gentlemen," he announced, "dinner."

Throughout the meal, Three continued to lobby Durant, ignoring the sullen mood of the group. By dinner's end Durant was furious at a man he'd never met, an obstinate recluse named Drake Green whose short-sighted belligerence blocked delivery of a much-needed resource to rate-paying users.

"Hell, Armand, of course we'll help. Just as soon as I get back I'll tell Nor-Cal's lawyers to get started on a pipeline condemnation action across the bastard's property. We do it all the time. Once there's a pipeline, you can open your wells and go after all the gas over there. Consider it done."

Three raised his glass. "Gentlemen, this calls for a toast. Tonight we witness the birth of Stilton Gas. Somewhere, Dad's smiling, I know."

With the exception of Three and Durant, no one else was.

Saturday, December 8, 4:30 a.m.

Jim rolled over and shut off the alarm before it had a chance to go off. He wasn't sure when he'd slept, if he'd slept at all. A cold wave of panic gripped him, and he considered going to Three's residence to remove the gun from the cabinet. If caught, he'd simply say he hadn't had a chance to clean it properly and wanted to see to it before the hunters left for the blinds.

He lay in the dark, pondering this, when his room flickered with the glow of lights from across the grounds. He propped himself up and looked out the window. "Dammit," he said. Three was up, his residence lit.

Jim flopped back down. Three was many things, but a dummy wasn't one of them. Jim always cleaned Three's gun immediately after each morning's shoot. To show up at four thirty in the morning with a feeble excuse would only trigger suspicion.

At the boat dock, Jim concentrated on carrying out the usual routine. Later, when investigators would interview everyone, they'd all be able to answer that it had been just another morning at Gable Farms. The boats had been ready, motors running, and off they'd gone. Nothing out of the ordinary. Terrible accident. Makes us all remember the dangers involved. Can't take anything for granted.

After he bid Three and Chester Durant "good hunting," Jim lingered at the dock until he was satisfied everyone was out of sight and well on the way to their blinds. The boat he used to clean and repair the blinds was tied up at the end, and he stepped in. He looked at his watch: 6:43, ten minutes until legal shooting time. For Three, the fine distinction drawn by Fish and Game as to when one could start killing ducks—or, in Three's case, shoot at them—had no meaning. If a duck flew within ten minutes of the legal time, Three shot. Jim sat and listened, his ears honed in the direction of Doghouse, Three's favorite blind, and the one to which he'd headed with his well-heeled pal, Chet.

At 6:51 Jim heard a fusillade of five shots. They came from the area of Birdhouse, the blind Three had declined, despite Jim's recommendation. Jim grunted. *Wouldn't even listen to me today of all days.* He drew his parka around his neck, taking care to keep it clear of his ears.

At 7:02 a muffled "whoomph" came from the direction of Doghouse. It sounded to Jim like an explosion deep within a mine. He stiffened and waited, imagining Durant clambering into the boat to seek help, dazed by the blast and panicked by the carnage. Instead, the walkie-talkie radio in his pocket crackled.

"Jim! Jim! Get out here!"

Three's voice? Impossible. The part of Three that spoke should be mush, or worse. Jim pulled out the radio and pushed the switch.

"Jim here. Whoever's calling, go ahead."

"You fucking idiot! This is Stilton! Get out here and help me. The Parker blew up and took most of Chet with it. He's dead. I'm sure of it. Oh, God, this is terrible. Help me. Oh, God, God..."

An hour later, four sheriff's vehicles and a coroner's wagon bearing the shredded upper third of Chester Durant crowded the parking area of Gable Farms. A deputy loaded a box containing the charred stock of Armand's Parker, as well as the fragments of the receiver and peeled barrels they'd retrieved from the gore-splattered blind.

The sheriff, a rangy character who years earlier had let out he was to be called "Duke," sat across from Armand Stilton and Jim Quesenberry in the clubhouse main room. Duke, an eager hunter, though poor shot, was no stranger to Jim. The sheriff enjoyed infrequent invitations from Drake to join Jim and Drake at Waterloo, where, after Jim and Drake killed the ducks, the three of them put away fair quantities of good bourbon while telling tall stories over a duck dinner.

"So, let me sum up here," Duke said, twitching one curl of the giant handlebar moustache he'd grown around the time he'd become Duke. "This fellow Durant was your invited guest. His own plane brought him into Colusa yesterday. Jim picked him up. Right so far?"

Jim and Stilton nodded.

Duke addressed Stilton. "He hunted quail in the orchard with you yesterday afternoon, had dinner here, played cards, went to bed around ten thirty."

Stilton nodded again, as he dipped a sponge into a bowl of soapy water on the table next to him. He squeezed the sponge and began to scrub hard at the blood spots on his vest.

Duke consulted his notes. "Didn't drink much. Only a couple of Old Fashioneds before dinner, a couple glasses of wine, maybe a brandy or two."

"Best as I can remember," mumbled Armand. "I wasn't paying attention to what he drank. He seemed fine."

Duke returned to his notes. "Got up at four thirty. Any reason so early? Shooting time wasn't for another two and a half hours."

Armand shrugged, still intent on his scrubbing. "It was him. Couldn't sleep, I guess. Maybe the time change, maybe…The man's been under a lot of pressure."

"Mmmm." Duke toyed with the other moustache curl. "You all went down to the boat dock around six."

"That's right. Takes fifteen or twenty minutes to get to the blinds. We like to be ready at shooting time."

"Oh, you'd have time to spare, all right," Duke said. Jim spotted the almost imperceptible wink.

Duke suddenly changed the pace and subject. "So, you and Durant shot some quail yesterday afternoon, right?"

"Yes," said Three, looking up. "We covered that already."

Duke smiled. "Carried twenty-gauge guns, I'll bet."

"Yes," Armand answered. He set down the sponge.

"Wear a jacket?" Duke asked. Armand nodded.

"Same jacket you lent to Durant this morning?" Again, Armand nodded.

"So, after you loaded your stuff and the guns in the boat, you set off for the blind, you at the motor on the stern seat and the deceased up front with the dog and decoys."

Armand looked up. "Chester Durant. He wasn't 'the deceased' then."

Duke ignored this. "When you got to the blind, you gave him some twelve-gauge shells?"

"Yes, a fresh box. He opened it and dumped them into the pockets of…my God."

Duke smiled. He spread his large hand across his mouth and accomplished a one-handed double moustache twirl. His voice lowered to accusation level. Jim sat forward.

"You didn't empty the pockets of that jacket after you boys shot quail, did you?"

Three's eyes darted from Jim to the sheriff.

"Why...y...yes, I did," he stammered. He drew himself up, indignant. "I always take old shells out of my hunting jacket. He glared at Jim, the message clear. Any contradiction and Jim would be packing.

"And, then, in the blind, you insisted your guest use your gun, correct?"

"Sheriff, they were both my guns. He didn't bring one. He saw the Parker, admired it, and I said, 'Go ahead, use it.' Next thing I knew, it blew up. God, what a sight...I never..." Armand buried his head in his hands.

Duke stood and walked over to the fireplace, where he struck a pose. *Christ, Duke,* thought Jim. *You've been watching too many movies.*

"It's clear what happened," Duke announced. "Somehow a twenty-gauge shell got mixed up with the twelve-gauge shells you gave Durant. Probably was a shell left in your jacket from quail hunting. He must have loaded it in, and then loaded a twelve-gauge in behind it. You saw what happens."

The Duke made a grand sweep with his arm. "Hell, I buy shells from Jim. I know how careful he is. The *only* way that shell got there was from your jacket." Duke's gaze bore down on Three.

"Could just as well have been you layin' out there in that meat wagon," said Duke.

Duke scratched his chin and chuckled. "Guess those folks back east will have to make do just talkin' about how bad the poor sucker was. Can't very well send him to prison now."

Jim nodded at Duke, careful to reflect his admiration at the sheriff's masterful powers of deduction.

CHAPTER 12

Signs of something terrible at Gable Farms swept across the Butte Sink like a freezing north wind. Drake, in a blind with Claire, heard the sirens and followed the flash of strobes that bounced eerily off the low clouds as the sheriff's cruisers sped along Butte Slough Road. All his members had begun to chatter on their walkie-talkies. Several flights of ducks cleared Waterloo before things settled down and the members returned to the business at hand.

"Let's pack it in," Drake told Claire. "They might need help with whatever's going on over there." He didn't try to explain that he never passed up an excuse to visit Gable Farms when Three was there. While Stilton could marshal an army of lawyers to torment Drake, Drake knew his mere presence raised Three's blood pressure fifty points.

Back at the Palace, Drake loaded his medical kit onto the ATV, and they took off. When they got to the road, he stopped next to Claire's car. "I'll call you," he said.

She shook her head. "I'm coming with you. Maybe I can help."

Drake thought about this a few seconds and decided there was no point in arguing.

On the way down the paved, all-year road into Gable Farms, the coroner's wagon passed them, headed out.

"That doesn't look good," called Drake, over his shoulder.

They arrived at the parking area to find deputies getting into cars. Jim Quesenberry, Duke, and Armand III were just coming out of the clubhouse. A subdued group of members huddled on the large veranda encircling the structure.

"God," said Claire, as she stepped off and looked around, "what a place."

"There's the owner," Drake said, nodding toward the clubhouse. "Wish you'd met him first?"

She gave him a kick.

"Let's find out what's happened," he said, and started toward the clubhouse.

"Morning, Duke, Jim," he said. He extended his hand to Three. "Armand."

Three ignored the gesture. "What are you doing here? We've had enough trouble for one morning."

"Came to see if you needed help," said Drake. He looked at the sheriff. "Duke?"

Duke took Drake by the shoulder and led him a few steps away. "Three's shotgun blew up. What happens when you shove a twenty-gauge shell in a twelve-gauge gun and follow it with a twelve-gauge shell. Killed his guest."

Drake frowned. He'd heard of such things but deemed them practically impossible, particularly with someone like Jim around, whose professionalism virtually blanketed the ineptitude of his boss. He filed Duke's account away, something to ponder. "Anything I can do?"

Duke shook his head. "Nope. Thanks, though. Pretty cut and dried. Hunting accident, pure and simple."

They stepped back over to the group, where Drake introduced Claire to Jim and Armand III. Jim took her hand, obviously pleased for a respite from the pall that had settled over the place.

Three merely nodded once in her direction. "Green," he said, "you're not welcome here. You know that. But as long as you're here, you might as well write a check for the Roto-Duck you destroyed. One hundred fifty dollars, including the battery. Then leave."

Duke's eyebrows arched. Drake smiled and said, "I didn't know the Roto-Duck season had opened, Armand. Look, I just came over to see if I could be of some help, one neighbor to another." He looked up toward the clouds. Normally he wouldn't give notice of his outlaw intentions, but Three's bad manners were impossible to ignore.

Besides, Three was upset over the accident, an opportunity not to be missed. "Lots more rain on the way, and that water's coming up nicely. In a day or so a man will be able to take a boat anywhere he wants around here. All perfectly legal, too, you know. Navigable waters."

Three reddened. "Now, listen here—"

Drake motioned to Claire. He winked at Jim and the sheriff. "You two be on your toes, now."

Armand III fumed the entire three-hour drive home. Not only had that klutz Durant cost him his precious Parker, he'd blown himself up before he'd acted on the condemnation project. Now Armand would have to find someone else to ramrod his pipeline across Waterloo. Without the pipeline he had no Texans, and without the Texans he had no gas. Oh, there were other gas entrepreneurs out there, Armand had met them—conservative, responsible businessmen who reported to corporate boards and preferred to deal directly with the owner of the land under which the gas lay. Deerlink's high-flying small band was different—colorful outlaws who appreciated Armand's scheme to drive Drake Green off Waterloo in order to acquire it for themselves.

The picture of Drake Green setting off in a boat loaded with decoys and skimming across floodwater toward Gable Farms fed Armand's fury. By the time he reached Ross, he'd worked himself into an apoplectic rage.

"Armand! What's wrong?" Donna asked as he stormed through the door. It registered only faintly that she seemed surprised to see him.

"Everything," he snapped. "Get me a drink."

She went to the bar in his den and came back with a straight Scotch. He tossed it down.

"Well?" she said.

"Horrible thing happened. Chet Durant loaded the wrong size shell in my Parker. Exploded and killed him. Stupid bastard."

Her reaction was not what he'd expected. She blinked several times, her face deadpan. She took the empty glass and headed back to the den. "Another?" she called. "I'll join you."

Everyone had cleared out, the members queasy about hanging around for their usual Saturday naps, domino games, dinner, and the Sunday morning shoot. Jim was grateful to have the place to himself—very grateful. His masquerade of professional detachment felt paper thin and was crumbling fast.

How could things have gone so wrong? To his knowledge Three had never lent the Parker to anyone. *Christ, why this time?*

He paced the empty clubhouse, reluctant to return to his residence, a large double-wide set on a permanent foundation behind a grove of oak trees, well out of the members' view. Even though the clubhouse was vacant and quiet, he felt connected there. Its furnishings, paintings, photographs, and other memorabilia of six decades of duck hunters surrounded him and brought comfort.

He pulled a beer from the bar's refrigerator and nursed it as he continued to pace and think. At least Duke didn't suspect the truth. That was one solace.

The ringing phone on the bar jolted him.

"Gable Farms, Jim speaking."

"Jim, I'm so glad you answered." Donna Stilton's voice was unmistakable. "Are you alone there? Can you talk?"

"Yes, yes, I'm alone. They all left. You've heard what happened?"

"Yes, Armand told me when he got home. Terrible. He's asleep now. He had a few drinks and took a pill. I think the whole thing unnerved him. I've never seen him so upset."

There was a pause, and Jim let it build, at a loss himself. How much did she suspect? Did she tie it in?

"Well," she said finally, "I just wanted to let you know I'm thinking of you. I know this must be terrible for you as well."

He caught his breath and stammered, "Thanks, Mrs. Stilton, uh, Donna. Yeah, I can't remember a day like this. Hope I never see another one."

"Jim, dear, that's mainly why I called. I hope you don't either. Remember what we all learned as kids. 'If at first you don't succeed...' Good night."

Jim stared at the receiver.

Drake waited until dawn had spread across the Sink and the watery playground created by floodwaters was open to him. While high water offered opportunity, it also shielded danger. Tufts of growth, mounds of land, and jagged snags of long-dead trees lurked inches below the temporary murk that, on its surface, invited unlimited exploration.

He loaded his gear and Tar into the eighteen-foot Boston Whaler outfitted with a new thirty-horsepower, four-stroke motor he'd bought just for these occasions. Tolerating San Francisco's traffic and bustle, Drake had shopped the annual Boat Show for the ideal combination of speed, stability, and stealth. Though Duke's deputies and the game wardens had more powerful boats, their added muscle provided no advantage in the shifting maze of floodwater. The pursuers were limited by the same hazards as those they pursued. Knowledge, experience, and stealth outran horsepower every time.

Drake could handle the deputies and wardens. They were what made hunting in high water pure sport. Time after time he'd eluded them as he stretched the "navigable waters" concept and trespassed even beyond Gable Farms to poach on clubs as far as twenty miles away.

It was Jim Quesenberry whom Drake dreaded on these ventures. Like Drake, Jim had grown up in the Butte Sink and had been schooled in high-water hunting by the master, Drake's father. Out of mutual respect and Drake's appreciation of Quesenberry's conflicted position as Three's employee, an unspoken pact had emerged. If Drake's forays into Gable Farms were detected by Quesenberry, Drake would wave in surrender and promptly retreat to Waterloo, the game over for that day.

With sheriff's deputies or game wardens, though, Drake adopted a no-holds-barred attitude and led them on chases that sometimes took days. He'd built a camouflage tent-like structure that he'd pull over the boat at night. He stayed out in the wet and cold, only to emerge like a phantom in the dark of morning to shoot ducks, wherever they may be. It drove the opposition nuts, and he loved it.

The rain intensified and a sharp wind raised a chop that slapped the boat's bow in staccato rhythm. Tar, usually nose in the air up front, huddled next to the stacked decoys, the dog's eyes on Drake's every move.

With the levees and main canal under water, Drake stuck to landmarks he trusted as reliable sentinels. Butte Creek, centuries old, now temporarily lost, still could be picked out by the cottonwoods and oaks that lined its banks. Drake steered close to the eastern line of treetops that wound through Waterloo and then Gable Farms as the creek carved its passage through the Butte Sink. Not only did the trees define his route, they provided cover.

Drake recognized the bend that told him he was passing over property that had once been a part of Waterloo, and the rush he always felt when poaching Stilton lands kicked in. Fifty years earlier, those very trees had provided shelter to the ancestors of wood ducks roosting there today. Somewhere beneath him, remnants of blinds Austin Green had constructed rose from the mud. When the floodwaters receded, they would again serve as reminders that long before the Stiltons, the Greens had hunted there. It pleased Drake to know the old blinds would still be visible when the Stiltons were long gone.

Ten minutes later, well into the heart of Gable Farms, Drake left the tree line and struck north toward a small rise. In normal times it was the crest of one of the few low hills in the Sink. He cut power and drifted in a lee that offered some calm from the wind as he began to throw out decoys. Tar rallied, the dog's tail drumming against the hull.

"You're wasting your time, Drake. Take 'em in."

Drake froze. Even Tar seized up before breaking out in angry, alarmed barks. An apparition rose from some brush fifteen feet away. Jim Quesenberry was visible only by his motion. He was clad head to toe in the 3-D camo gear favored by bow hunters. A few feet away, his camouflaged boat was barely visible through the tangled growth.

"Tar, down," Drake commanded. "Jesus, Jim, I wish you'd been in my company in Vietnam." Then he laughed. "You look like the Swamp Creature."

"Figured you'd head here," said Jim. "Drake, I just can't have it. Three's all over me about you. He'd can my ass off this place in a second if I looked the other way. If I catch you, I'm supposed to hold you and call the sheriff. You've got to get out of here before someone else spots you and turns you in. Three would probably fire me just because you managed to sneak in."

Drake reached for one of the decoys he'd thrown out. "Can't have that, Jim. You're the best thing that's happened to this place since my dad sold it off. I've got other spots. You know that."

In the late forties and early fifties, when Drake and Jim were school chums at the Colusa Elementary School, they'd led Huck Finn lives that included illegal high-water hunting. Time and again they'd breached the sanctity of the Stilton holdings, leading to hair-raising night-time retreats from Klaus Krenzler, Armand Stilton Jr.'s legendary enforcer. The angry German never caught them, a fact Drake came to appreciate more as he grew older and wiser. Krenzler had seemed capable of anything. He'd surfaced in Drake's dreams years afterward, the epitome of ruthless evil.

Jim smiled. "Yeah, I remember. We were crazy. Then *I* grew up and got respectable. Listen, there's another reason I'm glad I caught up with you today. The guy who was killed yesterday was some mucky-muck with Nor-Cal. Three had him talked into condemning a gas pipeline corridor across your property so he can connect his three test wells to the main distribution line. The guy may be dead, but Three's plan isn't. I heard him tell the members he's still going ahead."

Drake stopped wrapping line around the keel of the second decoy. *So now it's condemnation,* he thought. *Great. More lawyers, more money I don't have.* Besides the legal hassle, the mere specter of a pipeline traversing Waterloo's wildness sickened him. He sucked in a breath and let it out slowly as anger welled up from his gut.

He stowed the decoys and sat down at the motor. "I've handled Three's attacks in the past, I'll handle this one."

"I'll follow you," Jim said.

Drake shrugged. "As you like. Hell, I've lost my edge for hunting today. Come on over and we'll have a drink. Like to talk to you about yesterday anyway."

"Yesterday?" said Jim.

"Yeah, yesterday. Damned old Duke may be a good sheriff, and he's killed a few ducks, but he's sure as hell off the mark on this one."

Jim looked at Drake, questioning.

"Jim, the guy that died supposedly was an experienced hunter. Takes a pretty stupid one to load a gorgeous twelve-gauge Parker side-by-side with a twenty-gauge shell. From last night's TV news, I'd say the guy knew his way around a gun pretty well. Hunted all over the world and belonged to a high-toned duck club in Louisiana. My theory is that Three set the guy up, but that doesn't look so good after what you just told me. Something's sure weird here, though."

Jim looked down.

"Coming?" said Drake.

"Nah, I've got things to do."

Drake studied his friend. On Mondays Jim was always ready to let off steam. With the weekend's trauma, he should be looking for any excuse.

Drake shrugged as he cranked the motor. "Jim, we're going to talk about this, sooner or later. Your choice. Thanks for ruining my day."

CHAPTER 13

Pete Wooley scanned the profit and loss report from Riverbend Casino a third time. Unbelievable. His take this quarter would be slightly over $80,000. Added to the previous quarters, that meant he'd clear $300,000 for the year. Not bad for a guy who seven years earlier was living in a rundown HUD trailer.

He looked up from the table. "Mollie, I'm going over to the casino office for a bit. Need anything from the store?"

His wife, skin like Claire's and flashing dark eyes that could charm a snake, stepped away from the Viking stove and indoor grill that occupied an entire wall of the kitchen. "Charlie brought over venison steaks. He says he's also bringing a fresh salmon. I think we've got everything we need."

Pete grunted. Both deer and salmon season had been closed a month. But for Charlie Rainwater, that just meant less competition. While Pete disapproved of his son-in-law's lifestyle, he appreciated the constant bounty.

Pete was not looking forward to the reunion with his youngest daughter. They hadn't agreed on anything since she'd hit 13. He'd gone along with his wife's plan just to find some peace. Why couldn't Claire have been more like her older sister? Wanda hadn't been infected with the bug that bit Claire and triggered the itch that sent her away. Though Wanda's choice of husbands left much to be desired, at least she had one. Besides, Pete now had twin grandsons on whom his sun rose and set. Fortunately, Wanda's family was well provided for by the casino, Charlie Rainwater's flirtations with gainful employment having proved unreliable and even dangerous.

Pete was an activist for Native American rights, but his son-in-law's concept of action left Pete shaking his head and concerned that his grandsons would spend their teen years visiting their father in prison. Worse, they admired him and already showed signs of adopting his ways.

When Pete had organized a march to highlight the plight of Klamath River salmon, Charlie and his sons had taken concealment on a nearby hill, from which Charlie neutralized the opposition mounted by local farmers. With young Dennis and Randy as spotters, Charlie had used his "Poacher's Special," a Winchester Model 94 lever-action .22 Magnum rifle, fitted with a Weaver four power scope, to shoot out the tires of farmers' trucks blocking the marchers' path. Pete had grudgingly admitted the shooting worked since the protestors simply walked around the disabled trucks, but he'd chewed out his son-in-law for exposing the boys to such hazard.

There were other examples, ones that Pete tried to overlook, but because of their audacity, they kept Charlie Rainwater in the hearts of his community and the sights of local and federal law enforcement officers, particularly game wardens. Charlie clung furiously to the notion that Native Americans were entitled to kill any wild game, anytime, anywhere. He didn't care much for the casino and told his father-in-law so, though he had no problem with the money. It freed him to pursue his life as a world-class poacher.

Though the Rainwaters could afford anything at the supermarket, the family ate only meat, fish, or fowl provided by Charlie. And provide he did. Their casino-funded home included a walk-in freezer filled all year with venison, wild pig, wild turkey, ducks, geese, pheasant, quail, and, of course, salmon. Charlie's smokehouse occupied half the backyard, a wisp of alder or hickory smoke always curling from its stack.

During fall and winter, when salmon made their way upstream, Charlie Rainwater was their nemesis. With gill nets or on platforms from which he jabbed the migrating fish with spears, Charlie harvested hundreds, more than he and his family could possibly use. This, too, was an issue between him and his father-in-law. Charlie's illegal sales to restaurants and a few unscrupulous wholesalers earned him more than money. State and federal game wardens were drawn to him like the fish to their spawning waters. His few days in jail were far outnumbered by those he spent "exercising his rights as a Native American." In short, Charlie was a major pain in Pete Wooley's ass.

As Pete drove his new diesel 4-by-4 pickup into the casino parking lot, he thought of his youngest daughter again. His wife was right. It was time to mend that fence. The trouble was, how? She'd left the tribe, and the rules were clear. To receive casino money you had to be a tribal member when the casino was organized. Claire, impatient and scornful of her elders, had bolted to start a life of her own. Her mistake, now his headache. He sighed as he contemplated the unpleasant prospect of sharing with Claire a small portion of his casino earnings. Then the prospect of an evening with his grandsons shoved aside these weighty issues, and he smiled. His face darkened again when he thought of spending it with their father.

Claire's buoyancy and the music she'd picked for the drive were hard to ignore. Waylon Jennings and Willie Nelson were among Drake's favorites. Claire's new SUV, still fresh with the scent of leather and plastic that says all's well with the world, played its part. As Claire accelerated into the sweeping grades of the crags and forests along the Upper Sacramento River, Drake felt his irritation ease at losing a few prime days of high-water hunting. Even Three's condemnation scheme receded to a distant place, lost in the haze of miles and relaxation. He tilted the seat back, closed his eyes, and let the music and mountains weave their spell. Something new was happening. Its mystery warmed and frightened him. He liked that.

They passed the Castle Crags exit and were a few miles south of Dunsmuir when he sat up and said, "How about a short detour? I'll show you something."

"Sure," Claire said. "Tell me where."

"Next exit. Pull over after we're off the highway, and put it in four-wheel drive. Probably snow on the ground. At least there'll be mud."

She gave him a look. "Not that again."

Ten minutes later they were crawling up an unpaved track east of I-5. To their left, just north, a stream cascaded over snow-covered rocks and through the whitened forest.

"Castle Creek," Drake told her. "Full of small rainbows and brookies."

"It's a postcard," she said. "How much further? It doesn't look like anyone's been on this road since it snowed."

"They haven't," Drake said. "There's nothing ahead except a locked gate. It's just a light dusting. We should be fine."

"Seems like I've heard that before," she said, concentrating on every bump.

After a quarter mile they came to the gate, a crisscross log affair with a large pine slab overhead. On it, in pine branch letters was MOUNTAIN HOME.

"Your other place."

"Yep, hold on a minute."

He got out and dialed the tumblers on the large brass lock that secured the chain. The chain fell free, and he swept the gate aside, pushing back the slight layer of snow.

"Welcome," he said, climbing back in.

They drove another mile. As they climbed, the snow deepened. Drake reached over and laid his hand on the wheel. "Probably best to stop here," he said. "We can walk the rest of the way. It's only a few hundred yards."

She complied and stepped out. She stopped and listened. "What's that?"

"Bear River, the reason my grandfather bought the place. Come on."

"Now I know why I wore these boots." She laughed. "I must be getting to know you."

He took her hand and led her up the gentle slope, stopping at the crest. Twenty yards below lay the river, its water black against the snow that blanketed its edges. Volkswagen Bug size boulders rose from its middle. The rocks, topped with snow, glistened in the sunshine. Ahead, the road descended to a clearing and a snow-clad log lodge.

Claire shook her head. "I've never seen anything so beautiful." They stood, letting the silence of woods in snow speak for them.

"I have," Drake said. He put his hands to her chin, lifted it, and kissed her long and full.

Drake unlocked the door and stepped aside. Claire entered, stopped, and slowly turned, taking in the intimate charm of Drake's mountain retreat. Without a word, Drake built a fire in the rock fireplace, started water for tea on the stove and then sat down in front of the fire.

They passed Mount Shasta three hours later, Drake driving with Claire reclined in the passenger seat, asleep. As the majesty of the great mountain filled the rear view mirror Drake warmed in the fresh memory of their love making in front of his fire on one of Austin Green's bearskin rugs.

Riverbend lay just over the Oregon border, along the headwaters of the Klamath River and thirty miles southwest of Klamath Lake. At first, Drake thought it was a trailer park. Then the small, weary colonies of trailers and double-wides dwindled to the occasional tarpaper shanty, interspersed with rusted hulks of abandoned cars.

"It changes," Claire said. "You'll see. Turn left at the next intersection."

The intersection hosted a huge neon sign on its northeast corner. A twenty-foot-high Indian chief smiled down, coins and bills cascading from his extended fist. The other hand twirled a brightly scripted rope lariat that read, "RIVERBEND CASINO 1/4 MILE ON RIGHT."

Claire sighed. "We're almost there."

Drake nodded. "I had that feeling."

As they made the turn, another world appeared. Ahead, a broad boulevard beckoned. From its lush median strip and clean sidewalks sprouted vintage light poles with reproduction gas lights. The absence of overhead wires confirmed this was all new construction. Midway down, a block of signs marked the casino entrance. About a dozen tour busses were clustered in one section of the large asphalt lot.

"A slow day," Claire said. "There's usually at least twenty."

As they passed cross streets, Drake saw dozens of new two- and three-story suburban homes. Green lawns spilled to the streets, bracketing driveways that held boats, campers, and miscellaneous fast cars.

"Turn right up here," Claire said.

They entered a cul-de-sac dominated by a combination English Tudor/Western ranch home.

"Chief Wooley designed it himself," Claire said. "Try not to laugh."

"I can't promise," Drake said. He pulled into the driveway, between an enormous pickup and what Drake recognized under its winter cover as a tournament bass boat.

As he shut off the ignition, a car pulled to the curb—a fiery-red Trans-Am. Out of it stepped a woman, not as trim as Claire, but in her way every bit as attractive. Two young boys exploded from the back seat. A tall, lean man exited the driver's side, his skin dark and taut. He wore faded Levi's, a stained leather vest over a plaid shirt, well-worn boots, and a low-crowned, black hat. The Levi's were snugged at hip level with a tooled leather belt. On its silver buckle a golden fish arched as if jumping upstream. The man opened the trunk, lifted the lid of an ice chest, and pulled out a large king salmon.

The two women stood apart a few seconds and then embraced. Claire pulled away, blinking back tears. "Drake, meet my sister. Wanda, this is Drake."

Drake smiled and took Wanda's hand. The man came over, carrying the salmon by the tail. Drake guessed it to be at least forty pounds.

"And, this is her husband, Charlie. Charlie Rainwater."

Charlie stepped forward, flashing a broad grin and extending his free hand as the salmon's nose brushed the pavement. Drake took Charlie's hand, smiling and thinking, *I just know I'm going to like this guy.*

CHAPTER 14

Armand Stilton drummed the desk with his fingers, and frowned at the speaker phone. *That's the trouble with lawyers,* he thought. *When you're paying by the hour for advice, the adviser can't shut up.* A steady rain beat against the paned French doors of Armand's study, deepening his black mood.

"So, Armand, to sum up..." said Louis DuBois. Armand sat forward. *Jesus, at last.* "The bankruptcy referee needs to be convinced that condemning a pipeline across Waterloo is necessary either to preserve Nor-Cal assets or to result in cash flow that will be immediately available toward amelioration of its debts. Now, considering the fact that wholesale prices for natural gas are one-tenth what they were two years ago, the latter is probably not an option."

"Does the guy like to hunt ducks?" Armand asked, half serious.

"Pardon?"

"Forget it, a joke." *Actually,* thought Armand, *it wouldn't hurt to find out.*

"Armand," DuBois said, "I've talked this over with some of my colleagues. The consensus is that you need to make peace with your neighbor. Convince him the gas wells and a pipeline will benefit both of you."

Seven hundred dollars an hour and I get "Make peace?" The guy just doesn't get it. "Louis, I don't care about things that benefit Drake Green. I want the goddamned real estate. This isn't a question of neighborly relations. That five hundred acres is the last piece of the pie my father started to put together years ago. When I get it, I'll tear out everything

Green has done, sell off or butcher his goddamned noisy cows, sink as many gas wells as the place can hold, and plant rice over the rest. Now, I know you don't hunt, but if you did, you'd know what that meant. A feeding bowl for ducks."

There was silence as Armand let his lawyer digest this.

"I'd forgotten about the cows, Armand," DuBois said, his voice weary. "Armand, why don't you just make him an offer?"

Great, the clock just ticked off another seven hundred, and he tells me to do what we've been trying to do for fifty years. "Yeah, Louis, wonderful advice, brilliant. Why didn't I think of that? Hey, Louis?"

"Yes, Armand?"

Stilton bristled as he pictured DuBois congratulating himself on solving yet another complex legal problem and preparing to regale his partners at their club lunch with his accomplishment. He leaned into the speaker phone and shouted.

"You're fired! You and that billing machine you call a law firm. If you can't come up with a better answer than this, you sure as hell shouldn't be representing Stilton Industries. Pack up the files. I'll instruct our in-house lawyers to pick them up and find them a home with someone more tuned in to my problems."

He slammed the receiver down and sat back, pleased that he'd at least spoiled someone else's day. Armand knew he couldn't fire DuBois. Orland, Mulvaney & Merck held the keys to too many closets secreting Stilton Industries' skeletons. But neither would DuBois be able to face his partners and tell them that they had just lost 25 million a year in billings simply because he had failed to provide Armand with a creative solution to the Waterloo issue. Armand pictured DuBois canceling lunch plans and tearing his coifed gray hair for an answer. The world was right again.

The *Double Gun Journal* lay on his desk, and he opened it, looking for a gun to replace the one Durant had destroyed. As he read, he thought, *A twenty-gauge shell in a twelve-gauge gun. Christ, how could the man have done it?*

A front-page article in the *New York Times* had suggested suicide, citing Durant's mounting legal problems. *Hell,* thought Armand, *if he'd wanted to kill himself, he could have picked a cleaner way, one guaranteed to get the job done.* Shoving a twenty-gauge shell into the gun, while undoubtedly capable of causing death, could just as well have blown off part of his face without killing him. No, Chester Durant was no suicide. Of that Armand was certain.

He set the magazine down and focused on the events of the past weekend. In the four days since then, he had shut the subject out—the mess and shock too much.

Yes, they'd hunted quail the day before and had carried twenty-gauge guns. They'd walked back through the orchard, hung the birds in the shed, and gone into Armand's place to shower and change for dinner.

Armand closed his eyes, and the scene replayed itself like a film.

Chet had sat down at the table, slipped out of his boots, and asked where the booze was. Armand had opened the bar cabinet and told him to help himself. Durant had pulled out a bottle of Knob Creek and poured some over ice. Then he'd taken off the jacket—

Armand straightened. He'd told the sheriff he'd lent Durant that jacket the next morning. That's not what happened. He'd given Durant the jacket before they went out for quail. *Armand didn't empty the pockets on that jacket, Durant did.* He'd taken a handful of shells from each pocket and put them back in the box Armand had given him earlier. It had been a fresh box of Quesenberry's reloads, twenty-five shells. Hell, Durant had only fired the gun twice and killed a quail each time. If he messed up and left some twenty-gauge shells in the jacket, they should still be there, less the one that blew up the gun. Between what was in the box and whatever might still be in that jacket, they should total twenty-two shells. If not—

While Armand had no reason to doubt the sheriff's conclusion, he made a mental note to check the jacket and count the remaining shells when he returned to Gable Farms on Friday.

He turned a page and an ad for a Holland & Holland Royal twelve-gauge, single-trigger in the maker's case caught his eye. He picked up the telephone.

If the Devil has a rotisserie, he's got me on it, thought Jim Quesenberry as he set out on the quarter-mile walk to the club mailbox. Sleep had been out of the question, and his high-water encounter with Drake Green had only served to turn up the heat. Drake's parting comment festered, and he knew it was something Drake would pursue. Drake was like that—determined. Worse, it meant that at least two people knew or suspected the shotgun explosion had not been an accident. Donna Stilton's sweet reminder ticked like a stuck record. *If at first you don't succeed...*

Christ, he thought, *what does she expect me to do? I'm just damned lucky Sheriff Duke is such a hip shooter. One bite at this apple is about all anyone gets.* As it stood, Jim had a nagging unease that it had all been too easy, that there was something he'd missed. The whole thing would have gone off like clockwork if Three had just hung on to the gun he always used—that damned, beautiful Parker. All he had to do was break open the gun, shove in two shells—

Jim stopped in his tracks. *By God, that was it, the loose end.* Once he tied it up, Donna Stilton and the whole unhappy scheme would be behind him.

His mind began to clear, and he focused on the coming weekend, on all the details and fine points that had to be in place when the members rolled in Friday afternoon. Though Chester Durant's death was still front-page news, Jim had no doubt that Gable Farms would pick up where it left off. It was the middle of duck season, and the storms had brought down thousands of new birds. These men were hunters, not hand wringers.

He'd call the market and order one of the dinner favorites—a large crown roast of prime rib. On Saturday, he'd serve them a club tradition, Fire House Chili. There was the bar to restock, kennels to clean, fresh towels and linens to see to, firewood to bring in...the list went on. At the top, though, would be a quick visit to Three's residence.

By the time Jim reached the mailbox, he began to feel better about things. After all, what could Drake Green suspect? Suicide, like the papers had hinted? That Three had set it up? No, Three had needed Durant for his condemnation plan. Whatever Drake would be thinking, it wouldn't make a difference. Drake Green was the last person on earth to cause Jim trouble. As for Donna Stilton, she could think what she wanted. He'd tried, and it hadn't worked. That was that.

He opened the mailbox and sifted the contents. Normally Jim detested the two hours a month it took him to keep the club's lights on, the phones connected, and the grocer paid. For once, the thought of putting his mind to desk duties sounded pretty good.

Toward the end of the pile, he stopped. He held up a simple envelope with the return address of Cedar Hills in Little Rock, Arkansas. Letters from the director rarely brought good news. Jim opened it and began to read.

Dear Jim,

I hardly know how to say this. I have no explanation but felt you must know the answer. I won't pry; suffice to say we are all deeply grateful, though wondering what comes next.

Yesterday I received a call from our bank. They have received a deposit of $50,000 from the Stilton Foundation into a new account opened as the "Cedar Hills Performing Arts Theatre" account. You are designated as signatory. The instructions from a bank in San Francisco stated that the sum of $450,000 would follow and you would know when. Our bank is sending you a signature card.

I had a short chat with our contractor, and he's confident we can build an excellent facility for $500,000 by remodeling the vacant storage barn out back. It's a solid structure and just the right size. I hope you approve.

Jim, as always, thank you. You and God do work in mysterious ways.

Clinton J. Williams, Director
P.S. Your sister is doing well and was very excited when I explained the project to her.

Jim flushed with new heat. The Devil had just dumped half a million gallons of gasoline on the fire.

"Claire tells me you like to hunt." Drake chose his words carefully, Claire having briefed him on the family's renegade. Charlie Rainwater looked up from his venison steak and nodded. "You could say that."

Pete Wooley frowned.

"And you, Drake," said Mollie. "Aren't you a hunter too?"

Drake smiled. "You could say that."

All except Charlie and Pete laughed.

"Drake owns a duck club," Claire said. "He lives there."

Charlie perked up. "No kidding. Where?"

"Butte Sink," said Drake, reaching for more salmon.

"Never hunted down there," said Charlie. Then he laughed. "Never needed to."

From his seat at the head of the table, Pete Wooley's disapproval hovered like a rain cloud. He hadn't said a word since they'd sat down.

"What's the matter, Dad?" asked Charlie. "Don't like the venison?"

Wooley glared at his son-in-law. Then he brightened. "You're right, Charlie. I don't. It's too out of season." With that everyone laughed, and the table chatter took off in earnest.

Mollie was the model of a mother seeking details about her daughter's friend without appearing she was prying. Drake played along, entertaining the group with stories of hunters he'd known and a life spent hunting and fishing. Even Claire's dad jumped in, unabashedly asking how much each hunter at Waterloo paid and how much it cost to run the duck club, and making little effort to mask his mental calculations based on Drake's answers.

Drake finally sought to change the subject by commenting on the news coverage of the conflict between the farmers and the Klamath Indians. It was as if he'd pulled out a soapbox and invited Wooley to step up.

Fifteen minutes later Wooley was still filibustering on everything from the sacred suckerfish to militant farmers unwilling to live within the bounds dictated by nature. The twins, who Drake guessed to be about ten, were launching peas off their knives, drawing scowls from their grandmother. Charlie retreated twice to the kitchen for beer, motioning the second time to Drake, who nodded. Mollie, Wanda, and Claire spent the time nodding respectfully, quietly finishing their dinners.

When Wooley paused for a drink of water, one of the kids launched a multiple warhead that went wild, pelting his grandmother with peas and a glop of mashed potato. Mollie seized on the assault as a respite from her husband's diatribe and conducted a drumhead court martial. The culprits were banned from the table. Their joyous "Yeeayyy" as they raced for the family room and its video games lightened the mood and marked the end of dinner.

Two hours later, Drake lay staring at the ceiling of the guest room where Claire had placed him in the name of propriety. The old chief was quite a character. But Charlie Rainwater was a man in a league of his own. An unfamiliar peace settled over Drake, and sleep came easily.

CHAPTER 15

Friday, December 16.

Most of the members had arrived, and two lively domino games were underway in the game room of the Gable Farms clubhouse. Nick Pappas, whose California Grizzlies had lost their bid for a wildcard slot in the playoffs, circulated a pool on Sunday's game, a thousand dollars a square.

"Armand coming?" he asked Jim, who was tending bar. "We want his money."

"Far as I know," said Jim. "He usually lets me know if he's not going to make it."

One of the domino players shifted his cigar. "Wonder if he's bringing a guest."

His partner played the double five for four points, then celebrated by saying, "If he does, I hope the poor sucker brings his own gun and shells." The others laughed, and Jim shook his head. In less than a week the incident had been transformed from gore and gloom to cocktail humor. Still, he doubted the wisecrack would have been made in Three's presence.

Just then the dogs kenneled outside began to bark, heralding Three's arrival. Jim went outside to help him unload.

"Goddamn traffic in the Bay Area was all messed up," said Three. He swung his legs out from the Hummer and kicked his feet, reaching for the ground. He turned on his stomach and, with one hand on the steering wheel, the other on the special grab bar, he lowered himself. Jim never tired of the spectacle.

"Well, you're here now. All the boys are inside, a full turnout." Jim hesitated. "Anyone joining you?"

"No," Three answered. "I want you to shoot with me tomorrow. We'll see about Sunday."

"Fine, Armand. We'll work some more on your calling. Oh, your attorney phoned. Said for you to call him at home, no matter what time."

Three grunted and set off toward his residence. Over his shoulder he called, "Bring my stuff. And, oh yeah, there's a couple of tennis nets in the back. Find a place to store them. Next spring, we're putting in tennis courts."

Jim lifted Three's duffel from the Hummer and took in the two large boxes stowed in back. *Tennis courts,* he thought. *Wait till the members hear that.*

Three opened the door and stopped in the vestibule that served as a mudroom. Several pairs of waders hung from cleats. Next to them on pegs hung an array of hunting jackets, vests, and parkas, a selection to match any weather. Three took down a jacket and proceeded into the main room, where he laid it on an octagonal table that mirrored the shape of the structure. Then he went to his gun cabinet, took out a box of shells, and sat at the table. "Been thinking about this all week," he muttered.

Jim placed Three's bag on a couch. "Well, I'll be getting back to the clubhouse," he said. "Gotta check the roast."

Three looked up. "Stick around a minute. The roast will keep."

He spread open the jacket and turned the pockets inside out. A gum wrapper, a box of matches, and an old Iverson duck call tumbled out. Satisfied, he shoved the jacket aside. He opened the box of shells and spilled them onto the table. Then he began to count, moving each shell to a separate pile. "…nineteen, twenty, twenty-one, twenty-two…"

He looked up. A blank expression filled his face. "I'll be damned. The dumb bastard really must have left one in the jacket, and it killed him, just like that Colombo of a sheriff said."

"Need me for anything else?" Jim asked.

Three brushed him away. "Go check your roast. I'll be over soon."

Jim left Three's residence and set off for the clubhouse. He didn't feel his feet on the gravel. Instead, they stung as if he stood at the edge of a cliff. What angel of fate had directed him to Three's residence Wednesday to remove a shell from that box? Could he count on her again?

"Tar! Settle down!" Even as he shouted, Drake's gruff reproach melted. Everything about the black lab pleased him: the dog's shine, its rippled physique, and coal-black eyes, but most of all its joy. Eight months of restless romping and retrieving Frisbees against the strong currents of Bear River and the Upper Sacramento kept Tar honed for one thing: duck season. Eating and sleeping had become tiresome lapses tolerated between the new adventure of each hunting day.

Tar's tail drummed against the rail, and Drake unfolded from his deck chair. He shielded his eyes from the lowering sun, then stepped to a tripod-mounted telescope and twisted the eyepiece. He saw two large SUVs and two pickups, both fitted with camper shells.

"You're right, Tar. It's them."

Drake followed the course of the small caravan and watched it stop at the gate at West Butte Road. The lead driver got out, unlocked the gate, stepped back into his rig, and the convoy resumed, slower now because of the mud. The rains had eased, leaving Drake's road a challenge but passable. Any worse and the hunters would have had to pack in on ATVs. They wouldn't mind, though. The hunting was that good.

Tar's barks quickened to excited howls and, in spite of his melancholy mood, Drake smiled. *If I were a dog, I'd howl too,* he thought. It was the middle of duck season, the best part of the year. *Why don't I feel like howling?*

"Go on, Tar. Say hello," he said, releasing the dog from its invisible tether. Tar bounded down the stairs, raced down the hill, and then along the levee of the canal before it curved to divide Waterloo and Gable Farms. The dog stopped and made his stand as greeter and guard at Green's Crossing. Yelps rose from portable kennels in the vehicles, now stopped at the locked bar across the far end of the bridge. Again, the lead driver did his job and, one by one, the four vehicles crossed the narrow span. Tar looked toward Drake, who had reached the bottom of the gravel track that led up to the Palace. Drake motioned, and the dog loped back toward him.

To a chorus of barks, punctuated by blasts of horns, Drake and Tar led the procession up the hill to begin the ritual observed on and around Waterloo for over seventy-five years. Drake sighed as he trudged the hill. *This is supposed to be fun,* he thought. Instead, the weekly shedding of care he'd provided his members for almost thirty years suddenly had the rancid taste of monotony. *What the hell's wrong with me,* he wondered.

Traveling kennels were unloaded and the dogs resniffed old friend-ships or grudges while their owners unpacked. One or two of the dogs, including Tar, found something objectionable with one or two more, and the usual standoffs followed. Bottles were opened, cigars lit, and the weekend commenced. A long and boisterous dinner tapered to stories, some new, most not. It didn't matter. Like a tribe's oral history, the sto-ries were part of the ritual, and all who told them knew their role. Two newcomers sipped brandy and absorbed. Their turn would come.

At ten thirty, Drake looked at Tar, stretched out near the big wood stove. Quivers punctuated the dog's sleep.

"I'm calling it a night," Drake said, standing. "Four thirty's coming on fast." He saw Henry Neeley's raised eyebrows. This was early for Drake, who usually regaled his members and guests with stories and Scotch well past midnight. The late nights and early mornings were integral to the joy and pain of the sport.

"You OK?" Neeley asked.

Drake shrugged.

Neeley lifted his glass. "Our leader's in love. Got his mind on other things besides shootin' the shit with a bunch of smelly duck hunters."

Drake pointed a finger at Neeley then slapped his leg. Tar rose and followed him. Over his shoulder Drake called to the group, "You boys should follow my good example. Don't burn the place down."

Armand III left the clubhouse shortly before eleven, mellowed by a successful evening at dominoes, three Wild Turkey highballs, Jim's perfect prime rib, and two snifters of Germain-Robin Mendocino County Alambic brandy. He puffed on a Cuban Upmann as he carried a third snifter to toast what was to come. DuBois would not have called him at Gable Farms unless the lawyer had come up with an answer. Armand had waited until now to return the call, partly to scramble DuBois from bed late at night, but mostly to savor whatever news the lawyer had as a final nightcap.

He stirred the fire and plopped onto the leather couch that dominated the main room of his residence. As a thick curl rose from his cigar, he punched the speed dial programmed to DuBois's number.

"Yes?"

Ahh, this is good. He was sleeping. "Louis, this is Armand. You called?"

"Armand, oh, yes, yes. I was just catching up on the paper and dozed off. Glad you called back." There was relief in the lawyer's voice, and Armand pictured him coming to attention, like a well-trained dog striving to please its master.

"Armand, I think I have just the, uh, vehicle you need to deal once and for all with your neighbor."

Armand closed his eyes. There was no music like a symphony of vexatious litigation.

"A vehicle, Louis?"

"Didn't you tell me that this man Green has cattle on his property?"

"Yeah, several hundred, I think. I've told him dozens of times to get rid of them. They drive off the ducks, and they're a waste of good rice land." Over the telephone, Armand heard the rustle of paper.

"I've a survey of the properties in front of me," DuBois said. "The parcels under Green ownership, all that you call Waterloo, are bordered on the west by Butte Creek and on the north by the canal. Am I correct?"

"Yeah."

"Armand, that cattle operation must be polluting the water. If so, he's in violation of the Federal Clean Water Act."

Armand sat up. "So?"

"Well, that legislation permits private lawsuits to enforce compliance with federal standards. It's like the Proposition 65 situation."

"Proposition 65?"

"Yes, Armand. Proposition 65. Three attorneys in our firm devote all their time representing Stilton Industries in Proposition 65 litigation. It has to do with harmful or toxic chemicals and substances."

"Oh, yeah,"

"The Federal Clean Water Act has similar enforcement provisions. A number of lawyers have emerged that, uh, specialize in filing lawsuits against violators or potential violators." There was something in DuBois's voice, like he'd just taken a bite of apple and discovered a worm in it.

"I take it your firm doesn't do this."

"File the lawsuits? On, no, no. Defend them, yes. But not file them. Some of the lawyers who do this may be well motivated, but most are not. They are bounty hunters, pure and simple. The law provides for attorney's fees, and they're in it to collect them. Between the fines and the fees, many small businesses either go under or pay exorbitant settlements to stay afloat. It's safe to say your neighbor would face financial disaster if confronted with this."

Armand leapt up. "If not you guys, then who?"

"I've already talked to him, Armand. Jackson Crackers. His office is in San Rafael."

"Jackson Crackers? What the hell kind of a name is that?"

"My associate who located him says he's called Cracker Jack. Be that as it may, he has an excellent record in the area I described. His reputation, well, that's another matter altogether. Armand, if you are looking for someone to cause your neighbor so much trouble and expense that he'll throw in the towel, this is your man."

Armand settled back into the couch. "Hire him."

Drake stepped to the deck outside his room. Coots scolded and skittered across a nearby pond. Somewhere out in the black night a diehard mallard called for a mate. A calf bawled, probably lost from its mother. *Neeley's right,* he thought. *My mind is on other things.*

Two miles north, lights from Gable Farms pricked the dark. Drake pictured Armand Stilton in front of a crackling fire, sipping rare cognac and planning his next move.

Stilton. In all the months of all the years ahead, Armand Stilton would be there, backed by unlimited money and nursing an insatiable hunger. Why couldn't the man be content with what he had? Even as Drake asked himself the question, he shook his head. There was one thing he and Stilton had in common—a core of resolve forged by their fathers. Drake's legacy was to protect Waterloo. Stilton's was to own it. The two sons and the two properties were on a collision course.

Suddenly Drake felt very tired. Yet a strange new restlessness stirred him. It had started with Claire.

Waterloo and Claire—did the clash between his lifestyle and the permanent company of a woman really exist, as he'd always supposed? What woman could live in a concrete-block bunker above a duck marsh? What woman could share her life with a man who divided his year between a mountain stream and an array of duck ponds?

Drake shifted, still gazing at the distant lights of Gable Farms. *Other things.* Maybe it was time to fold his hand. Though he was cash poor, he was property rich. Waterloo was worth 10 million, at least—chicken scratch for Three. With the money, Drake could build a new life, one that had room for someone else.

He stepped back into his room, leaving the sliding door open. He wanted to listen to Waterloo as he pondered for the first time the notion of selling it.

The letter from Cedar Hills lay limp in Jim's hands, having been read, reread, folded, and refolded countless times that night. Finally he crumpled it, opened the wood stove that heated his quarters, and threw it in. The letter rose, as if struggling, then settled and blackened. It was gone, but its message remained. Donna Stilton had spun an exquisite web that strangled all resistance. He had to find another way to kill Armand III.

Another exploding shell was out. Even Duke wouldn't buy that again. Drake hadn't bought it in the first place.

Jim crawled into bed, turned on his side, and stared at the blur of flame through the stove's glass door. How many accidents could a duck hunter have? Ones that were fatal and left no tracks.

The obvious—one hunter accidentally shoots the other—was out of the question. While Three was borderline dangerous every time he handled a loaded shotgun, Jim Quesenberry was not. Like Drake, Jim was known throughout the Butte Sink as a professional. If he killed his hunting partner, it would be a stretch convincing anyone it was an accident. Even if he pulled it off, there would always be that blot on his reputation.

He began to review other hunting fatalities he'd heard of. Two accidents he remembered had claimed the lives of hunters who carried loaded shotguns in their boats as they searched for downed or crippled ducks. In each instance their dog had stepped on the gun, disengaging the safety and jamming its paw against the trigger. Man's best friend had become his worst and last enemy in the space of a second. Jim's young Labrador, Jethro, while rambunctious enough, couldn't be counted on to perform with such reckless precision.

Then there were the heart attacks, always a grim phenomenon that stalked a sport where many adherents were overweight, ate and drank with bacchanalian excess, smoked cigars against doctor's orders, went to bed late, and got up scant hours later. This risk, viewed by many hunters as in the "as good a way to go as any" category had claimed its share over the years. Jim filed it away as a possibility. The problem was, he hadn't a clue how to stage a heart attack and wasn't prepared to wait for Three to bring one on himself. Jim's sister and her companions at Cedar Hills were on clocks wound tight with medical risks they faced every day.

Jim rolled over. In less than five hours he'd be making breakfast for the members, then rushing to the dock to start motors and make a final check of the boats. If there was one thing Three really obsessed about, it was his boat. Jim went to sleep thinking of Three's boat. A boat was simple. It did two things: it floated—or it sank.

CHAPTER 16

Saturday, December 17.

Three's new Roto Duck ensemble, overnight expressed from Cabela's, had all the bells and whistles. There was the Roto Duck itself, larger and with longer battery life than its vaporized predecessor. Then there was the spread of electric decoys that bobbed and quivered, sending ripples on demand across placid water, irresistible to cruising mallards. "Press a button and watch 'em work," the catalogue had invited. Duck hunting by remote control. *Next thing*, Jim thought, *he'll buy some R2-D2 gizmo to sit out here and shoot his ducks. Probably be better at it. Would sure as hell be better company.*

The morning wore long, as there was no wind, and, consequently, no ducks. Three's usual impatience at such inactivity was overcome by his fascination with his new toys. Like a kid with a train set, Three amused himself throughout the morning's doldrums by pushing buttons and watching his plastic minions work.

Even Jim felt drawn to the hypnotic rhythm of Three's miniature army of Trojan deceit. He took solace that the entire Butte Sink was quiet, meaning that for miles around hundreds of other camo-clad hunters hunkered in blinds, desperate like him for diversion.

Then, from nowhere, a flight of ring-necks dive-bombed the blind and were gone as fast as they had come.

"Goddamit," shouted Three, "You should've spotted those!"

Jim shrugged. He should have. His mind had been occupied by the image of Three disappearing below the murky green water, his boat capsized and his squadron of mechanical marvels cavorting in programmed celebration. "Sorry," he said. "They came on pretty fast."

Three grunted and set down the control. He shouldered his shotgun and stared off into the distance, apparently confident more would follow. A volley of shots from Waterloo shattered the morning stillness.

"Enjoy it while you can, pal," Three muttered, looking south. "You'll be out of there next season, I promise."

Jim yawned to cover his sudden snap to attention. He forced a what-do-I-care voice and asked, "Something brewing, Armand?"

Three's expression became that of a cat that had tired of toying with a mouse and was savoring the grim delight ahead.

"Brewing. Yes, Jim, that's a good word for it. By next summer that sonofabitch Green will be off that place." His grin broadened. "You could say he's about to meet his Waterloo."

With that Three burst into laughter. Jim joined him out of good manners then lapsed into silence.

"Can't tell you much right now," Three said. "I've got a new lawyer, a real Cracker Jack." More laughs. He settled down and turned to Jim. "Count on adding Waterloo to your responsibilities before next season."

Jim spotted a small flight of ducks to the north and nodded toward them. "Birds. One o'clock."

Three hunched down and began to tinker with his control box.

It struck Drake that whoever had named Butte City had either a sense of ironic humor or a form of ambitious arrogance well suited to people who went around founding cities. Butteville maybe, or Butte Town. "Butte City" was just too much for a crossroads consisting of two principal structures—Tony Figone's duck plucking shed and, conveniently located next door by some accident of dim history, the Butte City Club, a dilapidated country bar.

Patrons of the Butte City Club were greeted by the glum countenance of a 410-pound white sturgeon mounted over the door. Local lore had it that a long-dead farmer had spotted the giant fish sunning in the mud at a bend in the Sacramento River. Known for his practical approach to sporting ethics, the farmer had rigged up a heavy pole with a chicken carcass as bait. Once the sturgeon had inhaled the chicken, the sportsman-farmer tied the line off to a rope from a block and tackle attached to a sled pulled by a team of draft horses. Any further remnants of the story were tatters of legend no longer considered reliable by the regulars who, for as long as Drake could remember, called the fish "Moe."

The years had not been kind to Moe. The carcass had aged badly from the darts and the occasional knife sent in its direction. Still, perhaps out of remorse and collective guilt, but more likely from Moe's immense presence, patrons of the Butte City Club had taken to patting Moe upon entering, a talisman of continued good luck.

Drake parked diagonally at the curb, noting Jim Quesenberry's truck a few yards away, in front of the duck plucking shed. Tony Figone's services were much in demand, particularly from duck club members, who paid three dollars a bird to keep their hands clean.

For Drake and Jim, duck season Saturday afternoons at the Butte City Club were a special and private part of the entire ritual. While Figone eviscerated and plucked their members' ducks and geese, transforming them into smooth, shiny main courses, the two friends would engage in the post-kill dialogue relished by guides everywhere. The antics, accomplishments, and failings of those who paid to hunt at Waterloo and Gable Farms were analyzed and dissected as only professionals who care for amateurs can do.

Drake hefted the burlap sack of tagged waterfowl from the bed of his pickup and hung it in Figone's outer shed. He could hear the short, craggy Italian at work in the cleaning room and judged from the number of trucks at the curb that Figone was too busy for pleasantries. Even the modest shooting in the Sink that morning was enough to bury the master plucker in feathers for hours to come.

"Pretty slow morning," Drake said, sliding onto the stool next to Jim.

"Sounded like your guys had some action."

"Hmm, some. Sixteen birds altogether. Some nice mallards, even a couple sprig." The bartender brought Drake a beer. He continued, "Expected a better morning. No wind though."

"Yep, no wind."

"Three show up?"

"Yep."

Drake took a long drink, then set the bottle down. "Kind of surprised he would after last weekend's mess."

Jim looked at him. "Nothing about that man surprises me anymore."

Drake let Jim's comment hang as he considered what it meant. A good thirty seconds passed. "You buy into Duke's theory?"

Jim pushed his empty bottle forward. "It's as good as any, I guess."

"Hmm…"

"Drake, like I told you, Three had no reason to harm the man. He was going to use him to get at you with that condemnation deal."

Drake nodded, watching Jim's expression in the mirror of the back bar. "Could have been someone else that set that gun up."

In the mirror, their eyes met.

"Or," Drake continued, "it could have been an accident, just like Duke said."

"Yep." Jim took a drink and set the bottle back down on the bar, where he moved it in small circles.

Drake waited.

Finally, Jim spoke. "Say, I'm damned sorry I had to run you off the other day. It's just not like the old days though. Three's over me like a sack on a snipe."

Drake noted his friend's abrupt change of subject and decided to run with it.

"Better you than Old Man Stilton's Nazi, Klaus Krenzler. I'm convinced that if Herr Krenzler had ever caught us, we would have ended up duck food. What the hell ever happened to him anyway?"

Jim took a long drink. This time he clapped the empty bottle down hard, getting the bartender's attention. "All I heard was that Stilton retired him. Bought him a house in Grass Valley. Hell, that was back when we were kids. He's gotta be dead now. Let's hope so, at least."

"Hmm…Doesn't sound like something a Stilton would do. You expecting a house someday?"

"More like a hose," Jim said. "I tell you, I can't stand that man. Worse than his father ever was. At least the old man had a brain. And he could shoot."

"You shoot with Three again this morning?"

"Yep."

"Well?"

"Well what?"

"Jesus Christ, Jim. What do you think? How'd he do?"

Jim grunted. "Played with his new toys all morning. Like I said, no wind, no ducks." Then Jim downed almost half his fresh beer, looked around, and bent near. "Says he's got a new lawyer who's got plans for you. Told me that by this time next year you'd be off Waterloo and I'd be taking care of it as part of Gable Farms."

Drake pushed his unfinished beer forward and stood. *Other things.*

CHAPTER 17

Sunday evening, December 18.

"Is the dog that interesting?" Claire asked. Though she was adjusting to Drake's silent lapses, his two-hour mope since she had arrived was making her wish she'd stayed in Willows. A movie alone was better than an evening with a stump.

Drake looked up from the magazine that had been open to the same page for the last half hour. An intent-looking black Lab stared from the page, the dog's cool eyes focused overhead, presumably on ducks.

"What?" he said.

"The dog, in the picture. Is it more interesting than me?" She'd tried but failed to keep any peevishness out of her voice.

Drake tossed the magazine aside and stared ahead.

"Want to talk about it?" she said.

"Talk about what?"

She stood, her spent patience propelling her like a released balloon. "You, me, us, the man in the moon—whatever it is that has you so wound up."

Drake reached for her hand. "It's not you," he said. "In fact, to tell you the truth, if it weren't for you, it would be a lot worse."

This was the closest he'd come to expressing his feelings for her since their stop at Mountain Home. In the weeks that followed, she'd valued that moment even more as she'd come to realize Drake's emotions were pearls secreted in shells hardened by a history he had yet to share. Sometimes he was bright with wit and imagination. Other times he was lost in unfathomable gloom.

She placed her other hand on top of his. "Tell me."

He drew a breath, pulled away, and stood. He walked to the glass doors and looked out.

"This place. For years it's been my life. It's what kept me alive. I saw stuff in Vietnam that drove other men crazy. Got them killed. I always came back to this place. It shut out a lot of the horror, or at least gave me something to hang onto. The kids who went over there with no anchor were the ones most vulnerable.

"When I left the Marines and moved up here, everything seemed to click. Hunting and fishing. What could be better?"

She cocked her head.

"Then," he continued, turning to face her, "finally, after all this time, I found something better."

She drew a breath. "Drake, the words are, 'I love you.' Is that what you're trying to say?"

He lowered his head.

"Then say them."

He looked up. "I love you."

She walked over to him. "I love you, too."

They hugged. As she held him close, she felt his tension melt. "That wasn't so bad, now, was it?" she said.

"Bad? No, it was—wonderful. God, Claire I can't tell you how good this feels. It makes all the rest—" He stopped and turned away.

"The rest? What, Drake? What's wrong?"

He looked outside. "This," he said, sweeping his arm. "My neighbor's at war with me, and I don't have any army left. I just want peace."

He continued to stare outside. "I could never ask you to live here."

Claire frowned. "I thought you just did," she said, finally. She went to him. "Drake, Waterloo is as much a part of you as you want me to be. Don't give up on it. Whatever it takes to keep it, you have to do."

She looked around the Palace, seeing it for the first time for what it was—a place for men to gather, drink, and swap stories. Drake was right about one thing: she could not live there.

"As for us," she said, "let's just build our own place. This belongs to your members." She walked to the sliding door and pointed toward the ruins of the old lodge. "We could live there."

Drake smiled and shook his head. "You're amazing. You really want to live out here?"

"It's the only way I'd live with you, Drake," she said. "If you gave up on Waterloo and moved away with me to Mountain Home or wherever, the day would come when you couldn't live with what you had done. That day would be the beginning of the end of us."

Drake studied her for a few seconds and then sat down. He reached for the untouched glass of wine he'd poured an hour earlier.

"What about my neighbor, Stilton?" he said. "Word has it he's about to throw some new lawyer at me."

Claire shrugged. "The cavalry wasn't able to roust my ancestors. No lawyer is going to roust me. General Green, you've just enlisted a fresh recruit. Now, let's start planning our new quarters."

They sat and talked for another two hours about resurrecting the old lodge. When they retired, Claire knew it was only talk and that Drake wasn't beyond talk—not yet.

Monday morning, December 19.

Armand III sat forward and peered over the steering wheel of the Hummer as he scanned addresses. He'd ventured west on Third Avenue in San Rafael only once before, when he'd been looking for an exclusive wine warehouse mentioned by a Gable Farms member. Not to be outdone, he had bought out the entire stock of the vintage his member had coveted, ten cases at $1,000 a case. He'd turned the wine over to Donna to donate to a fundraising auction, and laughed himself to tears as his member bid against Armand's shill to recapture the prize wine at $4000 a case.

Passing the wine merchant's unimposing building, Armand chuckled and concentrated on the address he sought. The transition from downtown San Rafael chic, a mile behind him, to the tarnished sleaze of low-rent storefronts was apparent. Third Avenue narrowed to two lanes, which slowed traffic and made passing impossible.

"Ah, there it is," he said to himself. He stopped, intent on finding a place to park. Tires screeched, then the Hummer shuddered as something shoved it from behind.

"Shit."

Armand opened the door, rolled to his stomach, and lowered himself to the pavement. He stalked back to a crunched BMW, noting with satisfaction that the Hummer was unscathed. The driver, an attractive brunette, glared out from behind an inflated airbag.

She pressed a button, and the window came down. "You just stopped for no reason," she blurted.

"I'm parking," Armand said. "Look, there's no damage to my car. Call it a draw. Back up and let me park."

"That's no car," she shouted. "It's a tank. It shouldn't be allowed on city streets. What about the damage to *my* car? This isn't my fault."

Unsympathetic motorists trapped in the column of stalled traffic behind them began to lay on horns. Armand felt the first waves of irritation that soured him whenever he faced life outside his sheltered bubble. The honking reached a crescendo, punctuated by shouts and waving arms. The woman in the BMW started to cry.

Suddenly Armand heard a voice behind him, low and cool. "Get back in your vehicle and do what I tell you."

Armand spun around. Standing next to the Hummer was a man wearing faded jeans, saddle shoes, and a multicolor checked blazer over a red turtleneck. Best of all, from Armand's perspective, was the fact that Armand had to look down to make eye contact, the stranger being a good two inches shorter.

"Go on, get in," the man said again, stepping into the lane of opposing traffic and holding up his arms. Oncoming cars slowed, then stopped as Armand clambered back into the Hummer. He watched, amazed, as the short guy in the plaid blazer began to pump one arm toward the cars piled up behind the BMW while holding off opposing traffic with the other. The chorus of horns stopped, and cars began to snake by.

"I saw the whole thing," his savior shouted to Armand as he continued to direct traffic. "Her fault, totally. How's your neck?"

Armand blinked.

"Your neck. Hurts pretty bad, doesn't it?"

Armand's neck felt fine.

Traffic thinned and the short guy called to the woman in the BMW. "Ma'am, pull your car into that driveway. Get out your license and insurance information, would you?"

Armand watched in his rearview mirror as the woman dabbed her eyes with a handkerchief and followed the stranger's instructions.

"Mr. Stilton, back your truck into that space."

Mr. Stilton? thought Armand. *This guy knows me?* Armand did as he was told, killed the engine, and waited.

The stranger appeared at the window, reached up, and extended his hand. "Hello, Armand. I've been expecting you. Jackson Crackers. I saw the accident from my office." He gestured to the second-story window overhead. "Get lots of business off this stretch of roadway. Lots of business. Relax a minute and let me get this babe's insurance stuff, then we'll go on up. I've spent two days at your lawyer's office in San Francisco reviewing your problem. Your neighbor is about to get one hell of a shock for Christmas." He paused. "Oh, when you get out, kind of stretch and walk stiff. Rub your neck. See you in a minute."

Armand's new lawyer winked and sauntered over to the BMW.

CHAPTER 18

Tuesday morning, December 20

"**D**amn thing's got a mind of its own," Jim muttered to himself as Three's boat splashed back into the water. Three times he'd managed to get the bow onto the dock, only to have it slide off when he let go to grab the side. Exasperated and soaked in sweat, he collapsed. Every year after duck season closed, Jim paid two locals who hung out at the Butte City Club to come in and haul out the boats for storage. Jim wasn't sure what he aimed to do once he got Three's boat out of the water and upside down on the dock, but he knew whatever it was, he wanted no witnesses.

Rested and filled with new resolve, he stood and walked to his pickup. *Should have done this in the first place,* he thought, as he tied off a length of rope to the trailer hitch. He backed the truck down to the dock then secured the rope to the boat's bow cleat. In minutes the boat straddled the dock. He removed the rope, slid the boat around lengthwise, and lifted it at the bow to turn it over.

He paced the boat's fourteen-foot length, searching for a weakness. Finally he squatted at the stern and sighted along the narrow keel. The boat simply had no secrets. Its construction was straightforward and solid.

What sinks a boat? he thought. *Water. And how does water get in? Over the top or through a hole.* Knowing he couldn't expect Three to oblige by bailing water into the boat, Jim tapped the hull as he contemplated drilling a hole and then covering it in some manner that would come apart after Three was far from the dock. There were open stretches of water over twenty feet deep on the way to most of the blinds. Even the narrow connecting channels averaged ten feet, plenty deep enough to drown a capsized hunter.

But how to fashion and conceal such a hole, only to have it open at the right time? What kind of plug would—woah. That's it. The plug.

The drain plug was near the base of the transom. Like the rest of the boat, it was simple in design—a tapered, two-inch round of hard rubber secured to the transom by a rubber strap attached to a screw eye in the plug's head.

Jim pulled the plug out and examined it. *Yes,* he thought. *This will work. Tie a cord to the metal eye and fasten the other end to the dock.* As Three pulled away from the dock, the cord would tighten, finally pulling out the plug. Once he was out of sight, Jim would untie the cord and plug from the dock and toss them. So long as Three maintained speed, water would stay out. Once he slowed to navigate the channels or put out decoys, water would come in. Fast. Stuffed in his waders and wearing a parka, he'd sink like a rock. He and his Roto Duck. It would look like the plug had worked its way out as Three motored along. An accident.

Jim stood. It seemed too easy. There had to be a snag. He paced the dock, the lesson of the shotgun shell fresh and sharp. After two minutes, he stopped. He had it. The damned strap. If the plug had worked its way out, it would still be attached to the boat.

Jim scratched his head, closed his eyes, and pieced the scene together, bit by bit, sensing that he had tumbled onto the end solution. All it needed was some tweaking. The lilt of Donna Stilton's words over the telephone floated up from the back of his brain. *If at first you don't succeed...*

He replaced the plug, pulled it out, and stuck it in again. He pulled it out one more time and let it dangle from the strap. He smiled.

He twisted the plug back into the drain hole then stood up and stretched. As he turned Three's boat back over and began to slide it into the water, he began to whistle "Anchors Aweigh."

Tuesday was Drake's favorite weekday. Rested from his weekend labors, he entered Tuesday refreshed and buoyed by the prospect of three full days until his members returned on Friday. He loved every minute of the hunting weekends, but had come to recognize the toll they claimed on his time and health. The long dinners, the booze, the physical effort of ensuring his members had the best shooting situations he could provide—all of it served to remind him that his thirty-five-year-old heart was writing checks his sixty-two-year-old body was pressed to cover.

On Tuesdays, Drake reorganized, laid out tasks, planned, reflected, and maybe even spent time with a book. Wednesday and Thursday were action days, when he'd shop, repair things, and work on blinds. Tuesdays he did what he wanted. He hadn't opened Tuesdays to Claire yet, though he knew it was only a matter of time.

It was 11:00 on what had, until that moment, been a perfect December Tuesday morning. Tar stirred from his place by the wood stove and began to circle. Drake frowned and set down his copy of *Moby Dick*, which he made a point to read every five years. He picked up his binoculars and stepped out to the deck. He watched with mounting irritation as a man climbed over the locked bar that spanned Green's Crossing and set off at a determined pace up the hill toward the Palace.

Clearly this was no poacher. He was in his thirties, dressed in jeans and a heavy shirt, wearing boots suited to the trek he was now making. He carried a thin satchel.

Drake guessed the intruder was either a salesman or a Seventh-day Adventist. As the man got closer, Drake studied his face through binoculars and ruled out the religious connection. He'd seen that look before, on men hunting other men. "Easy, Tar," he told the agitated dog. "I agree with you, though. Whatever this guy's selling, I'm not buying."

The man reached the top of the road and stood twenty yards from the Palace. "Drake Green?" he called.

"Can I help you?" Drake replied.

"You can if you're Drake Green."

"Do I know you?"

"Probably not. I have something for you."

"And what might that be?"

The man reached into the satchel and pulled out a large manila envelope. He held it up.

"This."

"What is it?"

"Personal, for you."

"Don't need it, thanks," Drake said. "Now get the hell off my property."

"Look, Mr. Green. You can either come down here and accept this from me or I'll leave it right here on the ground. Doesn't matter to me. Either way the law says you're served."

Drake groaned. Of course. A process server. Should have known.

"OK, I'm served. Good-bye."

The man laid the envelope on the ground, then turned and waved as he started back down the road.

So much for Tuesday, thought Drake.

Drake finished his third reading of the complaint, folded it, and slid it back into the envelope. *Goddamned cows, should have got rid of them years ago.* Every time he'd sold them off, he'd regretted it and replaced them, even adding to their numbers. The fact his father and grandfather had run cows on Waterloo, coupled with Three's objections, had been all the justification he needed. Not once had he imagined that what little of their piss ran off into Butte Creek or Canal 442 could cause the global catastrophe described in the lawsuit filed by the Law Offices of Jackson C. Crackers.

With his lawyer retired and his access to judicial favor gone, Drake felt like David facing Goliath, only this David's slingshot was empty. Though it was only noon, he poured himself a generous measure of the single-barrel bourbon a member had left. Two hours later, with the bottle half empty, he'd made a decision.

"Drake?"

Drake stirred, tried to open an eye, decided against it, and drifted back off. The dream was delicious. Claire standing over him, slipping delicate straps over her gorgeous tawny shoulders, her mouth a pout, her eyes a promise…

"Drake." Not a question. "Wake up."

He shook himself and attempted both eyes. It was Claire all right, but fully clothed. Red anger glowed from her eyes, and her voice was anything but inviting.

She held up the bottle. "Having a party?"

He swallowed, his mouth dry. "What time is it?" he managed.

"Six thirty," she answered. "I came out to surprise you. I guess I'm the surprised one. Is this how you spend your precious Tuesdays? Comatose?"

He sighed. *That's one of the trouble with women,* he thought. *They just don't know how to wallow when things go bad.* "Problem," he said. "Big problem."

She waved the bottle and laughed, caustic and without real humor. "Oh, 'big problem.' And this is how you face it? Honestly, Drake Green, you remind me of my father. When things got rough for old Chief Wooley, before the casino came along and turned him into Big Chief Lotsabucks, this is exactly what he used to do. Big problem. Big drunk. I don't see any casinos in your future, so I guess you'll just have to cope. What is it, or is it any of my business?"

Drake unfolded from the chair, aching for water. He walked to the sink, poured a glassful, and downed it. Then he belched. "Back to square one," he said. "Stilton's filed a lawsuit that claims my cows have polluted Butte Creek and the canal. Claims I owe millions of dollars in clean-up costs and attorney fees. I don't have a lawyer anymore and don't have the money to hire a new one."

Drake sat back down and covered his head with his hands. "I'm tired of fighting the bastard. I should sell. You and I could go have a real life."

He lowered his hands and looked up. "There."

Claire circled the room, her lips pressed thin. All the while her eyes never left him. Finally, she stopped. "All right, sell. Quit. Take the easy way. Only I guarantee you one thing. Like I told you before, that's the beginning of the end of us. In fact, let's just fast forward to the end right now. If you don't have the gumption to fight this thing and make the stand to save this property, then you're not the man who pulled me from that canal or the man who I thought I was beginning to love. I don't know where he went, but I know where he isn't. Call me if he turns up, OK?"

She spun around and left.

Drake took a deep breath and let it out. Claire's words stung him like dry summer nettles. He could handle losing Waterloo, but he wasn't sure he could handle losing her. He sank back into the chair and measured what was left in the bottle.

Drake woke at four thirty Wednesday morning. After relieving himself off the deck, he stood and listened to thousands of waterfowl as they began to churn the dawn. The incessant cackle soon produced tympanic results, and he rubbed his aching head, making what he guessed to be his four-hundredth promise not to drink straight bourbon alone again. He retreated to the medicine cabinet and downed a breakfast of three aspirin.

Claire's parting shot penetrated, and he rubbed his head again, not for the headache.

He began to count the spouting perks as the pot of coffee on his gas stove came to life. By one hundred the coffee was ready and so was he. The summons attached to the complaint said he had thirty days to answer. *Hell,* he thought, *the whole course of history has changed dozens of times in less than thirty days.*

By ten, Drake and his old D-7 Caterpillar had cleared away brush and growth, leaving a twenty-foot perimeter around what had been Waterloo Lodge. The exposed, charred timbers lay in a crazed patchwork of ruin and somber memory. Still shrouded in tangles of gnarled growth, Austin Green's two magnificent river-rock fireplaces marked the main room and dining room. Piles of rock from the upstairs fireplaces lay where they had tumbled during the conflagration.

Drake climbed down from the tractor and leaned against it, the Cat's guttural rumble somehow a fitting backdrop to the soliloquy that claimed him.

Why had he waited so long to do this? What had he been afraid to see? The day when Adam's girlfriend had driven him back to Waterloo from Mountain Home, they'd stood beside the still-smoldering wreckage with Drake's uncle. The hands of each adult rested on Drake's fifteen-year-old shoulders. It had been another world, one Drake spent years attempting to shed, only to return and live next to as if it never really existed. But it did exist, and not just in the past. With Claire, it could live again, well into the future. He shook his head and went to call her.

"Walmart."

"Camera department."

"Please hold."

Drake's throat tightened.

"Cameras." Claire's voice.

"I found him."

"Who?"

"That guy you thought you lost. He never was really lost. Just a little tired. He spent the morning bulldozing a clearing around your home site. He suggests you give notice today and spend the next six months building your new home."

He counted five seconds of silence. Then he heard her say, "Oh, Joan, would you watch the counter a few minutes? I need to speak to the manager." Back on the line, low and definite, "See you soon."

CHAPTER 19

Friday, December 23.

Jim stood back from the eight-foot Christmas tree and nodded, satisfied. Decorated with pictures of dogs, ducks, and other game birds he'd cut from outdoor magazines and pasted onto paper plates, its base was wrapped with the camo-patterned covering from his turkey hunting blind. Though the tree may have been Martha Stewart's worst nightmare, Jim saw it as one of his finest efforts in years.

Three was due, of course, since he made it a point to shoot each year on the day of Christmas Eve as well as Christmas Day itself. Jim was sure this was one of the many reasons Three's marriages kept getting shorter. *Hell*, he thought, *I'm doing the man a favor.* Jim's handiwork with the drain plug of Three's boat would bring Three's current marriage to a quick end without the usual courtroom hassle.

Only two other members were expected, bringing their sons as guests and departing Christmas Eve afternoon. That left Three for Sunday, Christmas Day, and he'd made it clear that he expected Jim to hunt with him. Jim had agreed, smiling in his knowledge that it would never happen.

The aroma of slow-roasted prime rib on a bed of carrots, potatoes, and red onions filled the Gable Farms main room, adding to the Christmas aura. Jim turned and looked at the big clock in the kitchen—2:30. He'd lost track of time, actually enjoying the tree trimming. He had one more thing to do before Three arrived and scant minutes remaining to get it done.

He left the main lodge, checked down the road to make sure no one was approaching, then trotted across the gravel parking area to his quarters in the double-wide tucked in the trees. He emerged twenty minutes later, limping and using a cane, his left foot and ankle wrapped in an elastic bandage over a stocking. *None too soon,* he thought, as the unmistakable crunch that preceded Three's Hummer bore down the road.

Two of Drake's members had opted to hunt only the morning of Christmas Eve day, leaving the rest of the weekend to him and Claire. She arrived at four o'clock, chased by the long shadows of the setting winter sun.

"What's all this?" Drake asked, taking in the tree tied on top and the cargo compartment crammed with packages. The fact she had gone to such extremes warmed him. He couldn't remember the last time he'd celebrated a real Christmas. It had been his pattern to spend the whole of Christmas Day in a duck blind. Whether or not the ducks were flying, it beat the loneliness of his empty concrete bastion. Tar and the dog's predecessors had been all the company he'd thought he needed or wanted.

"Christmas," Claire said. "Santa's helper craves an eggnog. I brought all the makings. Let's get this sled unloaded."

They decorated the small tree, and she arranged the packages around its base. Drake cooked them a duck dinner, and they spent the rest of the evening with her curled at his feet as he read to her the entirety of *Tortilla Flat.*

He finished and they sat, letting Danny's final and fatal triumph retreat back into the history that Steinbeck had immortalized.

Finally she sighed, then spoke. "That was beautiful. I can see why it's one of your favorites."

"Tell me," he said. "I've always wondered."

She looked up at him. "I don't believe that. If it's true, it's because you try to avoid knowing yourself."

He shrugged.

"OK," she said. "Danny sees all and knows all. But he doesn't really try to affect the outcome of events around him. He's a fatalist. A romantic and wonderful fatalist."

"And you think that's what I am?"

She nodded and smiled. "Until now. Danny let his world go up in flames. That happened to you once, before you could do anything about it. You're not going to let it happen again. I know that."

He chuckled, bent down, and kissed her.

"Want to shoot some ducks tomorrow?" he whispered.

"I can't see spending Christmas Day any other way," she said.

CHAPTER 20

Sunday, December 25.

It was 5:05 a.m. and Three's petulance hung over the table like a mass of valley fog. Jim hobbled from the stove to the refrigerator, preparing his boss's breakfast and pretending all was well, which he knew irritated Three even further.

The two other members and their sons had departed early the previous afternoon, Nick Pappas swallowing his displeasure over Three's intrusion into the one morning Pappas had set aside to hunt with his son. While the other father-son team had come in with limits apiece, Three's persistent squawks through a duck call and constant futzing with his remote-controlled decoy spread had spooked any ducks that had shown signs of temptation.

"Never again," Pappas had muttered as Jim helped him load up to leave. Jim had simply nodded, content in the knowledge that Pappas's statement would soon be a literal truth.

With considerable difficulty, Jim approached the table, the coffee pot in one hand, his body balanced by the cane in the other. The pot quivered as he filled Three's cup.

"Oh, for Christ's sake," snapped Three. "Let me do that before you scald me to death. *Scald,* thought Jim. Now, there was one he hadn't thought of. He relinquished the pot to Three.

"Can't you at least come out to the blind with me?" said Three. "Just sit there and call. I'll do all the work, put out the decoys…everything."

"Sorry, Armand. Doctor says I have to stay off it and keep it elevated. It's a seriously torn ligament. If it gets any worse, I'll need surgery."

"This happened yesterday at the dock?"

"Yeah, while I was gassing the boats. Slipped and twisted it completely around. Thought I broke my leg at first. It was all I could do to get to my truck and drive to Colusa. Supposed to stay off it for at least a week. If not, surgery's a sure bet."

Their eyes met, and Jim knew he'd made his point. While his employment relationship with Gable Farms was unfettered by the layers of procedure and administration that muddled most businesses, he was still an employee and, as such, covered by workers compensation, which Three regarded as a Marxian encumbrance designed to cripple free enterprise and redistribute the wealth.

Three sipped his coffee and nodded toward the kitchen. "Don't burn my bacon and get my eggs off. I want them over easy."

As Jim limped back to the stove, Three added, "You got my boat gassed before you screwed yourself up, didn't you?"

Jim turned and smiled. "Armand, your boat's all set. Good hunting. Oh, supposed to be a stiff north wind today. Wear those six-millimeter neoprene waders, and that new parka of yours, the heavy one. You'll need it."

After Drake had the guns and decoys loaded, he motioned to Tar. The dog sat on the boat's middle seat and faced forward, radiating anticipation and energy.

"OK, Claire, you're next," Drake said, extending an arm. She took it and slid down onto the front seat.

"Which blind are we hunting?" she asked, arranging things around her.

Drake stood at the stern, surveying the dark morning sky. "We have the place to ourselves so we'll take Number Three. It shoots the best in a north wind like this. We shot there the first time I brought you out."

"Oh, yes," she said. "Where you shot your neighbor's duck thing."

Drake winced, convinced his fun that morning had triggered his latest conflict with Stilton. "That's the one."

He cranked up the motor, backed from the dock, and set off into the maze of channels that snaked through the thick tules between

Waterloo's ponds. While others used powerful flashlights to find their way, Drake navigated the complex network in the dark, each turn scribed in his memory by thirty summers of keeping the channels clear, carving new ones, and sculpting ponds to match the flight patterns of the ducks.

After one of her first trips on Waterloo, Claire had told Drake that their plunge into the dark puzzle was like riding a roller coaster blindfolded. For Drake it always brought the same rush he'd felt swooping down jungle canyons in a death-spitting helicopter. He stood at the stern, steering by means of a four-foot extension pipe connected to the outboard's control handle. As the tules whipped by, he boomed into the wind: "Dum dum da da dum dum, dum da da dum dum..." recalling the scene from *Apocalypse Now* where Robert Duvall terrorized targets below to the amplified "Ride of the Valkyeries."

Claire, her head down as they raced through the darkness, managed to turn back and stare. "Oh, please..." she shouted, laughing at Drake's joy and the spectacle of his looming bulk, his bellowing tribute almost lost in the wind that slammed against him.

"Oh, you like that?" he shouted. "Second verse, twice as worse. Dum dum da da dum dum, dum da da dum dum, dum da da dum dum, dum da da daaaa..." Tar joined in, and the dog's howls turned the moment to pandemonium. Drake finally had to stop the boat. He collapsed in laughter.

"Duck hunting's not supposed to be like this," he managed to say.

"Fun, you mean?" she gasped, also doubled over.

"No," he said. He leaned forward around Tar and pulled her face to his. "I mean this." He kissed her and held her close a full ten seconds before returning to his position at the stern. "Enough playing around. Time to shoot ducks."

Jim drove his glowering employer to the dock and, with considerable difficulty, helped load Three's gear into the boat.

"Jethro," Jim commanded, and his dog jumped in.

"You'll do fine with him, Armand. All you have to do is shoot the ducks. Jethro knows what to do."

127

"Still don't like it," mumbled Three. "You seem to be getting around well enough."

"Armand, I'm sorry, I just can't. I'm going to my trailer, taking a Vicodin, and getting this foot elevated. Call me when you start in, and I'll be here to meet you."

Three stepped into the boat and sat down where he always did, in front.

Jim shook his head. "Armand, the dog's pretty good, but he hasn't learned to drive the boat yet. You'll need to sit in back by the motor. You're on your own today, sir."

"Shit," Three said, and scrambled to relocate himself.

"Just pull the cord. Should start right up," said Jim.

It did.

"Now, put the gear selector forward and twist the throttle. All there is to it. When you get to the blind, push that button on the end of the handle. That's the kill switch."

Armand mumbled something, and the boat moved slowly forward. Jim watched the thin cord trail from the dock. As the boat disappeared in the dark, the cord held taut above the water for an instant then abruptly went slack, its job done.

Jim waited and listened as Three's motor accelerated, finally fading to a distant buzz. Satisfied, he knelt on the dock and retrieved the cord, all fifty yards of it. He reached the end and held up the wooden plug he'd carved to replace the rubber one that now dangled uselessly from the transom of Three's boat. *Nice*, he thought. *I should frame this.*

Drake throttled back and let the boat glide into the pond. Ahead, the dark mound of the blind was silhouetted in the dawning light. "OK, partner," he said, "You know the drill."

He slowly circled in front of the blind as Claire unwound the cords that tethered lead weights to the decoys. She tossed each decoy over the side, where it landed with a small splash, wobbled, then righted itself.

"Perfect," said Drake. "You're a pro at this."

"I learned from the master," she said.

Drake killed the engine and poled the boat into the slot at the foot of the blind. Claire tied off the bow line. Drake said, "Tar," and the dog jumped up into the blind, then over to its hide. Claire crawled from the boat into the blind.

"All set?" said Drake. She nodded, and he passed up the guns and rest of their gear. Then he stepped up and stood next to her, peering into the mist. He raised a call to his lips.

Armand Three cursed Jim as he headed up the third wrong channel. "Should fire the sonofabitch," he muttered, his pique at being lost in his own duck club mounting. With each wrong turn the boat became harder to steer, adding to his list of scores to settle with Quesenberry. Finally, as dawn spread over the valley and familiar shapes formed around him, Three spotted the wooden sign marking the entrance to Doghouse, his destination. He pushed the motor's control handle to make the turn, and the boat came around sluggishly.

"Like steering a goddamned cow," he said, then smiled. Jackson Crackers had called him on his drive up to report that the lawsuit was underway. The thought of Drake Green's pissing cows finally delivering Waterloo into Stilton ownership served to lift his brooding over Quesenberry's treacherous clumsiness and shoddy boat maintenance. He brightened even more as the channel fanned out to form the pond surrounding Doghouse. He cut back on the throttle and reached for his Roto Duck pole, which Jim had laid carefully next to him. But the pole wasn't there. Just water. He looked down, shocked to see the entire bottom of the boat full of water, a fact he'd missed because he was wearing the extra-thick waders.

"What the hell...?"

He plunged his hand down again, this time connecting with the pole, a good six inches under water.

Confused, he struggled with the pole, still intent on sinking its base into the mud at the edge of the pond. He dismissed the water in the boat as something having to do with...*Hell, it doesn't matter.* He'd put out his Roto Duck, spread his mechanical decoys, then radio that malingering bastard Quesenberry and tell him if he wanted his job one more day he'd get his sorry ass out to the blind and fix the god-damned boat.

He pulled the control handle to turn the boat toward the pond's edge, but it wouldn't budge. Instead, the stern began to settle down, and the water reached his knees. Jethro barked once and stepped gingerly over the side into the pond. Armand watched, transfixed, as the dog paddled toward the blind.

"Goddamn you, get back here!"

The dog kept swimming.

Armand clutched the aluminum sides of the boat until the icy water flooded over his hands. Then he scrambled to the front, which seemed higher and dryer. The whole boat settled lower, water now spilling over its entire length. Within seconds the boat disappeared beneath him, and he began to kick in his struggle to stay afloat. But the custom-made, extra-thick neoprene waders and his triple-insulated Gore-Tex parka formed a death suit that immobilized him and drew him under. Water seeped over the chest bib of the waders, and hundreds of tiny cold needles jabbed him into panic as he flailed his arms.

"Help! Help me! Oh God, help!"

Drake watched from under the brim of his cap as the five mallards he'd been calling locked their wings and began to drop. "Any second now, I'll tell you when," he whispered. Suddenly the ducks flared and veered away to the west.

"Christ, not again," Drake said, rising. He stared north toward Gable Farms, surprised he hadn't heard shots when the ducks had dropped over Doghouse, the blind just over the levee. "Something sure scared them," he said. "Wonder what…"

Then he heard it, faint but unmistakable. A shout.

"Shhh, listen."

"Help, help…" Dwindling, then nothing.

"Tar, come. You, too, Claire. Someone's in trouble over there. Let's hustle."

They scrambled into the boat. Claire cast off the bow, and within seconds Drake had them racing toward the levee. He cut the engine just feet away, letting momentum drive the boat well up the slope. Claire grabbed the bowline and searched for a spot to tie it.

"Forget it," he said. "It'll stay. Come on."

He clutched her hand and pulled her along behind him, taking the bank in three strides. He stood at the top and scanned the pond.

"There, the far edge," he said. "See that?"

Claire crawled up beside him.

"Yes, yes, I see it. What is it?"

"Not what, but who," Drake said, stripping off his jacket. He slipped the straps of his waders over his shoulders and began to peel them off.

"You're not going to…" Claire began.

"The only way," he said, sitting and pulling his feet out of the wader boots.

"Tar, fetch." He pointed toward the commotion at the edge of the pond. The dog dove in. Drake followed.

Too weak and numb to call out anymore, Armand yielded to unfamiliar instincts as his brain, not schooled in physical effort, took over in a fight for survival. His stubby legs scissored in an irregular rhythm while his arms windmilled in ever slowing arcs. Suddenly one of them caught on something. His hand opened automatically and seized it, his fingers finding openings like four keys in four locks. *The bag,* his brain told him, *the decoy bag.*

Armand spit water and turned his head toward his hand. Sure enough, the mesh bag containing his prized remote-controlled decoys had floated away from the boat as it sank, the mass of buoyant plastic birds now bobbing on the surface. With his last strength, he flung his other arm over and grabbed the bag with both hands.

When he dug his fingers into the mesh and burdened the bag with his weight, it began to sink. Once more he felt himself slipping under—this time, he knew, for good. Still he clung to the bag, sensing that at least it slowed his descent. Besides, if there was one thing he would have picked to take with him into eternity, it was his electric ducks.

Drake swam with long, paced strokes, following Tar's wake as the dog beelined toward the edge of the pond. Every third breath Drake managed to look ahead, staying true to the dog's course. The splashing slowed then stopped altogether. Something bulky marked the spot then it too began to disappear. Drake saw Tar go under. With a final burst, Drake covered the last twenty yards in five strokes.

The dog surfaced feet from him, a rope in its mouth. Drake grabbed the rope and felt a great weight. He gasped some air and dove. Four feet under he bumped into what he recognized by feel to be a decoy bag. Then his groping hand connected with an arm. He struggled to the surface, hauling the body with him.

"Tar," he shouted as he emerged. "Here. Hold." He thrust out the arm and the dog took it in its mouth. Drake followed the line of the man's shoulders and found the other arm. With his free hand Drake motioned toward the blind. "Tar, there," he said, flattening his hand and scribing a hatchet chop. Together they swam, the body heavy and motionless between them.

Inside the boat slip, Drake took both of the man's inert hands and raised them one on top of the other up to the floorboards of the blind. Quesenberry's dog, Jethro, greeted him full in the face with a happy Labrador tongue, the dog obviously cheered by the sudden arrival of all this interesting company. Drake pushed the animal aside and, putting his weight on the victim's hands, lifted himself into the blind. Then he grabbed the man by the armpits, pulled him up and turned him onto his back. He stared for a second and shook his head.

"I was afraid it was you. My bad luck."

He tilted Stilton's head back and forced his mouth open, confirming that the tongue hadn't been swallowed. He knelt close and checked for breathing, then a pulse. Nothing. He covered Stilton's mouth with his own and blew in two sharp breaths. Again, he checked for pulse and breaths. Still nothing. He placed the heels of both palms over Stilton's sternum and leaned into five sharp compressions. He stopped and bent down to blow in more air when Stilton suddenly coughed and a trickle of water drooled from his mouth. He coughed again, this time followed by a green stream of water and vomit. Drake rolled him over on his side. As Stilton emptied onto the rough boards, Jethro, tail wagging, lapped it up as fast as it poured out.

After much wretching and swearing, Stilton pulled himself free of Drake's support. He sat on the floor and looked up.

"You," he coughed.

"Yeah, me. Merry Christmas, asshole."

Drake stood, crossed his arms overhead, and called to Claire. "Take the boat and go back. Go next door and tell Jim to bring two boats out here. Three's boat sank. He's OK, I think, just waterlogged. Have Jim call 911 and get an ambulance with paramedics."

Claire waved and disappeared as she left the levee. Drake knelt down, inches away from Stilton's wan face.

"You scared my ducks away. Again. Make it the last time. Understand?"

CHAPTER 21

J im Quesenberry sat in the dark, too stunned and depressed to function. Over and over, the caustic irony played itself out in a dirge of failure and frustration.

Three had sat huddled in blankets on the ride in, shivering and silent. Jim couldn't tell which of his boss's emotions would prevail, his anger or his fright. Either way, Jim knew he'd come out the loser.

The paramedics had been waiting at the dock. They'd swarmed over Three, checking his pulse, respirations, and blood pressure. Satisfied that the only thing drowned was Three's ego, they'd pronounced him fit but recommended a good night's sleep. Three had told them they didn't know shit and ordered Jim to drive him to the clubhouse. He'd put on fresh clothes, climbed into the Hummer, and sprayed gravel in an angry departure. He didn't thank Drake Green. He never acknowledged his presence.

As the Hummer dwindled in the distance, Drake turned to Jim and said, "That man's either the dumbest or the luckiest man I've ever known. Probably both. He really should give up duck hunting."

Jim, still reeling from the disastrous turn of events, stood there, hoping at any second he would wake from his nightmare. He was supposed to be mounting a concerned search for his employer that would end with a call to Sheriff Duke to report Three and his boat were missing. Jethro would, of course, have been waiting at Doghouse blind, eager for someone to come out and shoot a duck.

"Jim," Drake continued, jolting him back to reality, "how the hell do you figure the man's boat just dropped out from beneath him? Hell, even Stilton can drive a boat, can't he?"

Jim shrugged. "Barely," he said in a rasp.

"What?" Drake asked.

"I said barely," Jim answered. "I usually take him out, or he goes with a member. The only other time he's been on his own was that mess a couple of weeks ago. I was supposed to go with him today, but I couldn't."

Drake threw Jim a quizzical look. "Oh, yeah, I forgot. You hurt yourself. Glad to see you're better."

In all the excitement, Jim had left his cane in his trailer. Grimacing, he remembered that the last time he limped that day had been when he helped Three load up at the dock.

Jim tried to shrug it off, afraid to say anything else. He headed for his trailer, careful to put on a good limp.

"Hey, Jim," Drake called. "I thought it was your right ankle."

"Shit," Jim muttered to himself, stumbling.

Drake poured two glasses of red wine and handed one to Claire.

"The hunting day's shot," he said. "Might as well make the best of what's left. Merry Christmas, again."

They touched glasses and sat down on the couch. She reached over and absently stroked his beard. "So, tell me, do you just go around saving lives?"

He took a sip, swished it, then swallowed. "You do what you have to."

She set her glass on the table and grew serious. "Honestly, now. Was there just a second after you realized who it was that you..." She paused.

Drake let that sit, then laughed. "Honestly?" he said. "Hell, let me think on that."

He took another drink and sat back, his eyes closed, as he replayed the whole rescue scene. Then he chuckled. Yes, he'd known who it was from the moment he'd raised Stilton's other arm while they were still in the water. The squat, heavy shape of his troublesome neighbor was unique. Danny DeVito in waders. Drake had met all the Gable Farms members at one time or another, and it could have been no one else.

"I guess I knew it was him before I got him to the blind," he said. "There was no way I could just let the man die. Without him, my life would be some kind of fairy tale. Couldn't have that."

She rolled her eyes.

Darkness magnified Jim's paranoia, and the night monsters began their tormented dance.

How could he have screwed this up? But then, the bigger question loomed to haunt him: How could he have ever tried this in the first place? He was no murderer. Jim paced the clubhouse main room, its ordinary shadows and familiar objects mocking him.

He'd let Donna Stilton's money and his sister's plight lead him to this. While Three would never suspect it had been attempted murder, the fact that the boat had sunk would be enough. It didn't matter why it sank; it just did, probably taking Jim's perfect job with it.

Jim collapsed to a chair and fumbled with the TV remote control, hungry for something, anything, to take his mind off the miserable turn his life had taken.

The telephone rang. With a sense of foreboding, he lifted the receiver. It had to be her. She always called after he tried to kill her husband.

"Hello."

"Jim?"

"Yes."

"I know what happened. He told me when he got home. I'm down the street at a friend's place. I had to talk to you. Can you talk?"

"Yes, no one's here. What's there to talk about? It's over. I tried twice and failed. It's not in me to try again. Besides, I'm pretty sure that after he gets himself sorted out, I won't be working here. Thanks for what you've tried to do for my sister and Cedar Hills, but call your bank and take the money back. I'll tell the director the funding just didn't work out. They'll have to release what you've already paid, won't they?"

There was a long silence before she spoke again.

"Jim," she said, finally. "Are you a baseball fan?"

Jim shook his head, not sure he had heard correctly. "What?"

"Are you a baseball fan?"

"Well, no, not really. Not until the World Series. I usually watch part of that, if it's close and gets exciting."

"Do you know who Barry Bonds is?" she asked.

Jim searched his memory. "Can't say I do. Sounds familiar though."

"It should. He was the world's leading home run hitter. He played for the San Francisco Giants. I went to many home games where he played. Guess what I saw him do."

"What?"

"It was the bottom of the ninth, and the Giants were behind, seven to four. There were two outs and the bases were loaded. Bonds came to bat. He swung at the first two pitches and missed. The third pitch came toward the plate, high and outside. It would have been called a ball but Bonds stepped into it and blasted it into San Francisco Bay, a grand slam. The Giants won, eight to seven."

Jim sat quiet, finding her account interesting, but suspecting it to be the rambling of a rabid baseball fan who had too much to drink during an off-season night.

"Jim, are you with me?"

"I'm here."

"No, Jim, Dear, are you *with* me?"

"With you? What do you mean?"

"Jim, there are two outs, the bases are loaded, and it's the bottom of the ninth. There are two strikes against you, but you're still at bat. We need a grand slam. For your sister." Her voice dropped to a husky whisper that stirred him where it shouldn't, at least where she was concerned. "And, Jim, for me."

The line went dead.

CHAPTER 22

The week between Christmas and New Year's settled over northern California with a balmy quiet. The rains stopped, flood waters receded, and warm, clear days brought families out in droves. Homebound kids delighted in showing off new bikes and other booty while most adults were just glad for the pause before January 2, when whoever or whatever happened to be their particular Simon LeGree would raise the whip that sent them back to work.

People streamed to parks, theatres, and restaurants, celebrating the good weather and freedom from relatives for another year. At least that's how it played out in the cities and towns. Miles from such bustle and surrounded by watery barriers the Butte Sink remained stalled in its timeless isolation.

Drake told Claire that Monday was one of his customary rest days and that he saw no reason to treat this one any different. His close encounter of the wet kind with Armand Stilton had left him on edge. Stilton's hostile reaction was to be expected, but Quesenberry's weird behavior raised a question mark in the middle of a paragraph without beginning or end.

Claire left him to vegetate while she paced off the rough-cleared building site and planned their next moves. At the head of her list was the Dumpster they would need for all the debris. Inside the barely visible outline of the old foundation remained a pile of charred wreckage.

Within an hour the scope of the project began to overwhelm her. She'd never built a house before and was amazed at Drake's casual attitude toward such an undertaking.

"Relax," he told her from the deck, where he was reading. "Once we get the place cleared off, you'll see how fast things go. I figure we'll use the same foundation. Framing goes fast. We'll have the siding on by May. Then you take over."

"Don't we need plans?" she called up, shielding her eyes from the sun.

Drake made a thumbs-up. "Taken care of. One of my members is an architect. I asked him to put something together. He'll get a free season out of it. I gave him our sketches. You'll be the final judge, don't worry."

She nodded, probing the rubble with her shoe. Then she asked, "Where can I find a bucket?" He pointed to his work shed and returned to his book.

The day passed as Drake read and Claire busied herself prowling Waterloo's ruins. He peered over the book occasionally, each time finding it harder to ignore what she was doing.

At four thirty he set the book down, stretched, and stood. Claire was barely visible on the far side of the site, on her hands and knees, deep in her work.

"Hey, you," he called. She waved an arm, but didn't get up.

"Claire," he called, again. "It's after five somewhere. Sun's over the yardarm."

She waved back but stayed down.

"Dammit," he called. "It's time for a drink."

This time she stood. He noticed she required both hands to lift the bucket. "Be there in a minute," she called back. "Make mine a gin and tonic. A big one."

He grunted and went inside, where he poured himself a bourbon and soda and cut up a lime for her drink. He'd defrosted four green-wing teal for dinner. He sprinkled them with a mixture of wine and soy sauce, then rubbed them with his special blend of paprika, pepper, garlic, and dill. He was starting to wash and drain some rice when he heard her on the stairs. He filled a large beer glass with ice, squeezed in half a lime, poured in a six-count of Beefeaters and topped it from a fresh bottle of tonic. As she reached the top of the stairs, he handed her the glass.

"Perfect!" she said, and took a long, slow drink. She set the bucket on the floor and wrapped her arms around his neck, laughing as he shied from her soot-covered face.

"What a great day I've had," she said. "This place is so peaceful. Just the sounds of all the birds—the ducks, geese, everything. You'll have to teach me how to tell what kind they are."

"Sure," he said. He eyed the bucket but quickly looked away. "Let's take our drinks outside on the deck and see what's flying."

She shook her head and spread her hands. "Look at me. I'm a mess and need a shower. Then, if it's still light, let's do some bird watching. Hope there's lots of hot water." She turned and headed for his room and the shower.

His eyed drifted back to the bucket. "What's in there?" he said.

She turned back. "Oh, just stuff I picked up. Things I thought would interest you. Wait and I'll show you. Promise?"

"I promise," he said, keeping the irritation out of his voice. It wasn't her fault. He should have told her the rules.

She returned and picked up the bucket. "I don't trust you. It's coming with me." She disappeared into his room and closed the door.

She emerged forty-five minutes later, scrubbed and fresh. She held out her glass. "Can you do that again?"

Drake punched off the evening news he hadn't been watching and made her a fresh drink. While he did that, she shook out her long, dark hair, and he was amazed how it tumbled into place. He set the drink on the table and turned on the oven.

"So?" he said.

She picked up the glass. "So, what?"

"The bucket, Miss Archaeologist. Where is it?"

"Oh, I forgot. Wait, I'll get it."

She went back to his room, brought it out, and set it on the floor next to her. "We'll need some newspaper and gloves," she said. "This stuff's all rusted and filthy."

Drake's patience had thinned. For decades he'd resisted the urge to dig among Waterloo's ruins, willing the past to stay where it was. And here Claire, free of his mental baggage, had picked up a bucket and plunged in. He'd planned to simply scrape Waterloo's ashes aside and haul them away, rather than sift for things he did not want to know.

He went to the wood stove and pulled some papers from a pile, then opened a drawer and pawed through it until he found a pair of garden gloves.

"Here," he said, handing her the gloves. He spread the papers on the table.

"Hey, why so glum?" she said. "This is fun, like a treasure hunt."

She reached into the bucket.

Donna Stilton sat at her end of the ridiculously long dining table and prepared her arsenal of responses—nods or shakes of the head, gasps, ahhhs, and an occasional exclamatory "No!" demonstrating her awe at whatever conquest of field or stream Armand happened to be claiming at the time.

"So, I told Jim," he said between bites of braised Belgian squab, "'Hey, take the morning off and rest that foot.' Poor guy was in real pain. Hell, there was no reason for him to suffer. He really wanted to come along, but I insisted. Didn't even let him load the boat. Once I got going, everything seemed fine. Got right to the pond with no trouble and started putting out decoys. All of a sudden, no boat. Period. Damn thing just went under without any warning whatsoever."

"No!"

"Yep, dropped like it had no bottom."

She was torn between a gasp and an ooh. She chose the gasp. It was the right choice, since his expression registered satisfaction at her shock.

"Well, first thing I did was see to it that Jim's dog, Jethro, got to safety. I pointed to the blind and ordered it away. I knew I could take care of myself, but I just couldn't face telling Jim something terrible had happened to the dog."

"Ahhh…"

Armand stared down the table. She decided to ease off a little.

"Next I took stock of where I was and what I could do about it. Damned hard swimming in waders and a parka, so I looked around for something to hold onto. My decoy bag was floating a few yards away, so I swam over and grabbed it. Remember *Papillon* and the coconuts in the sack? Well, that's what I had in mind. And, by God, it worked."

"Thank God." His reference to the Deity had inspired her. She'd wait a few minutes and use it again.

"I was paddling my way toward the blind when all of a sudden that idiot Green shows up alongside me, he and his goddamned dog. First thing I know, they're all over me, forcing me under, getting us all tangled together."

She gasped.

"I managed to get them sorted out, but by this time I have to admit I was getting pretty tired. After all, I'd been in that freezing water a good ten minutes, saving that damn mutt of Jim's, and working my way to safety. Suddenly Green panicked and assaulted me again. By this time both he and his dog looked like they were going down. I held on to each of them and kept kicking toward the blind. They were too much weight for the decoy sack though, and it started to sink."

"Thank God."

"What was that?"

"I said, My God…"

"Oh. Well, anyway, I had a choice to make. Them or me. I chose me. Hard, but that's how it is in the wild sometimes. Eat or be eaten. I kept going toward the blind, and they got there just as I did, so no harm done. Next thing I know, Green attacks me again, blowing in my mouth and punching me in the chest. I figure he was trying to impress me with some kind of macho hero life-saving act to get me to ease off on him. Well, he didn't fool me, not for a minute."

Armand drank some wine, then continued. "As a matter of fact, just before dinner I talked to my new lawyer, Crackers. We're turning up the heat. He says I'll have that property of Green's by April." He resumed eating, but then paused between bites.

"One more thing."

"What's that, dear?"

"Jim Quesenberry. I'm letting him go. He's just not up to the job any longer. I know how you like to shoot with him, but I'll find someone just as good, I promise. Probably even better. As soon as this season is over, he's history."

It would have been another gasp, this time a real one, but she stifled it.

Claire asked Drake for a fingernail scrub brush and the basting brush he used for cooking. Then she mixed a solution of water, kitchen detergent, and heavy-duty cleanser. She had him go downstairs and bring up some solvent from his shop, and she poured some in an empty can.

With care she began removing items from the bucket, one by one, dipping them in either the wash solution or the solvent, depending on their condition, then brushing them and wiping them down with a dish towel. The bucket yielded old nails, nuts, bolts, ceramic shards, stuff that either had escaped the fire's intense heat or was impervious to it. After half an hour, Drake was wondering why he'd resisted combing the ruins all those years. Junk was junk.

He was considering turning the TV back on when she stopped and stared down into the bucket.

"Oh, I forgot about this one. It's special, I think." She reached down with both hands and brought them up behind her back. "Which hand?"

Drake shrugged. Either way she was about to foist some particularly foul old piece of scrap on him. He tapped her left arm.

"You win," she said, and brought around her closed fist. She began to uncurl her fingers, one by one, pausing a few seconds between each. He watched as, with maddening slowness, a dark metal shape began to appear—square or rectangular, he couldn't tell which yet. It had rounded corners and was almost half an inch thick. As she lifted her third finger, he saw a line across the shape, no, not a line, a break, straight across, with a small hinge at one end. She lifted her last two fingers at once to reveal an old metal Zippo lighter, blackened but intact.

"Here," she said, holding it out to him. "I figured it was your father's."

He stared at it a full ten seconds before he spoke. "It's not my father's. He didn't smoke."

He took the lighter and examined it. She pushed the can of solvent toward him and handed him the rag.

"There's something on the side," she said. "See it? Some writing, or a design."

"I know what it is," he said. "A duck. Inscribed over it there's a G and an F. I'd bet on it."

He dipped the rag into the solvent and began to clean the side of the lighter.

"There," he said. Sure enough, engraved into the metal was a duck in flight with the initials GF scrolled around and through it.

"Gable Farms," Drake said. "They gave them to their members. When I was a kid, Stilton had this Kraut for a caretaker, a scary dude named Klaus Krenzler. Besides always chasing me and Quesenberry off the place when we were poaching, he used to come over here and pester my dad with complaints from Old Man Stilton. He had one of these. Creepy old bastard smoked like a chimney. A few days before the fire, my dad threw him off the place and told him he'd load his pants with bird shot if he ever caught him here again."

Suddenly Drake stiffened. "Jesus."

He turned the lighter over and went to work on the other side. When he was done, he exhaled and shook his head.

"What's wrong?" Claire said.

"Look," he said, pointing to the engraved initials he'd exposed.

"KK. This was his lighter, Krenzler's. Has to be."

Drake stood and began to pace. "My uncle tried to get the fire department to investigate. They wouldn't. Too small. Just a bunch of volunteers with an old handed-down truck. The 'chief' was a tractor dealer in Colusa. He told my uncle that Dad must have been burning tules or stubble and the fire got away from him. Ridiculous. My dad was too careful. When he burned, he always had hoses hooked up and used me to help. He wouldn't have sent me off to Mountain Home with Laura if he was going to burn."

Drake stopped pacing and stood, looking out over the lodge ruins. A full minute passed before he spoke again.

"A couple of days ago Jim Quesenberry told me Old Man Stilton had retired Krenzler and bought him a house in Grass Valley." He turned the lighter in his hands. "I'd bet anything that was right after the fire."

CHAPTER 23

Tuesday, December 27.

For Jackson Crackers, there were three exquisite pleasures:

Number three: catching some unsuspecting entrepreneur or major corporation with their legal pants down, and nailing them for a shakedown settlement of a million dollars. California law required warnings posted if any of a litany of chemicals buried in the statute's fine print were used or produced on an employer's premises. The fines for failing to post accrued at $2,500 a day. One year's failure meant potential penalties of over $900,000. Most business that Crackers targeted had been in technical violation for years, facing fines in the millions. Crackers would file a lawsuit in the name of some allegedly aggrieved party and then, for a million dollars, agree to go away. This legal blackmail was expressly condoned by California's infamous Proposition 65, palmed off on the voters by well-meaning environmentalists and embraced by legal bounty hunters who saw it for what it was—a statutory jet stream to easy money, and lots of it.

Number two: sniffing out and extorting settlements from individuals or businesses in violation of the Federal Clean Water Act. Like California's Proposition 65, this legislation had spawned a host of brief-slinging lawyers who collected monetary scalps by exposing and pretending to correct violations. In most instances, the defendant ponied up a quick settlement for Crackers *et al.* to disappear, then continued to pollute.

But, for pure ecstasy, nothing beat number one, a tactic Crackers frequently employed in the service of numbers two and three: sneaking into court on an *ex parte* application for a temporary restraining order to shut down some business or activity, having given the minimum twenty-four-hour telephone notice. Crackers would sweep into the judge's chambers at the appointed hour, armed with sworn declarations of the calamity and disaster that were sure to follow if the defendant's illegal, tortious, and noxious activities were not immediately halted. Most of his applications were denied, but the process tended to make instant believers of the defendants, who got to witness Crackers's fervor and imagined how perilously close to financial extinction he could take them. Even if they survived the temporary restraining order, Crackers's targets generally fell in line and instructed their attorneys to pay him and make him go away.

In the case of Drake Green and Waterloo, Crackers was, for the first time, working for a real client. He would never collect a settlement from Green, who didn't have that kind of money. Instead, Armand Stilton III had agreed to pay Crackers his million. All Crackers had to do was push Green over the misery line, making life at Waterloo so intolerable that he'd sell the place to Stilton. Crackers had told Stilton that with a chemist and a courthouse he could oust the Devil from hell.

Crackers checked the large clock on his wall. At exactly 9:55 a.m. he picked up the phone and dialed. He was delighted when he heard an answering machine.

"This is Drake Green. Leave a message."

Crackers drew a breath.

"Mr. Green. This is Jackson Crackers, attorney for Armand Stilton III and all property owners affected by the discharge from your property of pollutants into Butte Creek and Canal 442. This call is to give you notice that at ten tomorrow morning, Wednesday, December 28, I will appear in Department One of the Sutter County Superior Court to seek a temporary restraining order preventing you from engaging in activities that discharge pollutants into Butte Creek or Canal 442. It is now nine-fifty-eight a.m. on Tuesday, December 27."

Brevity being the sting of notice, Crackers hung up..

Charlie Rainwater threw the Trans-Am into a 180 turn, expertly steering into the skid that launched him into a head-on, ninety-mile-an-hour collision course with his pursuers. The Fish and Game pickup, burdened with a camper shell, was no match for the nimble Pontiac. Charlie muttered a satisfied grunt as he flashed by the fishtailing pickup and watched in his rearview mirror as it disappeared in a hail of dust over the shallow embankment. Seconds later, his scanner picked up the doleful announcement: "We've, uh, lost him about six miles west of Bald Eagle Butte."

The broad lava formation known as Bald Eagle Butte, just inside the California state line, had long been one of Charlie's favored poaching grounds. Following his usual routine, he had paid little attention that morning to boundaries, relying instead on his knowledge of where his quarry likely would be.

Sensing there would be more on the radio, Charlie slowed down. If there were serious injuries, he'd have to go back and help, which would not only ruin his day but end his probation and land him in the state hotel at San Quentin for at least a year. As far as he knew, the hunting and fishing opportunities in prison were negligible, though, as a precaution, he'd read up on sturgeon fishing in San Pablo Bay, within the shadow of San Quentin's walls. The radio crackled.

"Oh, and send a tow truck. We ran over the edge and something up front snapped. Damned truck won't steer. Suggest that all other units concentrate on picking him up on Highway 97. It's a red Trans-Am. Not hard to spot. Set up a roadblock, though. It's the only way you'll get him."

Charlie grunted and gunned the engine. The last place he'd be that day in the Trans-Am was Highway 97.

He drove west a mile, then pulled over at an innocuous wide spot bordered by thick shrubs. He searched the bushes for a moment, found what he was looking for, and turned the car directly into them.

What looked from the road like an impenetrable tangle of dense growth parted, as if by magic, and the Trans-Am passed through. Clear of the brush, Charlie steered up a rough track some fifty yards and stopped at another tangle. He was at the base of a dark rise of lava rock, which he'd calculated some time ago to be in Oregon. Again he nosed the Trans-Am through the brush, which concealed the opening of a cave four times the size of the car. In it was a faded-blue '66 Ford pickup that looked as though it had been painted with a paintbrush. It had. Mounted over the bed of the truck was a green camper shell, the contrasting colors testimony to the fact that the shell had been scrounged from a scrap pile.

Charlie opened the trunk of the Trans-Am and hauled out the carcass of a 125-pound black-tail doe. He dragged it to one edge of the cave, where a boxed metal frame supported several heavy hooks. After hanging the deer from a hook, he removed his knife from the sheath on his belt, and went to work.

An hour later, Charlie eased the pickup from the cave and picked his way back to Bald Eagle Butte Road. He planned to return in a week to repaint the Trans-Am and put on other plates from his collection. His encounter with the wardens who'd surprised him while he was dragging the doe to his car suddenly lent merit to his wife's proposal that they drive down to visit Claire and her new boyfriend. Hunting ducks during the legal season wasn't Charlie's usual MO, but from what he'd seen of Green at Chief Wooley's, the guy was all right, just the type who would appreciate a nice venison steak from the loin of an illegal doe.

Drake pressed "Repeat" and reached for a pad to take some notes. Round whatever of the never-ending bout with Armand Stilton III would begin tomorrow at 10 a.m. He picked up the lighter with the KK initials. As he had the night before, he began to turn it over in his hand. He wished Claire had stayed, but she had gone back to Willows.

Each roll of the lighter strengthened his resolve. It had been used by the Stiltons' jackbooted caretaker to murder Adam Green. That the evidence was purely circumstantial and would never have flown in court didn't matter. The lighter and Drake's instincts were proof enough.

A grim smile creased his face as the irony of it all sank in. A few weeks before he had been prepared to walk away, his will to fight smothered by the incessant barrages of Stilton's lawyers. Now a tarnished lighter had ignited a new fire, one that would, somehow, consume the enemy. He picked up the telephone and dialed Todd Millar's number. Though retired, his lawyer could still talk.

At 9:45 the next morning, Drake arrived at the courthouse. There was ample parking, it being the week between Christmas and the New Year. He edged his truck into a diagonal slot and stepped out. He stood on the sidewalk a minute, watching and waiting. Millar had told him to size up the opposition before entering the courtroom, and the make and model of a lawyer's car said a lot. Drake recalled the various minions from the big San Francisco law firm whom Millar had sent scurrying from the courthouse to their staid Toyota Camrys or Honda Accords. "Hot shots don't drive a Camry," Millar had once remarked as they watched a well-tailored young woman march to her car in frustration.

Then there had been the time when their ally on the bench served up a ripe slice of hometown favoritism to some Orland, Mulvaney & Merck heavyweight. The furious lawyer burned rubber from the front of the courthouse in his new Corvette, only to be nailed by a local cop. "At least this one drove the right kind of car," Millar had quipped. "He really should have won, you know. Drake, this can't last forever." It hadn't.

Drake kept an eye on his watch as he leaned against his truck. At 9:50, he started up the steps, but a rumble from down the street caught his attention. What he saw next stopped him in his tracks.

A gunmetal gray Dodge Viper pulled up and parked in front, its driver careful to span two diagonal spaces. Once still, the machine seemed to be snorting. The noise stopped, and the driver stepped out. He barely topped the car's low-slung roof.

"Ahh, Mr. Green," the man called out. "Right on time. Perfect day for some injunctive relief, don't you think?" He swept past Drake. "Come along, now. We don't want to keep Her Honor waiting."

Her Honor? Millar had said the judge would be Dwight Hanford, the rice farmer who'd replaced Stanley Bell when he retired. While

Hanford was not in Drake's circle of friends, he'd been a farmer, and Millar seemed to think this weighed in Drake's favor. Sacramento Valley farmers constantly were at odds with some regulation or overzealous bureaucrat. A little cow piss was unlikely to incite much judicial ire from someone who'd watched years of pesticides run off his fields into the surrounding waterways.

The short Viper driver had vanished through the doors and out of sight. Drake suddenly felt that same empty hole in the pit of his stomach as when he'd led his men into battle.

"All rise! The Superior Court in and for the State of California, County of Sutter, is now in session, the Honorable Margaret Bromley presiding."

George Stubbens, the rotund bailiff whom Drake hosted twice a year for duck hunts, shrugged at Drake and stood next to a door in the wall. It opened, and a prim, gray-haired woman Drake guessed to be in her early seventies strode out, stood briefly behind the bench, then took her seat.

"Be seated," George announced to the all-but-empty courtroom. The lawyer from the Viper was standing at one of the tables up front. He nodded and smiled at the judge, then sat. Drake, who had been sitting behind the rail, moved up and sat at the other table.

"Good morning, gentlemen," Judge Bromley said. "I am prepared to hear the application for a Temporary Restraining Order in *Stilton et al. v. Green*. Please state your appearances for the record."

"Good morning, Your Honor," boomed the lawyer, standing. "Jackson Crackers appearing for plaintiffs."

Drake stood. "Drake Green, ma'am. I represent myself."

Judge Bromley's eyebrows rose. "Indeed?" she said. "Well, you know what Abraham Lincoln said about that."

Crackers chuckled discreetly, but just loud enough to let the judge know he appreciated her wit.

"Gentlemen, I am Margaret Bromley, recently retired after twenty-two years on the Superior Court in Santa Clara County. I have been temporarily assigned by the Judicial Council to Sutter County, pending the absence of Judge Hanford, who is on vacation."

Vacation? thought Drake. *Christ, why now?* Any cows they had in Santa Clara County had been butchered long ago to make room for software mills.

"In light of the fact you are just learning of my assignment, you each have the opportunity to make a peremptory challenge in accordance with California Code of Civil Procedure, section 170.6." She paused.

Peremptory challenge? Millar hadn't mentioned it. Drake looked toward Crackers, who was smiling.

"Your Honor's reputation and abilities are well known to me," Crackers said. "The plaintiffs welcome your participation in this very serious matter."

Crackers had known. *The weasel.*

"Mr. Green?"

Drake looked up. *Come on,* he thought, *how could this kindly looking grandmother hurt me? She looks sharp enough to see through this guy's bullshit.* He thought he might even be better off with her than Hanford, who, according to Millar, had become an anti-gun activist recently, something that was sure to cost him when he stood for reelection.

Not sure what to say, Drake simply smiled and shrugged.

"No challenge having been made by either side, we will proceed," the judge announced. "Now, I have reviewed the application and supporting documents. I must confess, I am deeply disturbed by the evidence before me. Mr. Green, I am also concerned that you are not represented by counsel. The question of a polluted water supply is a matter of gravest importance. That said, I think it best that you, Mr. Green, address the elements of plaintiff's application. First let's get you sworn. Madam Clerk?"

The clerk rose from her seat at the base of the bench and instructed Drake to raise his right hand. After he swore to tell the truth, Judge Bromley said, "Very well. Let's start with the basics. You have cattle on your property, is that correct?"

"Yes, ma'am."

"The application says several hundred head. Is that also correct?"

"I believe at last count it was something near two hundred seventy five."

"They roam free, on the banks of what is known as Butte Creek and this irrigation canal…" She lifted some pages. "Canal four four two?"

"Well, free, Your Honor? There is fencing. They stay on my property."

"But their urine and their feces, Mr. Green. Does it?"

Drake shook his head. This was ridiculous. He'd never tracked their piss, though he'd stepped in enough of their plop. "Well, Your Honor, as for their, their…uh, feces, it stays where it lands. On the ground. Their p…uh, urine, I guess it just soaks in."

Jackson Crackers slapped the table. "Just so," he said, standing. "And that, Your Honor, is the problem. The declaration we have provided from Dr. Wharburton, a chemist at the University of California, demonstrates that the count of bovine fecal and waste material found downstream from the Green property both in Butte Creek and Canal four four two are at levels posing extreme danger to anyone drinking the water."

With that, Drake laughed out loud. George, the bailiff, even snickered.

"Hell, Judge," Drake said, now confident he was on solid ground, "No one, I mean no one, has drunk water from Butte Creek or that canal in decades. They'd be dead fools if they did. Sometimes that water almost stands still, it's so full of pesticides from local farms."

Judge Bromley frowned. "We're concerned here only with your cattle, Mr. Green. Apparently you concede they contribute to the problem. Clean-up of our precious environment must start somewhere, and, in this case, it starts with you, or to be more exact, your cattle."

Chastened, and alarmed by her tone, Drake kept silent.

She continued. "Given that it is undisputed your cattle are a source of dangerous pollution to these two waterways, and, I presume, the waterways to which they connect, I agree this is an appropriate instance for immediate relief in the form of a temporary restraining order. The proposed order submitted with the plaintiff's application appears satisfactory. I assume, Mr. Crackers, that your client is prepared to post a bond sufficient to protect Mr. Green in the event he ultimately prevails?"

"Absolutely, Your Honor."

"Good. Mr. Green, I'm going to sign this temporary restraining order. It prohibits further discharge of pollutants from your property into Butte Creek or Canal four four two. How you accomplish this is up to you. Have you a suggestion as to the appropriate amount of a bond?"

Drake's mind was a blur. What he was hearing made no sense. How do you stop cows from pissing? He'd have to round them up and move them off the property. That would take a good week or two, smack in the middle of duck season. He'd have to close down the club, something his members would find intolerable.

"Judge," he stammered, "Your Honor, it's just not that simple. These cows are in pockets all over the place. I have members who have paid good money to shoot ducks on my property. A cattle drive in the middle of duck season is out of the question. It would kill the hunting."

Judge Bromley stared down from the bench. "And that might not be a bad thing, Mr. Green. I never understood how people could shoot those beautiful creatures. You'll just have to refund some of the money you've collected. I'm going to order a bond of ten thousand dollars. That should be sufficient to protect you." She bent over the papers in front of her and began writing. After several seconds she handed the papers over the bench to the clerk.

"Here is the signed order. Mr. Green, the clerk will hand you an endorsed copy. Failure to comply with the order will result in contempt of court proceedings and a very serious monetary sanction. I suggest you saddle up and, as they say in the movies, 'Move 'em out.'"

Drake, dazed and flabbergasted, took the order from the clerk. He was vaguely aware of an irritating presence next to him. He looked down to a maw of sparkling white teeth.

"Mr. Green," Crackers beamed, "let's talk outside."

CHAPTER 24

Drake's fury on the drive back almost landed him in Butte Creek. He spun out on a sharp curve and regained control just as the truck was heading for the edge. He stopped well off the road and killed the engine. The restraining order lay on the empty seat next to him. He snatched it up, crumpled it into a ball, and threw it against the closed passenger door. Jackson Cracker's parting words on the courthouse steps completed the boil, and he slammed his palms against the steering wheel.

"Shit!"

He opened the door, jumped out, and began pacing around the truck.

"Mr. Green," Crackers had said, "sooner or later you're going to sell him your place. Why not make it sooner and save yourself a lot of grief? Believe me, I've only begun. You may have heard about the pipeline that was in the works. It was temporarily stalled by Mr. Durant's unfortunate accident, but is now back on line. There is natural gas on my client's property and the people of California need it. I've spoken with Gas-En's lawyers and the condemnation suit will be filed next week."

Drake had stood, staring down at the Dwarf from Hell, speechless as Crackers continued.

"Get realistic and sell to Mr. Stilton now while you still have bargaining strength. Once your property is burdened with pollution injunctions and a pipeline right of way, it'll all be over. You won't be able to give the place away. I'm authorized to offer you five million dollars.

The offer is good for one week, off the table as of January third. Good day to you, sir."

Drake had fought the urge to pick the diminutive lawyer up and hurl him down the stairs. Instead, he had watched Crackers slide behind the wheel of the Viper and ease the ominous-looking vehicle down the street. The message was not lost on Drake: he'd only felt a small sting from Stilton's as yet unleashed strength.

Condemnation? That's back again? How had Stilton worked that? Christ. Drake climbed into the truck, pulled onto the road, and continued home.

When he pulled up to the Palace, Claire's SUV was parked out front. Beside it was a Pontiac Trans-Am that looked like it had been a painting project at a day care center. He stepped from his truck and looked around.

"Drake! Over here." Claire was at the partially cleared site, with her sister and Charlie Rainwater.

Great, thought Drake. *Company. Just what I need.* He walked over to them.

"Wanda and Charlie are staying with me this week," Claire said. "I was just showing them the building site. Charlie brought his shotgun and wants to hunt with you."

Drake extended his hand. "Good to see you again," he said. "Afraid there won't be any hunting this weekend, though." He looked at Claire.

"Let's go inside and make some coffee. I'll tell you all about it."

When Drake finished the account of his morning in court, he sat back with his hands clasped behind his head. "So, that's it. I've got to call off my members, arrange for cattle transportation, climb on an ATV, and round them up. Right in the prime of the season." He lifted his cup. "Happy New Year."

Charlie, who had kept quiet throughout, finally spoke. "Got another ATV?"

"Pardon?" said Drake.

"Another ATV. I herd cattle all the time."

Drake caught the nervous nod Wanda shot in Claire's direction and decided not to press for details. He'd seen the sides of beef in

Chief Wooley's meat locker. "Sure," he said, already calculating how they would split up the work. If they got started right away, maybe, just maybe, he could salvage his members' hunting season.

Claire took Wanda back to Willows, leaving Charlie to help Drake. The sisters were to return that evening, when Charlie would prepare them a venison steak dinner. As Charlie stood on the Palace deck surveying Waterloo's acreage and ponds, Drake sat down with a telephone book and began looking for a cattle transportation trucker to haul his herd away to a feed lot.

Armand Stilton nodded in satisfaction as he listened to Jackson Crackers's telephone account of the morning's courtroom triumph. He should have hired this guy years ago. DuBois and all his high-priced meter wizards had never accomplished so much in so little time. No wonder lawyers like DuBois wrinkled their noses at lawyers like Crackers. Results like this would put them out of business. DuBois *et al.* couldn't begin to formulate a creative solution to their client's problem until hoards of them had fattened at the billing trough.

"So," Crackers was saying, "he's running scared. No question. The trick now is to hit him while he's down, and hit him hard. You say those Gas-En lawyers are ready to go?"

The cellular connection began to break up.

"Yes," Armand shouted, willing volume to overcome physics. "Their team will be in San Francisco tomorrow morning at DuBois's office. I want you there."

There was a garbled response, then silence.

"Armand?"

Donna was standing in the doorway of the paneled room that served as his office and study. While, at the moment he felt like a general in his command center, usually he went there to nap. His father had methodically built a structure for Stilton Industries that shielded the conglomerate from Armand III's limited executive talents. But for all his planning and precautions, Armand Jr. seemed to have forgotten about Gable Farms.

Armand smiled at Donna, filled with the power of destiny met. "I've done it," he said.

"What's that, dear?"

"Green," he said. "I've boxed him in. He'll have to sell, and at my price."

She pondered this then smiled. "That's wonderful, dear, but don't you think that's a good reason to reconsider getting rid of Jim Quesenberry? After all, he grew up out there. He knows both properties so well. If you take over Waterloo, you're going to need his experience."

He knew she had a point. Besides, he'd enjoyed the heroic spin he'd put on the sunken boat episode, which he'd told to a slew of wide-eyed holiday party crowds. It would hardly do to fire Quesenberry. Instead, it would improve the story and show his largesse by keeping the fallible caretaker on board. But overriding everything else was Armand's crusade to own Waterloo. Jim Quesenberry was Drake Green's friend. That just might prove useful.

"You know," he said, "I never really intended to fire him. Just letting off a little steam, that's all. One thing Dad taught me was to keep key players in place, even if they make an occasional mistake." He looked at his watch.

"Say, aren't we due at the Fairchild's in an hour?" Yet another urban audience waited to be mesmerized by his tale of courage and perseverance in the wild.

CHAPTER 25

Each time the phone rang, Jim Quesenberry hesitated before answering, sure that it was Three calling to lower the axe. The fate of those guillotined during the French Revolution had always fascinated him, and now he realized that the true horror in the process occurred while the victim lay with his head on the block, waiting the clatter of the guillotine blade's awful plunge.

The phone rang a lot as members eager to flee the post-Christmas chaos of home and family called to check on the weather and numbers of ducks. Without exception they asked for Jim's version of Three's dunking, the story having obviously made the rounds. Reluctantly, Jim mumbled through his explanation that the plug in Three's boat must have worked its way loose. The reactions ranged from outright laughter to disappointment Three had managed to survive. Nick Pappas even suggested Jim should think about equipping Three's boat with a worn plug in hope history might repeat itself. Jim caught his breath at that one and covered a moment of guilt-stunned silence with a forced laugh.

When Three finally called, the warmth and jovial tone in his voice caught Jim off guard.

"Jim!"

"Armand?"

"Yes. Say, old boy, I apologize if I seemed out of sorts with you the other day. I shouldn't have taken it out on you. Damned fluke, that's all. We'll all be a bit more careful in the future, right?"

Future? Particularly a future involving Jim and Three together—that wasn't what Jim had been braced to hear.

"Yes, yes..." he stammered. "Boat plugs, Armand. They're on my checklist now. Believe it."

"I do, Jim. Now, listen up. This is important. I'm going to be needing your help. I've got that bastard Green right where I want him. I know you two are old buddies, so don't try to kid me. I want you to help convince him that I'm determined to see this through, which I am. I'll pay a fair price...now. If he insists on dragging this out, all bets are off. You tell him that."

"Armand, I hardly see the man—"

"Bullshit. Jim, you hustle your ass over there right now and deliver the message. To tell the truth, if it weren't for my wife, I'd have sent you packing. Now, do this and do it right. Like it or not, you're part of my team. Do your part."

"Yes, sir," Jim said, cringing at the thought of Drake's reaction.

Jim found Drake at Waterloo's equipment shed, gassing the two ATVs Drake kept for his members to use when Waterloo's access road became an impassable sea of mud.

"Hey, Jim," Drake said, ruefully. "Just in time for the great roundup. Meet Charlie Rainwater." Jim shook hands with Charlie Rainwater and immediately decided this was a man never to be crossed. Charlie's eyes danced in narrow slits of taught, sun-hardened skin. They conveyed a message of ruthless humor.

"Uh, Drake, it's Armand I came over to talk about."

Drake set down the gas can and faced Jim. "He have another *accident?*" Drake said. "Hey, glad to see your ankle is better."

Jim twitched. This was not going well. The last thing he'd been prepared to discuss was Three's recent run of bad luck in the field.

Without giving Jim a chance to respond, Drake turned to Charlie. "What do you make of this? Jim's boss, Armand Three, invites some eastern big shot out to hunt, hands him a gorgeous Parker twelve-gauge side-by-side, and the guy gets blown up. Somehow there's a twenty-gauge shell stuffed in the chamber. Two weeks later, Three goes out hunting alone, something he never does because, number one, he can't call ducks, and, number two, when someone calls for him, he can't hit them. Jim's laid up with an ankle injury that can't make up its mind which ankle it belongs to."

Drake winked at Jim, then continued. "So, old Three sets out alone, but before he reaches the blind, his boat sinks. The drain plug has somehow come out. Lucky for Three, I'm hunting just over the levee. I hear him screaming and get there in time to haul him out. Now, I ask you, is Three the unluckiest hunter you've ever heard of, or what?"

Charlie made a show of pondering this while Jim, desperate to steer the conversation back to the purpose of his visit, shrugged Drake's question off in a show of nonchalant indifference. Finally Charlie said, "Sounds like someone's got it in for the sucker."

Drake nodded. His expression tightened, but he couldn't hold it. As Jim started to pale, Drake exploded in laughter and laid a light punch against Jim's shoulder.

"Jesus, just kidding. Don't take things so seriously. Now, what is it you wanted to talk about? We've got cows to chase."

Jim looked skyward, struggling to recall the short spiel he'd rehearsed on the way over. "Armand said to tell you that you should sell to him now. He'll pay you a fair price. But if this goes on any longer, all bets are off."

Drake climbed aboard one of the ATVs. "Jim, with that man's luck, the only safe bet is that he won't be around much longer. Then I won't have to think about it. Tell him that for me. Might make him more careful." He turned to Charlie. "Ready, partner?"

Charlie mounted the other ATV, and they rode out of the shed, leaving Jim shaking his head.

The cows, accustomed to a semiwild existence, did not take well to the notion of a roundup. For every two or three Drake and Charlie managed to drive into the makeshift holding pen, another ten lumbered away, wary of the chugging ATVs and determined not to join their few imprisoned companions. After three hours and multiple escapes, the two drovers pulled alongside each other and switched off the machines.

"This isn't working," Drake said.

"No shit. Going to take at least eight other guys to get this done."

Drake nodded. There weren't eight guys. Maybe Quesenberry, and that was it. "Let's take a ride," he said. "You'll enjoy this."

Jim stood in the doorway of the Gable Farms clubhouse and shook his head. "Drake, I'd love to help, but I can't leave the place right now. Junior Grimes is due here any second to help me haul out the boats. I want to get them out before this next storm hits. It's supposed to be a doozy." Jim looked down, and Drake sensed his friend's real dilemma—Armand III. As Three's campaign to acquire Waterloo escalated, so had Jim's problems based on his friendship with Drake.

"Hey, it's OK," Drake said. He looked over Jim's shoulder into the cavernous main room. "Mind showing Charlie around?" he said. "He's never been inside a billionaire's duck club." Actually, Drake doubted Charlie had ever been in any duck club, other than his current visit to Drake's.

Jim shrugged and swept his arm in a gesture of entrance. "Be my guest."

Drake led Charlie in, pleased that he had at least provided Jim with something he could do. There was no one prouder of the Gable Farms setup than Jim Quesenberry, who took great pleasure in serving as a tour guide when he could.

As Jim explained the museum-quality display of antique decoys, vintage shotguns, and decades-old photographs, Charlie's interest sharpened and he began to ask questions about the club's layout and design. When they reached the aerial photograph of the property that spanned one wall of the game room, Charlie stopped, transfixed. The photograph provided graphic details of the club's fifteen ponds and blinds, including the routes to each.

After a full minute, Charlie stood back from the photograph. "You can get to most of the ponds by roads?" he asked, still staring ahead.

Jim nodded. "Those are work roads," he said. "For maintenance and summer work. The members use the water channels. That way they get right up to the blinds. The roads don't go near the blinds. They just cut alongside some of the ponds, making it easier to haul in materials."

Charlie continued to study the photograph, and Drake finally coughed, signaling it was time to go.

After they stowed the ATVs in the equipment shed, Charlie lifted his hat, pulled a bandana from his jeans, and wiped it across his forehead. He cocked his head in the direction of the Palace. "Got any cold beer back there?"

Drake nodded. "Good idea. Give us a chance to rethink how to do this." What he really had been pondering was driving to Yuba City, kidnapping the Honorable Margaret Bromley, and strapping her to the back of an ATV so she could apply her twenty-two years of judicial wisdom to the concept of corralling 275 recalcitrant cows.

Charlie's first two beers were gone in five minutes. When he popped the cap off a third, he studied the bottle with an appreciative gaze. "You know, Drake, this is one hell of a place you got here. Ridin' around chasin' those damn cows gave me a real good picture of why your neighbor is so set on buyin' you out." Charlie swept his bottle in an arc. "Them's some of the finest duck huntin' ponds I've ever seen, and, brother, I've seen a bunch, mostly without invitation."

Drake, not halfway through his single beer, nodded. "Thanks. It's taken years to get it this way. But it's not the duck ponds he's after. He wants to run a pipeline across this place to connect gas wells on his property to the main gas line for the valley. If you take the binoculars there, you can see the three wells he's put in. They weren't on that photograph we just saw, because they went in early this year. Gas people call them 'Christmas trees' because of the way they raise up from the ground and twinkle at night. I think they're just a goddamned ugly mess of pipes, and pipes are what this trouble is all about. The only way Stilton can get his gas to market is across this place."

Charlie picked up the binoculars and surveyed Gable Farms for a full three minutes. Then he set them down and began to rub his chin. The chatter of mud hens and the plaintive yodel of a passing flock of geese drifted in from outside.

"Funny, isn't it?" he said, finally. "The wildlife, they don't know property lines. They just come and go where they want, when they want. I suppose it's the same with gas."

Drake set his beer down and stared at Charlie. Some cows joined the racket from outside, as if daring Drake and Charlie to try again.

Gas. Under Waterloo. The few times Drake had entertained the notion, he'd immediately dismissed it—the prospect of pipes, valves, and pipelines a nightmare of contradiction to the quiet simplicity of the place as prime waterfowl habitat. He was sure the three test wells Stilton had let the Texans sink accounted for the poorer hunting that season at Gable Farms. During their weekly sessions at the Butte City Club, Drake and Jim had always compared the numbers of ducks killed at their respective clubs. This season Waterloo's hunters were outgunning their high-rent neighbors two to one.

Drake continued to study Charlie, not sure where this was headed, but fairly certain that the professional poacher had just shared a fundamental block of his outlook on life.

"Doesn't matter to a duck or a deer who or what owns the property," Charlie continued, "just so long as there's good food, good water, and a place to bed down. Seems to me gas must be pretty much the same. If the geology's right, it don't care where it lies." He raised his bottle and pointed it toward Gable Farms. "I don't see much difference between your property and his. If there's gas there, then there's gas here."

Drake said nothing. Of course there was gas under Waterloo. He'd always known there was. He just didn't want to face it. Like the rubble of Waterloo Lodge, its unseen presence held too many hard choices. What if he'd gone sifting through those ashes years earlier and uncovered that lighter? What was he supposed to do? Go find old Klaus Krenzler and kill him? Better that the ashes kept their secret, just like it was better to maintain Waterloo as a prime place to hunt ducks instead of turning it into a gas farm.

Charlie downed his beer, stood, belched, and crossed to the refrigerator. He paused at the open door and held up a beer for Drake. Drake nodded. *What the hell*, he thought. *The guy's going to be sort of like my brother-in-law. Might as well get to know him. I doubt if he gets to phi-losophize much with old Chief Wooley.*

As if on cue, Charlie said, "You know, that casino may be a good thing for my father-in-law and our family, but I'll tell you something." He took a long drink. "It ain't for me, and I think it really ain't for him. Don't get me wrong. He likes all the money and stuff. Hell, for that matter, so do I. Means I can do what I know and do best. But Pete Wooley, hell, now he's a goddamned executive. Only real Indian thing he does is get all exercised over those Klamath Lake suckerfish. Doesn't fish or hunt anymore, but would drive ten thousand miles to stage a rally or demonstration to protect suckerfish."

Charlie tilted the bottle toward the ceiling, drained it, then slammed it down on the table. "For the life of me, I can't understand how something that's so full of bones and tastes like mud got so god-damned sacred."

Charlie stood, steadied himself, and walked toward the sliding door to the deck. Drake beat him there, opened the door, and watched as Charlie stepped out, unzipped, and began to piss under the railing as if it was the most natural thing in the world to do.

Charlie looked over Waterloo's ponds, and beyond, to Gable Farms. A broad smile cracked the Indian's leathered face. "Drake, much as I'd like to stay and chase around after cows and go hunting with you, I think Wanda and me will hit the road tomorrow. My boys probably have my father-in-law tied to a stake by now. Besides, I've got a job for 'em."

CHAPTER 26

Monday, January 2.

The dimensions and décor of law-firm conference rooms make statements that range from close-to-the-bone austerity to opulent reassurance that the client's investment has bought unassailable success. At Orland, Mulvaney & Merck, the main conference room, dubbed The Cathedral by the firm's associates, carried the latter message to its extreme. From rare hardwood paneling milled out of trees lifted by giant helicopters from ravaged South American rainforests to its massive polished granite table, the Cathedral served as a legal redoubt intended to incite confidence in the firm's clients and fear in its adversaries.

Louis DuBois swept into the room and ran his hand along the edge of the cold granite. How he had looked forward to this day. Finally, after years of babysitting Armand Stilton III's obsession with Waterloo, DuBois was poised to put the whole unpleasant business behind him and devote his full attention to the firm's centerpiece client, Stilton Industries. He mused how this day's meeting would be different from others he had presided over in his favorite of all places, his sanctuary, his Castle Keep. Today there were no adversaries, just allies all gathered for a common goal: the legal obliteration of Drake Green and the transfer of Waterloo to Armand Stilton Jr.'s troublesome heir.

On one side of the forty-foot table, in high-backed, deerskin swivel chairs, sat the eight lawyers from Gas-En and its wholly owned bankrupt subsidiary, Nor-Cal Gas and Electric. Armand III followed Dubois, with four Orland partners and seven associates trailing in their wake.

DuBois had gone all out, viewing Armand III's problem as a springboard from which he would capture the Nor-Cal bankruptcy and the looming Gas-En crisis as a prized plum for Orland, Mulvaney & Merck. After all, Nor-Cal was far from broke. It just didn't have the cash to meet its debts, thanks to the siphoning activities of Gas-En's merry band of thieves. Gas-En, for all its current troubles, still had the cash reserves to pay Orland, Mulvaney & Merck many hefty millions. When the money was gone, the firm would step aside to let the government and Gas-En's creditors gnaw the company's bleached bones.

DuBois took his seat at the head of the table, with Armand III on his right. The Orland entourage came next, an unspoken ranking dictating the order of their seating.

DuBois patted a thin folder in front of him and cleared his throat. "I see we're all here. Good, let's get started. First, I think it would be appropriate if we go around the table and introduce ourselves. To my right is the gentleman whose, uh, legal situation and objectives bring us all together—Armand Stilton Third. To his left, my partner, and one of our senior litigators—"

"Not so fast, Louis," said Armand, scowling. He looked down the line of Orland lawyers, then back at DuBois. "By my count, this room's costing me about ten thousand dollars an hour. I don't need names. I need results. And the one guy most important to what we're doing isn't here yet."

The conference room door opened and Jackson Crackers strode in, as if on cue. He wore faded jeans, Merrill moccasins, and a loose-fitting Hawaiian shirt. He paused and surveyed the layout, then walked directly to the empty oversized swivel chair at the far end of the table and sat down. He leaned back and scrunched into the huge chair as if testing it for purchase. He grunted, sat forward, laced his fingers in front of him, and proceeded to pop his knuckle joints, one by one.

Armand smiled as his champion spoke.

"Greetings. I'm Jackson Crackers, Mr. Stilton's chief counsel. Here's what we're going to do. First, all of you who haven't tried at least twenty-five jury trials, raise your hand."

The assembled lawyers exchanged nervous glances. Armand spoke up. "You heard him. Do it."

Slowly, hands began to rise. Soon every lawyer at the table, including DuBois and excluding Crackers, sat stone-faced with a hand in the air.

"As I thought," Crackers said. "All of you, out. We don't need you—except for the chief Gas-En lawyer and the Nor-Cal lawyer with the most condemnation experience. You two stay."

Crackers gazed down the table at DuBois, who looked like he was about to cry or throw up; it was hard to tell which.

"Dubois, you can stay, too, if you want. Understand, though, that my client is paying for only one lawyer this morning, and that lawyer is me. As you know, we have a contingent fee arrangement. You negotiated it. I'm not having my million bucks jeopardized by a passel of bag carriers who can't find the courthouse."

The room cleared, and Armand III moved down the table next to Crackers, who, for the next hour and a half, laid out his battle plan.

Though Armand had decided not to fire Jim Quesenberry, Donna Stilton knew her volatile husband well enough to realize this was etched in sand rather than in stone. The next tide of temper could easily wash it away.

Armand's recent immersion in the icy water of the Doghouse pond and his drive to bring the long-standing "Waterloo issue" to an immediate conclusion left Donna with one last opportunity to inspire Jim Quesenberry. Her seductive grand-slam suggestion may have stirred in Jim a momentary urge to try again, but she sensed his sole motivation to do her bidding had been her ability to tip his moral scale in her favor. With two failed attempts, Jim not only was running scared, he believed that fate was against him and that what Donna wanted was not meant to be. Armand's long hours with the nutty little lawyer from San Rafael had left Donna with time on her hands. She decided to use it well.

As the chartered jet pulled up to the General Aviation terminal at the Little Rock airport, Donna glanced at her watch. 11 a.m. The flight from San Francisco had taken three hours. Allowing for two hours on the ground, she'd be back in Ross by six, just in time for cocktails.

The town car she'd arranged met her on the tarmac, and twenty-five minutes later she was seated opposite Clinton J. Williams, director of the Cedar Hills Rehabilitation Center and Convalescent Home. A check from the Stilton Foundation in the amount of $450,000 lay on his desk.

"Mrs. Stilton, I don't know what to say. This is more than generous. It's...it's—"

"It's done, is what it is, Mr. Williams. Now build your theatre."

Donna sat forward, holding Williams's eyes with hers as she continued.

"Mr. Quesenberry is much too modest about his role in this. While the money comes from our foundation, his dedication and devotion has inspired this grant. Because of him, our foundation has decided to adopt your facility as a principal beneficiary. All you need do is provide me with a list of capital projects. Mr. Williams, the Stilton Foundation is prepared to make you the Mayo Clinic of rehabilitation and convalescent centers. You can thank Jim Quesenberry for it, which, by the way, I would be most grateful if you would do at once."

She crossed her legs and lowered her eyes. "The poor man works so hard with so little reward for all the good he does. I just know that another kind letter from you would mean the world to him. Who knows what it might inspire him to do next?"

The Gulfstream V began its descent from twenty-eight thousand feet, and Donna gazed down on the snow-capped Sierras. "Yes!" she shouted where no one heard. Soon. It would happen soon. Of that she was certain.

CHAPTER 27

Friday, January 6.

"If I see that process server out here one more time, I'll sell him a membership," Drake said. Claire huddled low in the blind. The weather had turned, and a stiff north wind drove a chilling drizzle that penetrated the few open slivers of their layered, waterproof clothing. Even Drake was tempted to pack it in, but the recent legal blitzkrieg launched by Jackson Crackers and the Orland law firm had forced him to seek refuge in the one place he felt safely isolated from the outside world—blind 4, or, as his grandfather had named it in a play on the Waterloo theme, Lord Nelson.

Over the past week, Crackers's process server had intruded five times to leave papers, notices, and orders with Drake. The last, an "Order to Show Cause re Contempt," charged him with willful disobedience of the court's temporary restraining order and threatened a fine of $5,000 a day until the cows were removed. It further threatened involuntary removal of the cows by the county health department under the watchful supervision of Duke the sheriff, all at the projected expense to Drake of $25,000. Drake was ordered to appear before Judge Bromley on Monday either to document removal of the cows or to face the fine and an indefinite term in jail.

Before the order to show cause there had been a complaint for condemnation and notices of depositions Stilton's lawyers planned to take, including Drake's, which was scheduled to run three days during the last week of duck season. There were also interrogatories—reams of questions conjured up by the Nor-Cal condemnation lawyers to pin a low valuation on Waterloo.

Drake stopped calling Todd Millar, who, exasperated, had finally reminded Drake of his retired status. Millar gave him the names of three lawyers who specialized in condemnation and told him to get together a war chest of at least $250,000 and plan on losing it. That's when Drake decided to go hunting.

"Without a lawyer, what are you going to do?" Claire managed through chattering teeth.

"Don't know yet," Drake said. "Tell you one thing, though. It doesn't take any lawyer to tell me what I already know."

Claire peeked up, willing to momentarily expose a cheek to the razor-sharp cold. "What's that?"

Drake patted his shotgun. "Possession," he said. "It's ninety-nine per cent of the law, isn't it? I'm here, and this says I'm staying."

Claire swept the parka hood clear of her face. "Drake! Get serious. Your romantic notion of the lone hero standing off the evil forces gets you nowhere. You need money and a good lawyer." She looked down. "Without those, you might as well give up and make the best deal you can."

Drake stood back and blinked. "Hey, wait a minute here, Miss Where's-the-Man-I-Thought-I-Loved? You're the reason I've fought him off." He fumbled in the pocket of his parka. "You, and now this." He pulled out the old lighter and held it up, inches from her face.

"You and I are building a place here to live in, and we're building it smack where Stilton's father had my father murdered. My world has come down to that. I'll die before I let Stilton take it from me."

Her mouth dropped as she formed a response.

"Teal, from the northeast," Drake said, raising his shotgun. "Coming low and fast." He fired three times and dropped three of the kamikaze-like birds before she got her gun to her shoulder.

"Tar!" he ordered, and the dog splashed into the water.

"See?" said Drake. Claire shook her head and looked away.

Though it was only an envelope, and an elegant one at that, with its flower garland border, Jim Quesenberry handled the letter from Cedar Hills like a rattlesnake. He drew his knife from the scabbard on his belt and, with a quick swipe, sliced the monster along its edge. He pulled out the contents, recognizing at once the cursive flourish of Clinton J. Williams. His heart raced and his breath came quick as he read of Donna Stilton's visit. The theatre project was a done deal. When he came to the part about the Stilton Foundation's commitment to a long-term capital renovation and expansion plan, using his sister as the Cedar Hills poster child, Jim leaned against the rock column supporting the mailbox.

Donna Stilton had swept past him, her charitable cyclone harboring a murderous cloud. He should have stopped her, but he hadn't, being content to stand by and let her bring some small joy into his sister's life. His arms fell to his sides, and he heaved a great sigh.

Short of outright murder, what could he do? There were two types of duck club accidents that claimed lives—shooting and drowning. Armand III had survived both, while the shadow of suspicion cast over Jim by each had grown.

Maybe Jim was just being paranoid, but Drake Green's barbed comments had struck home. If Drake, his close friend, suspected him involved in Three's "accidents," Sheriff Duke wouldn't be far behind. The moustache and posturing disguised a methodical plodder with little to do except sit around and ponder. When and if Duke got down to counting shotgun shells, puttering with drain plugs, or checking up on Jim's ankle injury, things could get ugly.

One more failed attempt was out of the question. Whatever Jim rigged next had to work. He owed it to Donna Stilton—and to himself. Only a fatal mishap free of all question would clear the shadow cast by his previous failures.

Jim stared at the Buttes, oblivious to the cold north wind and the building storm. It would have to be soon. Duck season ended in two weeks.

CHAPTER 28

Monday, January 10.

The wind lashed southern Oregon with a punishing vengeance. Sheets of ice-laced water whipped everything that moved, making driving almost impossible. Most of the state's snow removal equipment remained in sheds, the highway people waiting for a break before tackling the awesome task ahead. Schools closed, as did all but essential businesses.

Even the most hardened Klamath Basin residents had begun to think of it as the storm of the decade, too cold and too furious for all outdoor activity, including the duck and goose hunting for which the region was famous. Charlie Rainwater stood on his front porch, shielding a mug of coffee in his hands. "Perfect," he said.

Since Charlie and Wanda had returned home, he'd thought of only one thing—duck hunting on Waterloo. It was his for the asking.

While poaching claimed most of Charlie's time, it was limited to deer, elk, and salmon. Poaching ducks and geese had become nearly impossible. Public reserves were closely guarded, and, until he'd met Drake Green, Charlie had spurned private duck clubs; he was a loner, not a joiner.

Waterloo, however, was different, as was Drake Green. *There,* thought Charlie, *is a man I could hunt with.* He could even tolerate the notion of hunting by the rules with a man like Green. The trouble was, some fat cat neighbor of Drake's had designs on the property.

Charlie turned and went back inside. "Boys up?" he asked Wanda, seated at the kitchen counter watching local news coverage of the storm. She shook her head. "Nope, no school. I think they're watching TV in their room."

Casino dividends to the Rainwater family had made television sets in each room possible, including all four bathrooms, the laundry room, the garage, Charlie's workshop, and even the space attached to his elaborate brick smokehouse, where he skinned, dressed, butchered, and packaged the bounty of his endeavors.

Charlie grunted and headed up the stairs. He paused at the door to the double-sized room that housed his sons. He listened a moment, then opened the door, timing his entrance perfectly. A pillow launched a second earlier just cleared where his head would have been. The chaos occasioned by two snow-bound ten-year-olds littered the room, now a war zone. Upended toys, games, and clothing pocked the battlefield, while lumped bedding formed opposing forts that defined the front lines. Charlie took a sock bomb in the chest and then whistled— a piercing blast that triggered instant calm.

"Cease fire!" he yelled. "Enough!"

The grinning faces of his sons poked cautiously from behind each fort.

"You two have twenty minutes to clean this mess up and get dressed. Put on long johns and your warmest stuff—gloves, parkas, the works."

"Where we going, Dad?" asked Randy, while his brother across the room rolled another sock behind his back.

"Drop it, Dennis," ordered Charlie. "War's over. We're going fishing."

The two boys stared at each other, then spontaneously erupted as Charlie closed the door. He smiled as he descended the stairs.

"You're not," said Wanda, her eyes wide.

"I am. Do them good to get out of the house."

"Fishing? In this weather? For what? Snow trout?"

Charlie shrugged. It wouldn't do to tell her. Besides, she was used to his mysterious comings and goings and knew better than to probe. They had an understanding. The less she knew, the better. While the husband-wife privilege might deter investigative efforts, it was not inviolate and could be breached if the pressure was great enough. Best to keep Wanda out of the loop, particularly this time. The old chief was the last person he wanted to know, at least for now.

He went into the garage and began to load his "real" truck, a twin-cab, 4-by-4 diesel Dodge Ram fitted with an all-weather camper shell. This was his cruiser. Charlie's fleet of innocuous older wrecks, beat on the outside but racing sharp under the hood, were stashed throughout southern Oregon, ready when needed.

As Charlie stood by the open rear hatch surveying the gear he'd assembled, his sons burst from the house to the garage. They joined him at the back of the truck, bundled in state-of-the-art insulated parkas—camouflaged, of course. The boys peered into the back of the truck.

"Where's our poles?" asked Dennis.

"Won't need poles," said Charlie. "Not for this kind of fishin'. See those buckets? They're your poles today. Grab your hip boots. You'll need those too."

Waves like ocean surf pounded Klamath Lake's southern shore, and the twins' excitement mounted. When water actually broke over the highway, Charlie reached next to him and tousled Randy's hair.

"Great weather, hey, guys? Ain't going to be nobody at our spot."

Dennis peered around his brother, his eyes full of wonder. "Where's that, Dad?" he said.

Charlie chuckled. "You'll see. You've been there before."

This added mystery quieted them, and the dark miles ticked by.

Finally, Charlie turned off Highway 97 and headed north along Modoc Point Highway, away from the main lake body and toward what was known as Agency Lake. "Look familiar?" he said.

The boys stared ahead. In ten minutes they reached the marshy inlet fed by the Wood and Crooked Rivers. Charlie pulled onto a gravel road. He stopped and slipped the truck into four-wheel drive.

"Well, you great pathfinders got it yet?" he asked.

They both leaned forward, huddled a few seconds, and then looked up at Charlie. "It's where we came with Grandfather," Dennis announced. "When we got our pictures in the paper."

Charlie laughed. "Hey, you guys are pretty good after all. That's right. We're almost there."

Both faces clouded, and Randy spoke up. "Dad, there's nothing there but mud and suckerfish."

"Is that right?" said Charlie, smiling. "My, my."

They made three trips that day and four the next. When they finished, Charlie reckoned they'd harvested slightly over three hundred suckerfish. All of them were alive and well in the Rainwater's covered swimming pool, which Charlie had drained and refilled with fresh water. To maintain peace in the bedroom, he explained his plan to Wanda, who simply shook her head and walked away. "At least it's not illegal," she said. "I think."

With the boys, though, a simpler explanation was warranted. "You saw how much your grandfather enjoyed the whole suckerfish thing last fall," Charlie told them. "Well, I'm giving him the chance to do it all again. That darn casino has him and all his old pals walled in like a prison. They need to be out showing the world they're real Indians, not bean counters."

That seemed to satisfy them, particularly when Charlie described their role in the next phase of the operation. First they'd spent two glorious days out of school, up to their hips in muddy water netting suckerfish. Now they got to take a trip.

CHAPTER 29

The storm ripped along the spine of the Cascades and tore into northern California with the rumble and roll of ten thousand freight trains. Water levels that slowly receded during the lull began to rise again, and fast. Drake, who had set off for the courthouse at eight in the morning, only to sink his truck up to its doors in the mire of the Waterloo access road, slogged his way back to the Palace, where he slipped under the blankets and snuggled close to Claire.

"Mmmm," she said. "Thought you were due in court."

"I am," he said. "Too muddy. Besides, bad things happen there. I like it here better, where good things happen."

At precisely ten, Judge Margaret Bromley took the bench. She was greeted by the toothsome smile of Jackson Crackers.

"Where is Mr. Green?" she asked.

Crackers made a show of surveying the empty courtroom. He turned back and shrugged.

"Well," she said, "considering the weather, we'll wait five minutes."

The quiet courtroom was disturbed only by the click of the large clock's hands. At five after, Crackers cleared his throat and said, "Your Honor, I made it here from San Rafael with time to spare. Mr. Green lives only thirty miles away."

"Yes," she said. "I find the defendant, Drake Green, in contempt of court. A bench warrant shall issue for his arrest."

She turned to the bailiff. "Mr. Stubbens, as soon as the clerk has prepared the warrant and I have signed it, I want you to deliver it to the sheriff for immediate action."

She swirled from the bench, and Jackson Crackers left the courthouse smiling, as usual.

Armand III, snug in the squat, steel strength of the Hummer, barreled up I-5, oblivious to the weather's rage and intent on the details of his all-out war to claim Waterloo. Crackers had just reported the judge's action by cell phone. "There's no way he's getting those cows off there in this weather," Crackers had assured Armand. "That man's going to be eating jail food and reading condemnation papers for the next few weeks."

Armand chuckled at the image of Green behind bars and almost missed the Colusa turn off, his pleasure so complete.

Once east of Colusa and headed into the vast trough of the Butte Sink, the weather's demands on Armand's concentration increased. Many parts of Butte Slough Road and Pass Road, the narrow levee-top corridors that spanned the Sink before connecting to the higher ground of West Butte Road, were under a foot of water, perfect Hummer conditions. Armand steered the powerful all-weather vehicle through drowned segments of road, thrilled as watery obstacles were splashed to mist by the force of his unstoppable machine.

Fifteen minutes later he reached the elaborate entrance to Gable Farms and charged down the road. He brought the Hummer to an abrupt stop in front of his residence and sat behind the wheel, exhausted yet exhilarated. He was torn from his reverie by a pounding on the window.

"Armand, are you all right?"

He pressed the window button and let the glass descend just enough to meet Jim Quesenberry's eyes. The concern he saw made him laugh. *This is the stupid bastard who didn't check my boat's drain plug. It's time the dumb hick starts paying attention to caring for the man who signs his checks.*

"Yeah," Armand said, "just having fun. Get this rig unloaded. I'm going inside. Who else is coming?"

"I think you'll have the place to yourself, Armand. Before the storm knocked the phones out I heard from most of the others. They're staying home until the weather clears."

"Really? Good. You can help me get some nice limits."

Jim shook his head, rain cascading from the brim of his cap. "Armand, those ponds are small oceans. We'd be swamped as soon as we got away from the dock. I brought in some help and hauled all the boats out this morning. They'd have been torn away. We'll have to hunker down till this blows over. I'd have called you, but, like I said, the phones are out."

Armand frowned and considered driving back home. He peered out the slit of the partially lowered window. Though it was only three in the afternoon, the sky was black, and it was now hailing. What had been an odyssey of power as he'd driven north suddenly loomed as the drudge of retreat if he headed south. A few drinks in front of a warm fire, followed by one of Jim's home-cooked meals, held much more appeal.

"What's for dinner?"

"How about ducks, Armand? Still got a few in the freezer."

Armand wrinkled his nose. "Make it steak. Get my stuff inside. I'm staying."

Four hours later, with Armand well marinated and stuffed, Jim considered his situation. The weather was not expected to clear for two days, and Armand had talked himself into staying the week, grumbling something about "a break from all the social bullshit." With Armand prone to serious cabin fever, Jim knew he would be on Jim to take him hunting at the first break. *Somehow,* Jim thought, *out of all this there must be another opportunity.* All he had to do was spot it.

After Armand tottered from the clubhouse toward his residence, Jim returned to one of the large leather recliners in front of the fireplace. He stared into the fire for the next two hours. With each option that emerged, he shook his head. No, this time he had to be totally unconnected when it happened—not there, but miles or hours away. The fire failed him, and he drifted into a troubled sleep.

CHAPTER 30

Sheriff Duke held the bench warrant up to the light, scrutinized it, then turned it over and did the same thing from the back.

"She said 'immediate action'?"

"That's right, Duke," said George Stubbens, who fell into a chair across from his boss. Duke dropped the warrant and watched it fall to the desk.

"What do you suppose she meant by 'immediate'?"

"I think she meant yesterday, Duke. She's real pissed at him."

"All on account of his cows?"

"Well, she thinks their pollutin' our water. The ducks didn't help."

"Ducks?"

"That he shoots 'em." George adjusted his ample backside, leaned forward, and looked both ways, as if someone might be lurking in the corners of the sheriff's office. "Duke, the woman drinks."

Duke let this hang a few seconds as he considered its content and source. "Well, I drink too, George. Water, orange juice, beer, and good whiskey. Know anyone who doesn't?"

"That's not what I mean, Duke. She's hung a big plaque on the wall. It says she's Past National President of a Bourbon Society." George straightened and folded his arms across his chest.

Duke shook his head. "That's Audubon Society, George. Audubon. It's an organization of bird lovers. You saw the other things she's hung in there, didn't you? All those bird pictures?"

The bailiff shrugged.

Duke stood and peered out the window. He sighed. "Well, I just know that road of Green's will be a mess. I'll have to wait till it dries out." He gave his moustache a single twist and turned back to face his deputy. "George, you still go out there hunting?"

George nodded. "Was out there two weeks ago. Got four mallards and a couple of teal. He fixed me a real nice dinner, too. Rib eye steak."

"No kidding. Rib eye." Another moustache twirl. "He still got a radiophone out there for emergencies?"

"Yep, right next to the bar."

Duke shuffled through his desk and pulled out a tattered, brown leather notebook. "I got that number here somewhere." He winked at George. "Think I'll give him a call. Maybe he'll surrender and save the county some money." He stretched and sighed again. "I've been meaning to talk to him about that caretaker neighbor of his anyway."

Claire, startled, looked up from her book. "What's that noise?"

Drake finished feeding a log into the wood stove and stood. "The radiophone. Almost forgot it was there. Hardly ever use it." He moved to the bar and unhooked the microphone, just as the set crackled again.

"Drake, this is Duke. You there? Over."

"This can't be good," Drake said. He pressed the microphone switch.

"I'm here, Duke. Over."

"Uh, Drake, I've got sort of a situation I need your help with. That judge who's filling in for Hanford has instructed me to bring you in, like arrest you. She's found you in contempt of court. Over."

Drake looked at Claire. "Told you," he said. He pressed the microphone switch again.

"So, Duke, you know where I live. Over."

A few seconds passed. The set crackled again. "Well, Drake, that's not the problem. I'm pretty sure that road of yours is closed, and I was hoping you'd just manage to get out of there on your own and come in when you can. This can be worked out when you get here. Over."

Drake laughed. "Worked out?" he said into the microphone. "As in spending the next few days or weeks in your jail? No thanks, Duke. I'm comfortable right here. Besides, as soon as this storm lifts, I'll get out and finish collecting those damn cows. You tell that to Her Honor. Over."

Again, there was a pause. "Drake, I see your point and just wanted you to know what was up. So long as this storm's in, there's not much I can do. But once it's gone...Be a lot easier on both of us if you just voluntarily came on in. I was fixing to talk to you anyway about what's been going on out there. Over."

Drake frowned. "Going on? What do you mean? Over."

This time Duke came right back. "That, uh, shotgun incident with Chester Durant and this recent thing where Stilton almost drowned. I need some more information. Over."

Drake turned away from Claire and stared out toward Gable Farms. The jibes he'd thrown Quesenberry's way, innocent as they'd been, suddenly didn't seem funny anymore.

"Not much I can tell you, Duke. I showed up afterward, both times. You know that. Over."

"Even so, Drake, I'd like to talk to you. Rather not talk about it over the radio. Over."

"Damn," Drake muttered. He took a breath and responded.

"OK, Duke. Tell you what. Soon as this storm passes and my road dries out enough, I'll come on in and talk with you. One condition though. Over."

"What's that, Drake? Over."

"I'm not going to jail. Got it? Over."

"I'll see what I can do, Drake. Take care. Over."

"Over and out," said Drake. He clipped the microphone back to the set. "Damn!"

"Drake?" Claire said.

"It's Quesenberry, I'm sure of it. The sheriff thinks he's somehow tied into Three's accidents. Shit."

"Oh, come on," said Claire. "That's ridiculous."

Drake opened the sliding door and stepped out onto the deck. He stared north, into the darkening sky. "Is it?"

The lock quickly yielded to Charlie Rainwater's deft touch, as did most devices designed to keep him out of places where he was not supposed to be. Within minutes he was prowling the Oregon State Hatchery equipment yard, a compound tucked away in the foothills of the Klamath Basin. Not until spring would the tank trucks begin their runs from state fish hatcheries to the streams and lakes that Fish and Game kept stocked with trout to amuse the tourists and amateurs. It wasn't Charlie's kind of fishing, but he did appreciate the fact that his tax dollars supported activities that tied up game wardens, particularly now that he needed a temporary loan of a piece of the department's equipment.

He paused inside the chain-link fence a few minutes as he took stock of his choices and confirmed he was alone. His cousin, Arnold "The Ram" Sheepshead, who worked as a mechanic for Fish and Game, had assured him he would be. The department's employees had been transferred for the season to the highway department.

There were four large tank trucks and two smaller ones. Charlie calculated his load and decided on one of the large ones, just to be safe. He jimmied the door and hot-wired the newest one, reasoning that his schedule allowed for no breakdowns. He pulled out of the yard, relocked the gate, and set off for home. It was nine thirty, the night had cleared and there was a lull until the next storm, which was due to hit by daybreak—just enough time to load up and hit the road.

CHAPTER 31

Junior Grimes still could not believe his good luck. He let his right hand drift from the steering wheel to his rear pocket, from which he pulled out three twenty-dollar bills. Yep. He'd counted right. Three bills. Sixty dollars. Quesenberry usually paid him forty dollars for his help hauling out the members' boats. Two bills must have stuck together.

By the time Junior had discovered his unexpected bonus, a whole day had passed. Time, he reasoned, has a way of sorting things out. Besides, it was Gable Farms money, not Jim Quesenberry's. He peered ahead into a dark mini-burst of driving rain. The flatbed truck he used to make his living hauling hay, manure, junk, or whatever needed carting from one place to another, ground ahead, as it had day after day, month after month, year after year. Junior and the truck, an amalgamation fused from the residue of previous failures, were fixtures in the Butte Sink, a duo to be counted on when something heavy or unpleasant needed doing.

It wasn't every day Junior got so lucky. *Best to celebrate good fortune when you can,* he thought. He pulled up in front of the Butte City Club and parked; it had been his destination even before he had a reason to celebrate.

Junior recognized the massive, slouched shoulders of the bar's only customer as those of his sometimes partner. When Junior had something really heavy or stinking to do, he brought Lonnie along. Lonnie turned toward the opened door, and Junior knew from the stupid grin that the sixty dollars was in serious jeopardy. Though Junior possessed money during its brief passage from origin to disposition, he never really owned it. He reached overhead and stroked Moe, the huge, white sturgeon.

"Hey, guys, wake up. We're almost there." The twins stirred from their sleep and blinked.

Dennis rubbed his eyes. "Where are we, Dad?"

"Sutter County, California." Charlie Rainwater said with a laugh, amused his sons had slept the whole drive south. They'd left home seven hours earlier, and Charlie had stayed at an even fifty-five, counting on his adherence to the truck speed limit and the almost constant rain to discourage any highway patrolman's interest. Once he'd left I-5 at Corning and headed east into the labyrinth of two-lane valley roads, he relaxed and focused on the task ahead.

He looked at his watch: two o'clock, with a good three hours of daylight left. Perfect. He'd planned his arrival for late afternoon, reasoning that the operation should be carried out in daylight rather than at night, when the truck's headlights might attract attention. Now all he needed to do was find the place.

He crossed a barren intersection and pulled to the side to take his bearings. To the southeast, through the rain and low clouds, he made out the peaked, black rise of the Sutter Buttes. He unfolded the Sutter County map he'd picked up on the trip with Wanda and began to sort out the roads he needed to find. Five minutes later he pulled out, the convoluted route to their destination charted in his brain.

When they reached West Butte Road, Charlie's wariness as a professional poacher took over and his senses went into overdrive. The rolling hills to the east, the towering Buttes ahead, the flooded country to the west, and the undulating narrow road—they all blended into a kaleidoscope of consciousness, with him and the boys at the center. Nothing escaped him as pieces of the geography around them tumbled into place.

Slowing, he eased the truck to the side of the road, the muffled slurp of mudded gravel replacing the rough drone of rubber on asphalt. Finally, at the crest of a gentle grade, he stopped and surveyed the valley floor. He grunted, satisfied that he was looking over the same landscape he'd seen from the deck of Drake Green's Palace and the aerial photograph in the Gable Farms clubhouse. Gable Farms lay below, sleeping and vulnerable. The scene reminded Charlie, not a voracious reader, of one of the stories he'd read the twins: Gulliver— ripe for the Lilliputians.

In the far distance, through the haze of rain and scud, Charlie could just make out the faint vein of Canal 442 as it scribed the line between his target and Waterloo.

"This is it, men," he told the twins. "Time we go to work."

Drake leaned back from the table and stared at the pieces of the disassembled gas motor that powered the portable generator. It had come apart easily enough. Getting it together was a Chinese puzzle. A combination of boredom and foresight had compelled him to tear into it, the motor's hesitant coughs during the last power outage remind- ing him that the generator was overdue for an overhaul.

Claire looked up from her book. "Trouble?"

Drake rubbed his beard. "This thing has a mind of its own." He raised a hand.

"What is it?" she said.

"Shhh, listen."

Thirty seconds passed.

Claire leaned forward and whispered, "What are we listening to?"

"That's just it," he said. "Nothing. The rain's stopped."

He stood, opened the door to the deck, and stepped out.

"Ducks are working," he said over his shoulder. "Let's go on out. What do you say?"

"Sounds good to me. I was getting entirely too spoiled with all this nice, warm, dry comfort. Much better to slog around out there in the wet cold."

He cocked his head.

"Oh, just kidding," she said. "Of course I want to go."

"Just an hour or so," he said. "More for the change of scenery than anything else."

She pursed her lips. "Right."

Footsteps on the trailer's stairs woke Jim Quesenberry an instant before the heavy knocks on the door.

"Jim! Storm's over. Time to hunt."

He'd been dreading this—alone again in a duck blind with Three and no plan in mind. "Be right there, Armand," he called, resigned to his fate.

Fifteen minutes later they were geared up and on the dock. As Jim began to muscle Armand's boat into the water, Armand inspected the transom. "Looks like a new plug," he said.

"It is, Armand. It screws in. Can't come out unless it's screwed out."

Armand grunted. "Should've had that in the first place." He stood back and watched as Jim labored. Then he gazed up at the sky while Jim wrestled the heavy outboard from the rear of the pickup, dragged it to the boat, and managed to attach it without any help.

Is it all worth it? Jim wondered. *Maybe I should just quit and look for a job at another duck club.* But then he thought of Cedar Hills and knew he was only fantasizing.

Jim loaded in their guns, the decoys, and the rest of their gear as Armand leaned against the bed of the pickup and fussed with his Roto Duck control box.

"All set, Armand?" he asked when he was done.

Armand stepped forward and held out his arm. Jim took it and steadied him as Armand climbed in and settled into the front of the boat. Jim took his own seat in the stern and motioned to Jethro. The dog jumped in the center, and they were on their way.

From his perch on the crest of West Butte Road, Charlie leaned against the tank truck and watched through powerful binoculars as the boat left the dock. He continued to follow its course through the channels that separated the club's ponds. Even though it was lost at times behind tules or trees, he tuned in on the faint buzz of the engine and managed to track the boat's course. Finally, when it emerged into the clearing of the pond Charlie had picked out as its destination, he nodded and said to himself, "Uh huh, got you."

He swept the binoculars one more time over the entire Gable Farms layout, concentrating on each pond. Satisfied the boat he'd tracked held the only hunters out that day, he turned his attention back to it and watched as the figure in the stern put out decoys while a second hunter sat up front. After the boat pulled up under the blind, he tapped the truck's cab.

"OK, men, now the fun part, the reason we're here."

He started the truck and moved slowly along the edge of the road, stopping several hundred yards ahead at the intersection with a gravel side road. The photograph in the Gable Farms clubhouse had confirmed it was a secondary access road into the property. It was blocked with a padlocked chain, from which hung a metal sign:

POSTED
NO TRESPASSING
NO HUNTING
Gable Farms, Inc.

Charlie pulled up at the chain and stopped.

"Gee, Dad," said Dennis. "It's locked."

"Got my key right here," Charlie said, reaching behind the seat. He drew out a monstrous set of bolt cutters. "Now, I don't want to ever catch you guys doing this. Got that?"

He jumped out and applied the cutters. Seconds later the chain lay limp across the road. He slid in behind the wheel. "OK, we know where the enemy is. We head the opposite direction."

He steered the truck along the road, taking forks that led northwest, away from the pond with the hunters. Minutes later the road dipped and then leveled along a levee that marked the northerly edge of a pond.

"Might as well start here," said Charlie. He stopped the truck and got out, calculating the distance from the truck to the pond's edge.

"Afraid we can't use the hose," he said. "Time to man the buckets again. I'll get up on top and scoop 'em out. Randy, you take the bucket from me and pass it on to Dennis. Dennis, you dump 'em in the pond. Let's get started."

Ten minutes later, Charlie guessed they'd unloaded at least fifty fish and moved on to the next pond. This time he was able to get close enough to use the truck's planting hose and within three minutes had discharged another fifty fish. They had similar luck at the next two ponds, but then had to slow the process to use the buckets again. The sixth and last pond proved the hardest; they had to carry the buckets of suckerfish a good thirty yards.

Charlie stood with an arm on each of the boy's shoulders as they watched the last of the carp-like creatures fin away into the murk. "That, boys, was a good day's work," he said. "How about we go find us some great cheeseburgers?"

The twins dropped their buckets and let out a loud, "Yeayyy…"

"What the hell was that?" Armand said, standing on his toes, straining to see.

"Damned if I know," said Jim, who had known for some time that someone was intruding on Gable Farms property. No ducks had flown near their blind all afternoon. He'd decided that finding and evicting the trespassers with Armand in tow would only create a bigger problem. Whoever it was, they weren't shooting ducks. Maybe they were just birdwatchers. That happened sometimes, and Jim tended to overlook them, so long as there were no members around.

Two shots came from Waterloo. Jim turned in time to see two ducks fall

CHAPTER 32

Friday, January 14.

The storm's bite passed, leaving a cold, steady rain, which bade well for the second-to-last weekend of a disappointing season at Gable Farms. While Three napped, Nick Pappas headed a delegation that cornered Jim in the game room.

"Jim," Pappas began, stirring the ice in his highball with a finger, "we've all been looking at the numbers. They're lousy. According to the club's shooting records, this has been the worst season since eighty-eight."

Jim nodded. The drought of the late eighties had almost left the Butte Sink a dust bowl. Farmers desperate for water had lobbied to keep scarce reserves allocated to crops, rather than available to flood duck ponds for wealthy hunters.

"It's those goddamned test wells," Pappas continued, not one to circle to a conclusion. Jim wasn't sure he agreed, but he couldn't dispute that the number of ducks killed on Gable Farms was way off. Moreover, Pappas's theory was supported by the fact that Waterloo's hunters had enjoyed a good season. Waterloo had no gas wells.

Jim kept his silence, waiting to see where this was headed.

Pappas set his drink down and leaned forward. "We want you to talk to him. Tell him that most of us are prepared to pull out unless he dismantles those wells. Hell, I've as much as told him that already, but he won't listen. You're the waterfowl expert around here. He'll listen to you if you tell him the wells have screwed up the hunting."

Jim raised his eyes to the ceiling, feigning concentration on Pappas's proposition while, in reality, he searched for a solution to his other problem in the cigar haze floating above. He'd just spent four and a half days alone with Three and had come up with nothing. He felt stalled, impotent, his confidence drained. He'd love to tell Pappas to just be patient—that soon Three would be history, and with him the wells.

In truth, the prospect of sending Three off to the big blind in the sky had touched other nerves in Jim, nerves worn raw by Three's arrogance and lack of appreciation for the true potential of Gable Farms as a prime duck club. There were many changes Jim longed to bring about. Under Three, the place was deteriorating into a rich man's social club and losing much of its heritage as a pristine place to hunt ducks. There was no reason it couldn't be both. With Three out of the picture, the first things to go would be the gas wells and the Roto Ducks.

"Well, Jim?"

Jim looked around at four pairs of eyes that demanded an answer.

"Fellas," he said, "as much as I'd like to see those wells ripped out, I've got a job to protect. Armand's already on me about the boat thing. His gas project is one of his pets. If I started in on him about it, I might as well pack my bag. I think you boys would rather have me here than somewhere else."

Pappas sighed. "You're right there, Jim." He took a drink. "There's more, you know. His plan for tennis courts, for instance. This is a duck club, not a goddamn country club."

"Give it time," Jim said. "This season's shot anyway. A lot could happen before next season. Hell, Armand blows hot and cold on things, one after another. By next year he could be off gas wells and tennis courts and on to something else, maybe even something good for this place."

The door to the clubhouse main room swept open, and Three stepped in out of the rain.

"Evening all," he called, "who's my domino pigeon tonight?" He spied Pappas and rubbed his hands together. "Pappas, glad you're here. Hope you brought enough money." He peeled off his parka and made straight for the bar.

At first Armand thought the irritating noise that interrupted his brandy-soaked slumber was a bug. Half asleep, he waved a hand and pulled the blankets over his head. The bug got louder. He raised a corner and peered out. The luminous hands on the bedside clock read 11:47. He'd been in bed only twenty minutes, but it felt like hours. The $450 drubbing Pappas handed him at dominoes had led him to drown his anger in brandy, his second big mistake of the night.

The noise turned into a brash clang that stopped, clanged, and stopped again. Clawing for consciousness, Armand propped himself up on an elbow. It was the goddamned telephone.

"What the hell?"

He snatched up the phone. A dim flicker of thought reminded him of the frequent pleasure he derived from calling people in the middle of the night. Only a select handful had his private Gable Farms number, so it was unlikely that one of his tormented recipients was seeking revenge. "Who the hell is this?"

"Ar–mand? That you?"

The Texan's drawl and bifurcation of Armand's name identified the caller at once.

Deerlink—Armand's elusive key to exploiting the gas under Waterloo. In the background Armand made out the warbled twang of loud country music, mixed with the raucous din of a very crowded bar in full swing.

"Deerlink?" said Armand.

"Y'all got to speak up, Ar–mand," Dink shouted back. "It's pretty noisy here."

Armand sat up and again looked at the clock.

"It's almost midnight," he shouted into the telephone. "Is something wrong?"

"Wrong? Hell, no Ar–mand. Nothing's wrong. Homer, Clive, and me are just out on the town with a few of the Dallas Cowboy cheerleaders. Hell, the night's young. Thought y'all'd be up for sure. Had a hell of a time tracking y'all down. Finally got this number from your wife. Nice lady. Like to meet her sometime."

Armand's head began to clear as he pieced together what the Texan was saying. What could be so important that Deerlink had called

Donna for his exclusive number? Moreover, why had she given it to him?

"Ar–mand, here's the deal. We've kept the natural gas supply choked off long enough that prices just took an interesting hike, which made me think of you. I talked to your lawyer, Du-bwas, this afternoon. Me and the boys were thinking of coming out to San Francisco next week to meet with him and those condemnation lawyers from Nor-Cal. Y'all are still interested in gettin' your neighbor's property and layin' that pipeline, ain't ya'"?

Interested? This was too good. Armand stood as the adrenaline kicked in. He'd given up on the Texans, figuring they'd found an easier, quicker opportunity. Here they were, back, knocking at his door.

"We was wondering," Deerlink continued, "if we was to buy memberships in that fancy duck club of yours, it would give us more stake in the project. Get my drift? The boys and me like to mix our business with pleasure every chance we get. Keeps us young and interested. And, Lord knows, we just love eatin' ducks. Now, we'd like to take you up on that invitation to shoot ducks at your place, just to get the lay of the land. Next weekend work for you?"

Armand smiled, the irritation of being torn from his blissful, boozy sleep overcome by his sudden good fortune. With the Texans on board, he'd be unstoppable. Better to have Gable Farms members who shared his vision for the future rather than the whiners who wanted to drag the place into the past. He started ticking off the members ripe for replacement, starting with that domino-cheating troublemaker, Pappas.

"Dink," he said, "nothing would give me greater pleasure. You, Clive, and Homer will be my guests here next weekend. I promise you a shoot you'll never forget."

Jim listened, horrified, as Three's enthusiastic plans for the coming weekend and his wooing of the Texans to his cause invaded the sanctuary of their duck blind. More gas wells on Gable Farms. The complete obliteration of Waterloo as a duck club. Three's electric decoys sat still, their commander's attention focused on telling Jim all that was expected of him.

"These boys will want a duck dinner every night they're here," Three said. "Get out that old duck press of my father's and shine it up. Lay on our best wines. I'm going to sell them three memberships at two million each. Anyone who squawks can quit. The fact is, I hope this weeds some of them out—you know, the complainers. I'm tired of trying to please a bunch of old ladies who can't see the opportunity around us. Instead of griping about a few gas wells, Pappas and his buddies should seize this opportunity. You heard what happened when I offered them shares in my gas company. Assholes."

Several seconds passed, and then, as an afterthought, Three said, "And they can't tell me that gas wells scare the ducks. Hell, you saw all those ducks on that test well we passed on the way out here. Like flies to syrup."

"Those were mud hens, Armand," Jim said, quietly. "Mud hens. Coots. Junk birds. The things you keep shooting that even the muskrats won't eat."

Jim resumed his silence, numbed by the thought of more wells on Gable Farms. Then the image of gas well Christmas trees protruding from the barren, drained ponds of Waterloo struck him, and he dropped his head, no longer interested in spotting ducks for Three to miss. The wind had stopped, and the pond's surface was placid. Three's mechanical decoys stood out as ridiculous appendages, incapable of fooling anything. Were it not for the finned hump threading through them...

Finned hump? Jim stared at the decoy spread while Three rambled on about the rosy future of his gas empire.

Now there were two fins circling lazily among the decoys—no, wait, three. And another, curving out from the decoys toward the far tules. And then two more, coming directly toward the blind—slow, unerring torpedoes.

CHAPTER 33

Monday, January 17.

Drake and Jim Quesenberry pulled up in front of the Butte City Club within seconds of each other. After they'd deposited their members' Sunday ducks at Figone's duck plucking shed, they went inside. Jim waved to Junior Grimes and Lonnie, who were seated at the end of the bar. They waved back.

"To the ducks," Drake said, raising his bottle.

"The ducks," Jim said, clinking his against Drake's. "If only it could last."

Drake looked at Jim. "What's that supposed to mean?"

Jim emptied half the bottle, swiped his sleeve across his mouth, and turned. "Drake, he's coming at you with everything he's got. Now he's linked up with those Texans again. They want your place, and they aim to get it. According to Three, there's almost as much gas under Waterloo as there is dirt. Once they condemn that pipeline to connect the Gable Farms wells, they figure it'll drive you off and they'll turn your place into a gas farm. That and rice." Jim picked up his bottle. "There, I've told you. My conscience is clear."

Seconds passed before Drake finally answered. "Jim, I appreciate your going out on a limb for me, but I know about the gas. I've always known it, I guess. And I suspected those Texans were holding something back when they paid me a visit last month."

He pulled the Krenzler lighter from his vest pocket. "They'll never get the place, Jim," he said, placing the lighter on the bar. He studied it as he continued. "Not even after they condemn their goddamn pipeline. Hell, I'll paint it green or something." He chuckled. "Maybe camo."

Drake pocketed the lighter and turned on his stool to face the door. He stared outside. "Jim, you've always been honest with me about Three, even though it could cost you. It's my turn to repay the favor."

They faced each other.

"It's Duke," said Drake. "He wants to talk to me about Three's, uh, accidents. I think he's fishing. He'll want to talk to you next."

Drake let Jim digest this. "Now, Jim, don't get me wrong. I've cracked some jokes about those things. Hell, who hasn't? But not for a minute did I think you had anything to do with them. Just a run of bad luck, that's all."

Drake didn't like Jim's nervous twitch and the furtive look that suddenly filled his eyes. It was one thing to support a close friend's innocence. Preaching innocence while suspecting guilt was something else.

"Jim?" he said.

Jim looked away. "You're right. Bad luck. Let's drop it, OK?"

Drake's eyes settled on Moe the sturgeon.

"Guess we both should have paid more attention to Moe," he said.

Jim's head snapped up. "Jesus, that reminds me. You ever see any big fish in your ponds? I mean, big, ugly things like carp?"

Drake shook his head. "No. Oh, there've been catfish and bass that come in from the creek, but carp? No, I don't think so. Why?"

"Damndest thing," Jim said. "Yesterday, while I was out with Three, I saw a bunch of 'em. At least four or five. Probably in the six-pound range. Just swimming along. Uglier than sin. That's not all."

He finished his beer and motioned for another. "This morning I took a boat and checked all the ponds. Half of them are loaded with these things."

Drake continued to study the sturgeon. "You've never seen these before?"

"Never. And there's no way fish could get in our ponds from the creek or canal. We've got screens on all the weirs."

Drake nodded. It was an expense he'd foregone at Waterloo. "So, is it a problem?"

Jim shrugged. "I don't know. You tell me. Think ducks are put off by suckerfish?"

Drake turned. "You didn't say suckerfish, did you?"

"Well, hell, that's what they look like. I netted one. They've got these big, round mouths, like suction cups. I'm telling you, I've never seen fish like them around here."

Drake finished his beer and stood. "Hell, I wouldn't worry about it. They probably came over from the Sacramento River in all this high water." He looked at his watch. "I'm running late. Duke's expecting me. I've got to talk him into holding off making me a guest of the county while I get rid of those damned cows. If he asks about you and Three's accidents, don't worry. Three's always been clumsy and had bad luck. Thanks for keeping me posted."

As he drove toward Yuba City and the sheriff's office, the thought of suckerfish in Gable Farms ponds took his mind off all the rest. He pounded the steering wheel and laughed.

While Charlie Rainwater was many things, liar was not one of them. Pete Wooley had learned to take his son-in-law seriously, particularly when it came to creatures of the wild. If Charlie said he'd seen sacred suckerfish in the ponds of a Butte Sink duck club, then, by God, they were there. Stupid white men might have either planted them for amusement or maybe they were a whole different strain of suckerfish, indigenous to the Sacramento Valley. How they got there didn't matter. What did was the fact they were sacred.

Suckerfish were the cleansers, the fish that scoured lakes and streams and made them pure. They were the Jesus-of-the-Waters in that they took on the sins of their surroundings and turned them into salvation. Or at least that's what Pete Wooley preached to his followers.

"You say the fish are in danger?" said Wooley, studying his son-in-law's eyes.

"No doubt about it, Dad," said Charlie. "Once those fat-cat hunters discover that their duck ponds are breeding grounds for suckerfish, they'll drain the ponds and let the osprey and vultures feast on 'em."

Wooley winced. "What about the ducks?"

"Duck season ends there next weekend, Dad. When it's over, they usually drain those ponds anyway, for maintenance. Not a pretty sight when you think of all those suckerfish flopping around in the mud, getting torn to shreds by all those predator sons-of—"

"Stop!" said Wooley, raising his hands. "You can lead us to this place?"

"No problem, Dad. How many can you get to come?"

Wooley pursed his lips. Then, as he began counting fingers, Charlie felt pangs of disappointment. He'd expected more, many more. Finally, with both hands spread, Wooley answered.

"Probably around a thousand," he said. "Yeah, a thousand. Maybe a few more. Not much going on right now. I'll call that reporter from the *New York Times*. He'll like this."

Charlie relaxed, realizing that each finger represented one hundred, Wooley's mental inventory of activists from tribes throughout Oregon, Nevada, and California—his rapid deployment SWAT team. Charlie sat back and grinned. "Great idea, Dad. Let's get started. Give me a list of numbers. I'll help with the calls."

Duke tilted back in his swivel chair and, with one hand, spanned his whole moustache. He executed a perfect, single-handed double twirl.

"So, that's it, Duke," Drake said. "I'll bring in some help and have those cows moved by Thursday. I plan to stop by the Butte City Club and hire Junior Grimes and his pal, Lonnie. I just saw them there. They always need work."

Duke nodded, lost in thought. Finally he sat forward and spread his large hands on the desk. "Drake, that damn fool lady judge was in here not one hour ago haranguing me for not having you in the lock-up. Says if I can't get you in jail and those cows rounded up by this Friday, she'll call her pal the governor and get some state troopers in here who will. Now, I know it's not all that simple for you, but it does look like you've got a break in the weather."

He continued to twiddle his moustache, concentrating.

"Junior and Lonnie aren't the most, uh, dependable hands around, you know. They sober?"

Drake shrugged. "They were riding barstools all right a little while ago. Should be able to ride an ATV. Thought I'd have Junior use his truck while Lonnie and I flanked them on the machines."

Duke nodded. "You know, Judge Hanford broke his arm on a ski slope. Damn fool, skiing at his age. Anyway, he's coming back this weekend. He'll be back on the bench Monday. That should mean adios to Her Honor—she and her birdie pictures."

Duke paused. "How's the hunting been?"

Drake, surprised at the sudden shift, gave a quick and correct assessment. "Hey, it's been great. Like to come out and shoot this coming weekend? End of the season, you know. Come on out Friday and spend the weekend."

Duke smiled. "Why, Drake, that's mighty nice of you. I'd love to. George tells me you cook up a mean rib-eye steak, one of my favorites."

"Rib eye it'll be Duke. Friday night. Ducks on Saturday."

Drake stood, anxious to leave. "See you Friday afternoon then."

"Uh, Drake, there's something else."

Drake looked down at the sheriff. "What's that, Duke?"

"Sit back down. This will take some time. It has to do with Stilton and Jim Quesenberry."

CHAPTER 34

Inspired, Armand punched the Hummer's dash button that activated the built-in cell phone. "Dial DuBois," he commanded. He drummed the steering wheel as the connection was made.

"Louis," he said, when the attorney answered, "my friends from Texas are coming to town."

"I know, Armand. We're meeting here Wednesday morning."

"Good. Listen, I was thinking. It's about time you got your feet wet, so to speak." Armand laughed. For pure entertainment nothing beat his own humor.

"Pardon?"

"Louis, I mean you need to come up to Gable Farms. Deerlink and his pals are coming up after they meet with you. You should join them. Mingle with the people you'll be working for. View the property. Hell, I've paid you enough to represent it, now you should see it. You're going to be putting together this gas company deal. You need to be in touch with the real estate, and not just the people. Jackson Crackers may be a ball buster, but I doubt if he knows the first thing about SEC filings and all that silk stocking stuff you guys do. This is the last weekend of duck season. Maybe you can even shoot a duck."

Armand counted the silent seconds, chuckling as he imagined the attorney's anguish. The closest to the great outdoors Louis DuBois ever came was his weekly luncheon at the Olympic Club.

"Uh, Armand, I'm afraid Marjorie has plans for us this weekend."

"Cancel them, Louis. I'll expect you here. Hitch a ride with the Texans. It'll do you good to lose some of that starch."

Armand punched the button again and told the robot's voice to connect him with Jackson Crackers.

"Hello, Armand. Just thinking of you," the lawyer said. "I've come up with another angle. You'll love it. Tax evasion. Seems Green's old man put that property into an agricultural preserve status to save property taxes. The thing is, you need to farm something now and then to qualify. He hasn't. Probably owes back property taxes in the millions. We could force a tax sale."

God, I love this guy, thought Armand.

"Hey, Jackson, that's great! Now, let's talk about it at Gable Farms this weekend. I'm inviting you up for the season's closing. I know you don't shoot ducks, but it will be a great get-together. Everyone will be there. The Texas guys, DuBois, the whole team. What do you say? Great food, Cuban cigars, the best booze…"

"Women?" Crackers said.

Armand darkened. He should have known. *Oh, well, the guy's other talents make up for his lack of social grace.*

"Jackson, this is a duck club. Not a bordello. Women are welcome once a year, and that's just wives. No hanky-panky."

"Armand, I'd love it. Have someone fax me a map to the place. What do I bring?"

"Money. We play dominoes. Sometimes poker."

So intent on his plans for the weekend and so pleased with himself over orchestrating this assemblage of legal and financial strength, Armand didn't notice the silver Mercedes SL500 Roadster that bore north on I-5 as he came south. In all fairness, he could never have spotted Donna's car anyway; the four-lane interstate freeway was divided most of the way by a twenty-foot median. She counted on that, knowing that Armand always had his mind on business while cocooned with a huge Cuban cigar in his Hummer. Sometimes, when he was really worked up, he actually lit it.

Donna's mission, born of desperation, was simple and urgent. She had one last chance to kindle a fire of fatal heat in Jim Quesenberry. When duck season ended, Armand would be off to far pockets of the planet, killing things she couldn't pronounce or catching fish larger than he was. While there might be a guide or outfitter willing to do the job, she could not stand another month with Armand, his pomposity, rudeness, and only occasional interest in her as a woman. She'd be far better off with the $20 million in life insurance than Armand's unlimited wealth while he lived. The thought of life with him until next duck season was unbearable.

And the cigars. God. First thing she'd do after the funeral would be to take that humidor full of expensive cigars and send it to the duck club. It wouldn't hurt to keep a friendly alliance with the members. While she didn't care all that much about hunting, she loved the shooting.

With Pavarotti crooning Italian love arias from the CD player, Donna pressed on, determined that this time she would spur her champion to success.

Jim regarded Tuesday's chores as part of the price of admission. Changing sheets, dusting, cleaning toilets, and doing dishes were tasks of duck club caretaking that, if done right, went unnoticed, and if botched, drew sharp criticism.

Jim's several attempts to farm the work out to locals had met with miserable failure, their standards being nowhere near those set by Three and adopted by the members. Jim's labors after a hunting week-end had become a literal application of the maxim "If you want something done right, do it yourself."

He'd just finished the eighth residence and was walking toward the clubhouse when the sound of a vehicle on the entrance road made him look up. At first, he couldn't make out what it was, its low-slung, silver shape out of synch with the bulky SUVs that frequented the place. He stopped and watched as it drew closer. When the Mercedes was fifty feet away and he could make out the driver's features, he sucked in a breath. *Donna Stilton. Jesus.*

She stopped the car in front of him, stepped out, and leaned on the window of the open door. Her honey-blonde hair, always done up or stuffed into a hunting cap when he'd seen her before, now fell to her shoulders—a silky waterfall. He'd never seen hair that beautiful.

"Hello, Jim," she said. "We need to talk."

By four that afternoon, Pete Wooley and Charlie Rainwater had connected with all the Native American activists on Wooley's list. One after another, tribal leaders assured them of support, all viewing the outing as a grand opportunity for a long-deferred conclave at the base of the Sutter Buttes.

The Buttes, spires and domes that reached two thousand feet above the valley, formed from gas-charged, hurricane-force eruptions 1.5 million years earlier, had been sacred to the Maidu Indians, who had considered them the center of creation. The prospect of an inter-tribal conclave to demonstrate for protection of a newly discovered population of sacred suckerfish near their base and to honor the Middle Mountain—or Histum Yani, as the Buttes were called by the early Maidus—proved irresistible to Wooley's followers, whose restless political energy boiled for outlet after long months of winter boredom.

Wooley peered over the top of his reading glasses as he pushed away from the telephone and electronic calculator. "I make the count at just under twelve hundred," he said. A broad grin split his face. "Think of it, Charlie. Over a thousand Indians spilling in from all over the state—from out of state, even. My boy, I'm proud of you."

Charlie flashed a modest smile. It felt good, at last, to bask in his father-in-law's favor.

"Dad," he said, "I'm going home and get some rest. Been on the road a lot lately."

Wooley's face clouded.

"Visiting Claire and her boyfriend, Dad. Stuff like that."

Wooley's expression relaxed, but not by much.

"Besides, seeing as we're on the road early tomorrow, I want to make sure those grandsons of yours get a good night's rest. Pick you up here at five, right?"

At the mention of his grandsons, all trouble left Wooley's eyes. "That's fine, Charlie. See you then."

Charlie's suggestion that the twins accompany them, while at first rejected by Wooley, had finally won his approval when Charlie reminded him that the *New York Times* reporter had particularly asked about the boys. He'd liked the depth they'd given his earlier story—the

Native American elder passing the baton of tradition on to the youth. This time, though, he asked that they not pinch their noses while he photographed Wooley holding up sacred suckerfish. Charlie had promised they wouldn't.

On the way home Charlie stopped at the casino and drew $1,000 against his account. The demonstrating celebrants were to rendezvous at Rolling Hills, the new Indian casino just off I-5 at Corning. He'd have plenty of time for some blackjack before they set off for Gable Farms and the Buttes.

CHAPTER 35

Wednesday morning, January 19.

Dawn's shafts of color struck the winter frost that had glazed everything it touched. The valley sparkled in the cold, clear morning air.

Drake tossed the remnants of his coffee into the sink and pulled his wool cap over his ears. "Going to be cold as a witches whatsis out there," he said.

Claire stood. "Are you sure I can't help?"

"I'm sure," he said, heading for the door. "You really want to help me, just keep working on those house plans. Right now, that's all that keeps me going."

He buttoned his jacket and stepped outside. He took his time on the stairs because of the frost and then headed for the equipment shed, his boots grating a satisfying crunch as they pressed the frozen ground.

He slid open the large wooden door and mounted one of the ATVs. Tar stopped sniffing its morning rounds and barked approval when the machine fired up.

Drake nosed the vehicle through the door and set off toward Green's Crossing, where he had arranged to meet Junior and Lonnie. Tar jogged alongside. Something different was brewing, and the dog loved every minute of it.

They arrived at the crossing, and Drake frowned. No Junior, no Junior's truck, and no Lonnie. He looked at his watch: 7:10. They were supposed to have been there at 7 sharp.

He stepped off the ATV, unlocked the bar gate, and shoved it aside. "Damn drunks," he said. "Duke was right."

His words, frozen in frost, hung before him. He leaned against the ATV and decided to wait until 7:30. After that, he'd go out and try it alone. He'd leave the crossing open. When and if they showed up, they could come in and track him down. *I shouldn't be hard to spot,* he thought. *The only idiot on an ATV chasing cows around the banks and levees of a duck club on a freezing winter morning. Like Duke said, go through the motions. Shit.*

"Got him!"

Three began to jump up and down. He had actually downed a duck. Jim shook his head. The ducks had been high, too high.

"Jethro," he called, and the dog hit the water.

"Nice shot, Armand," he said. Actually, it had been an impossibly lucky shot, one accomplished only by the most skilled of hunters—or the most incompetent. True skill lie in knowing when *not* to shoot.

Three grinned and patted his new Holland & Holland. "Which is it?" he said. "The gun makes the man or the man makes the gun?"

Jim shrugged. He'd never heard either and was not about to cough up some witty response. Three's moments of exuberance were known for their brevity. Any attempt to steal his thunder over the lucky shot would likely be met with ice, and Jim was already walking on ice, very thin ice.

Donna's visit had propelled him into a new and far more dangerous turmoil. From the moment she'd stepped out of her car until the moment he'd watched her drive away, Jim had been on the other side of the looking glass, surrounded by grinning Cheshire cats and cupid-like mad hatters.

An exquisite pain had swollen inside him, a pain that made him want to sing, and Jim was no singer. Above the confused maelstrom of emotion whipped up by his obsession to improve Cedar Hills and his will to save Gable Farms, a strange new force gripped him, leaving him almost unable to function. His duck calling that morning had been atrocious.

"Well, that's a good start on dinner for my guests," Three said, as Jethro's head appeared over the edge of the blind, a gorgeous mallard in its mouth.

"Drop, Jethro," Jim said. The dog let go, and the duck fell to the layer of tules that circled the blind's rim.

Armand nodded his approval and then looked at Jim. "Only thirteen more to go," he said. "Get quacking."

A chain-saw-like sound came up from the south, a sound Jim recognized at once as an ATV. *Drake, out trying to catch his cows.* That wasn't going to help the hunting. Jim sighed. It was going to be a very long day.

The immense parking lot at Rolling Hills Casino was less than half full when Charlie pulled in. He scanned the lot, his poacher's eyes ever on the alert for signs of trouble or threat.

"Hey, there's Arnold!" he said, spotting his cousin.

Arnold "The Ram" Sheepshead was leading a group of eight, who had just disembarked a forty-three-foot Winnebago land yacht. Arnold was actually Charlie's cousin through Wanda, and, as such, also shared in the casino spoils.

Charlie, Pete Wooley, and the twins met Arnold's group with handshakes and hugs, Wooley beaming the whole time.

"It's only ten thirty," Charlie said. "Let's go in and get some breakfast." He winked at Arnold as he made a card-dealing motion with his hands. All areed and the first contingent of Save the Sacred Butte Sink Suckerfish marched toward the casino's restaurant. On the way, Charlie fell in step with Arnold.

"Everything go OK?" Arnold asked.

"Like clockwork," said Charlie. "Got the truck back the day before yesterday. Left it with a full tank. The State of Oregon owes me."

Arnold laughed. "That'll be the day. Hey, you sure we got time for cards before we do this thing?"

Charlie grinned. "Does a salmon swim?"

By one thirty, the Rolling Hills Casino parking lot was overflowing with Native Americans who had arrived in convoys of pickups, campers, RVs, trailers, and buses. A boisterous mood of celebration filled the air as old acquaintances were renewed and new ones made. People strolled among tailgate lunches and barbecues, fortifying themselves for the long days ahead. Native American costumes abounded, with spangles of beads, shells, and feathers.

As Charlie and Arnold stepped from the dark casino into the bright sunlight, each blinked and reached for their polarized sunglasses.

"Wow!" said Charlie. "Now, this is a sight."

Arnold shook his head in wonder. "Man, is it. Hope someone's taking pictures."

Wooley hurried toward them. "Charlie!" he called. "Where the hell you been?"

Charlie patted his rear pocket. "Just taking care of business, Dad."

Wooley shook his head. "Charlie, you just can't go flying off on one of your sprees. This thing is ready to go. That's the way of demonstrations. The people get all worked up and need to let it out. We wait too long and they lose interest. Besides, the casino manager wants us to get the hell out of his lot. He needs the space for customers. You should appreciate that."

"OK, Dad. Let's hit it. You got the boys?"

"They're in the truck," Wooley said. "I'll get on the PA system and tell people we're leaving. You know the route, so we'll lead."

Charlie nodded, gave Arnold a high five, and headed for his truck.

"I got them! A double!" Three sprang to his toes, his arms raised in triumph. Jim grabbed the waving barrel of his boss's shotgun and gently pushed it aside. Jethro looked up at Jim.

"Uh, Armand, those were mud hens—again. You keep shooting them at the rate you've been doing, and we'll be out of shells. I only brought three boxes."

The dog dropped its head and settled back down.

Actually, thought Jim, *if he shoots one more mud hen I'll kill him with my bare hands. No jury in this county would convict me, and it would solve all my problems.*

It was three thirty. Two mallards and one widgeon lay on the floorboards. Jim had quit counting the unretrieved mud hens when they passed sixteen. For diversion, he'd taken to watching the blurps and slurps of the strange new intruders that had infiltrated the ponds.

Three hadn't noticed them, and Jim's instincts told him that was a good thing.

"We've got two hours of light left," grumbled Three, "and we're using every minute of it. My guests want duck dinners this weekend and, by God, they're going to have them."

Jim shrugged. He was beyond caring.

A sound caught his attention—horns, lots of them, like a wedding caravan. He pulled over one of the blind's stools and stood on it. The horns were coming from West Butte Road, and were getting louder.

"What the hell's that racket?" said Three, now also straining to see.

"Don't know, Armand," Jim said. "Hand me up those binoculars."

Three passed up the binoculars, and Jim focused them in the direction of the noise. "Jesus," he said.

"What is it?" said Armand, who tugged at Jim's jacket. "Let me see."

Jim lowered the binoculars and stepped from the stool. "You're not going to like this, Armand," he said. "Looks like a parade of several hundred cars along West Butte Road. Lots of them have already turned off onto that north access road into the property. I don't know what's going on, but it sure as hell isn't good."

Three climbed onto the stool and raised the binoculars. "Goddamn it, steady me!"

Jim grabbed Three's legs and held on.

"Oh, shit. Shit, shit, shit..." Three said, mesmerized. He began to quiver. "It's a goddamned invasion! Christ! Goddammit Quesenberry, do something!"

Jim relaxed his grip on Three's legs and held up a hand. "Come on down, Armand. We'll take the boat and find out what this is all about. Maybe someone's having a big party or something, and they just made a wrong turn."

Even as he said this, Jim doubted his hasty conclusion. People, much less hundreds of people, did not have parties out on West Butte Road, particularly in the dead of winter.

As Drake pulled into the equipment shed, Claire ran toward him. "Drake," she called, "what's happening over there?"

"Beats me," he said. "Sounds like some kind of rally or something. I thought I heard someone on a bullhorn and then lots of cheering. Let's go check it out. I'm not doing much good here anyway." The cows, riding the crest of their recent victory, had proved even more difficult. The holding pen was empty.

He put Tar in the kennel, and they climbed into Drake's pickup. When they started across Green's Crossing, something caught Drake's eye. He stopped and stared into the grove of cottonwood trees on the far side. The front of Junior Grimes's truck formed a sculpted arc around one of the trees.

"Christ," he said. He eased his pickup across the bridge and stopped.

"I hear something," Claire said. "Singing?" Drake shrugged. It was hard to tell.

They got out and walked around to the other side of Junior's truck. Junior and Lonnie sat on the ground, their backs propped against the rear tire and an almost empty gallon of what appeared to be red wine perched on a flat rock between them. An empty jug lay next to the rock.

Junior looked up. "Mornin', Drake. Issit time to go to work?"

CHAPTER 36

"Now, Armand," Jim said, as they approached the levee road, crammed with cars, trucks, RVs, and people. "I don't know who or what these people are, but we've got to stay calm." As a precaution he emptied Three's shotgun.

Jim cut the engine and nudged the boat into the levee bank. He looked up into a sea of faces, many of them decorated with streaks of color. Silence settled on those closest to where Jim and Three had landed, and it began to spread down the road as word of their arrival spread.

"Greetings, neighbor. Here, let me give you a hand."

Jim looked up and recognized the flat, dark eyes that said, *Don't tread on me.*

"Rainwater?"

"Right, friend. Charlie Rainwater. Good to see you again."

Charlie motioned to his right. "This here's my father-in-law, Chief Pete Wooley. He's in charge."

Armand exploded from his seat. "What? Who the hell do you think you are? Get the hell out of here before I have the whole drunken bunch of you arrested and prosecuted for trespassing." Three turned to Jim. "You know this man?"

Charlie stared down at Armand. "Who's he?" he asked Jim.

"Uh, Mr. Rainwater, this is Armand Stilton the Third. He owns this property. I work for him."

The Indian nodded. "Oh, yes, I remember now. You mentioned him when you ran me off this place last week."

Jim relaxed a bit, thankful Rainwater had perceived his predicament. "Could you explain, please, just what is happening here?" he said.

With that, Wooley stepped forward. "We, representatives of the Native American tribes of California, Oregon, and Nevada, are here to protect the sacred fish that inhabit these waters. That and to honor Histum Yani." He swept his arms aloft, toward the Sutter Buttes.

Jim considered this a few seconds, a faint and dreaded light beginning to dawn. "Uh, what sacred fish might those be, Chief?" he said. He recalled Charlie's preoccupation days earlier.

"Why the mother of all fish, the purifier of waters and scavenger for the gods," Wooley said, his chest filling. "The sacred suckerfish."

A hushed chant started among those closest in the column of onlookers, soon taken on by the hundreds beyond, who spilled almost all the way back to West Butte Road, a good quarter mile away.

"SAVE THE SACRED BUTTE SINK SUCKERFISH, SAVE THE SACRED…" The chant grew to shouts, then cheers as signs and placards appeared and a small group broke off, dancing, circling, chanting, lost in the rapture of the moment.

Three's eyes widened. "My God."

Jim scratched his chin. "Uh, Chief, just how long do you plan to spend protecting the, uh, suckerfish and honoring old Histi whatshisname?"

Wooley glared down. "Histum Yani." Again he gestured toward the Buttes. "Those."

Charlie spoke up. "The chief and his people will demonstrate to protect these sacred suckerfish for as long as the fish are here. By my count, there are hundreds of them living in these ponds. Chief Wooley intends that this demonstration last four days, and after that, we will return to this sacred site on a regular basis—oh, say, once every two or three months, more during the winter months when the fish are breeding and more vulnerable."

Wooley stared at his son-in-law.

Three, now purple with rage, shouted, "You can't do that! I have shooting guests arriving tomorrow. Important people are coming here to hunt and do business. Now, clear out!"

He leapt from the boat, his stubby legs scrambling for purchase on the bank. Too quick for Jim to grab him, Three tumbled down the muddy slope into the water. The splash was greeted by a cheer that Jim swore could be heard throughout Sutter County.

"Hmmm," Claire said as they pulled into the Gable Farms parking area. "The last time it was sheriffs, now this."

Three television news trucks were parked at angles, their crews setting up lights and laying out cords. Drake recognized two attractive female newscasters, who were in the throes of make-up.

A young man in jeans and a sweatshirt raced over to them. "Mr. Stilton?" he said.

Drake shook his head. "No, just a neighbor. What's going on?" He looked around for Jim or Jim's truck.

"We're not exactly sure, yet," the man said. "All three channels received calls this afternoon of a large Native American demonstration and rally that's taking place on this property. We just got here, but it looks like whatever is happening is out there." He motioned west, toward the Gable Farms interior. "Can you show my crew the way?"

Drake shook his head. "I could, but I won't. Besides, you'd need a boat."

He tugged at Claire's sleeve and led her back to his truck. Out of earshot of the TV people he said, "Come on, let's go down to the boat dock. Maybe Jim's down there. Stilton's probably with him. That's his rig." He nodded in the direction of Armand's residence. The Hummer was parked in front.

Drake pulled up at the Gable Farms dock and parked alongside Jim's pickup. The sun was setting, casting long shadows across the water. Bright bursts of light began to flicker from several of the levee roads.

"Bonfires," Drake said. "Whatever this is, the ducks aren't going to like it one bit. Hold on, I hear a boat."

He peered down the channel and was able to make out a bow wave. "He's not wasting any time," he said, as the distance closed. "It's them."

When they were just yards away, Jim turned the boat and killed the engine. The boat came to rest against the dock, and Jim jumped out, Jethro behind him. Armand stood, and Jim extended a hand.

Armand glared at Drake as he stepped onto the dock. "Great. All I need. Does trouble follow you or you follow it?"

Drake tied off the boat. "What's up?" he asked Jim.

"Your friend Rainwater and hundreds of his pals. They say they're here to protect sacred suckerfish and to pay some kind of homage to the Buttes."

"You!" Armand cried at Drake. "They're *your* friends?"

"Easy, Armand, I hardly know the man. He's Claire's brother-in-law. I guarantee you, whatever this is, I had nothing to do with it."

"Right, and I'm the Prince of Wales. Quesenberry, get me back to the clubhouse. I'm calling in the law."

Drake raised a hand. "Armand, listen to me a minute. Your place is crawling with TV news trucks. As soon as you set foot back there, you'll be swarmed with reporters. These are Native Americans. This thing is going to be all over the six o'clock news. If you make a big deal of it, it's going to draw even more people out here. That's the last thing either of us wants. I suggest you play this down. Make light of it with the reporters. Then let's you and I go talk to Rainwater and his father-in-law, who's probably running this. Maybe we can reason with them and head this off before it spoils the weekend."

Jim nodded. "He's right, Armand. This is pretty much a no-win deal."

Armand's eyes narrowed. He stared at Jim, then Drake, then back at Jim.

"I knew it," he said at last, "You're in league with him. The two of you probably cooked up this whole thing. So Green, this Rainwater thug is your girlfriend's brother-in-law. My, what a small world."

He turned to Jim. "Well, mister, you get me back to the clubhouse where we can call the sheriff. You're so chummy with this Rainwater character, you'd better come up with a way to get him and his…his… tribe off my property. Either that or you go. I've about had it with you."

Three turned to Drake. "You want to help save your friend's job, you'd better help come up with a way to clear this mob out of here damned quick."

Jim began to shake his head. "Armand..."

Armand walked over to Jim's pickup and climbed in. "You heard me. Now, let's go."

CHAPTER 37

"**I** have no comment," Armand said, brushing aside microphones as he ran toward the clubhouse. Jim, impressed with the array of faces he recognized from the nightly news, straightened his cap and followed, but at a sedate pace. He stopped when Leslie Lodestar of Channel 7 stepped in front of him.

"Sir? Are you connected with Gable Farms?"

Jim smiled into the camera. "I'm Jim Quesenberry, the, uh hunting professional." Jim preferred the world knew him for his true talents, rather than his bed changing and cleaning skills.

"Mr. Quesenberry, what is your understanding of this demonstration out here this evening?"

Jim took a breath as he prepared for his television debut. Then he saw Three glaring at him from the clubhouse deck. "I'm afraid I don't have time right now," he said, and hastened to catch up.

After they cleared the door, Three said, "Lock it. And get that hick sheriff on the phone. Tell him to bring the SWAT team."

Duke pressed the mute button on the remote control. From the opening moments of the local news, he'd been expecting the call.

After his excited dispatcher told him of the call from Gable Farms, he gave instructions to have two of the four on-duty units meet him at the office. Together they would convoy to Gable Farms. Then he told the dispatcher to alert off-duty officers.

As he slid into the cruiser, Duke wondered what it was about Armand Stilton III that seemed to attract disaster. An old Al Capp fan, Duke recalled the character from *Li'l Abner*—Joe Btfsplk—the guy who always had a dark cloud over him. Only this time Stilton's dark cloud threatened the one weekend of duck hunting Duke was to have this season. Duke sighed. Stilton had become entirely too much trouble.

Drake and Claire cleared the news vans without stopping. They reentered Waterloo and were approaching Green's Crossing when Drake saw lights ahead. They were pointed toward each other, like some kind of cross-eyed monster. As Drake drew closer, he saw what it was: Junior's truck, now sporting a concave front end. Drake pulled to the edge, and Junior came to a stop alongside.

"Guess you won't be needin' us today?" Junior said.

"No, Junior, I don't think so," Drake said. A sudden malevolent impulse seized him. "You boys might find work over there though," he said, waving his arm toward Gable Farms. "Drive on over and tell the people out front you work for Mr. Stilton."

Junior gunned his engine, which was making terminal sounds as steam began to rise. "Gee, Drake. Thanks. Want me and Lonnie back here tomorrow?"

"No, Junior, I think everything's under control now. See you later."

Drake pulled away and burst out laughing.

"Drake, that wasn't nice," Claire said. Her own laughter came seconds later.

When Duke and his entourage pulled into Gable Farms, they were treated to the spectacle of three well-known television news reporters interviewing Junior Grimes.

Duke climbed from his cruiser and leaned against its side. "This is funnier than when the pigs ate baby sister," he said to the deputy beside him. Duke had heard the expression several weeks earlier at a lodge meeting and stored it away for the perfect moment.

"What is your capacity here at Gable Farms, Mr. Grimes?" one of the reporters asked.

Junior looked at Lonnie. Lonnie shrugged.

"My capacity?" Junior said. "Well I s'pose it's the same here as any-where else. 'Bout a gallon or so. After that, I'm usually pretty wasted. Wouldn't you say so, Lonnie?"

Lonnie nodded, smiling into the camera.

The reporter drew back, never losing her own smile. "Uh, Mr. Grimes, thank you. I see that some law enforcement officers have arrived. Perhaps we should talk with them."

The reporters fled Junior and Lonnie like fleas from a treated dog.

Duke stepped forward and donned his mirrored, one-way, official trooper sunglasses. By then it was dark, but he figured the lights from the television cameras were all the excuse he needed.

"Good evening," the reporter began, "you are Sheriff Duke Clements, is that correct?"

"That's affirmative, ma'am," Duke said.

"Sheriff Clements, are you able to tell us what this demonstration is all about? Does the demonstration pose any concern from the stand-point of public safety?"

Duke thought about this a few seconds, and said, "Well, the call we received said something about fish. Suckerfish, I believe. I gather they're endangered or something. As for public safety, the only dan-gerous thing I can think of out here this minute is them," he motioned toward Junior and Lonnie, "if they climb back into that truck." Two deputies moved to block their way.

"Sleep it off, Junior," Duke called. "Wouldn't want to see you wait-ing tables at the County Farm again this month."

Duke turned to the reporter. "Right now, I'm going inside and talk to the property owner." He tipped his hat and started for the clubhouse. On the way he tripped on some brick edgework, difficult enough to see in the dark, impossible through his trooper specials. He muttered something and took them off.

"So, that's it, sheriff," Armand said. "They're trespassing and destroying private property." Armand looked out the window. "You'll need reinforcements," he said. "I want you to drive them off. Arrest the leaders. I'll sign a complaint."

Duke paused in front of a display cabinet housing at least fifty wooden decoys. He went on to the wall that contained an array of vintage shotguns. "My daddy had a Model 21 just like that one," he said. "Wonder what happened to it—"

"Sheriff, I have guests arriving tomorrow. I want those Indians out of here tonight."

Duke turned. "Did you ask them to please leave?" he said.

Armand blinked. "Well, no, not in those words. I made it clear I wanted them gone, though."

Duke nodded. "Yes, I expect you did." He adjusted his wide leather Sam Browne belt, stroked the rich, dark stock of one of the Model 21s, and started for the door. "I'll go out there and talk to them, Mr. Stilton. But sometimes the best way to handle this kind of fire is to just let it burn out."

He motioned to Jim. "Jim, come with me and show me the road. Damned if I'm going boating tonight." He looked at Armand, whose clothes were soaked and streaked with mud. "Looks too dangerous."

Charlie watched the lone cruiser make its way out the levee road, along the column of parked demonstrators. His father-in-law stood below him at the edge of the pond, a large suckerfish stretched across his arms as he posed for the *New York Times* photographer. Wooley was flanked by his grinning grandsons. They were not holding their noses.

"Cavalry's coming, Dad," Charlie called.

Wooley knelt and released the fish. He climbed up the bank and stood next to Charlie. The twins stayed at the edge of the pond, and Randy swung a long-handled net to gather up another fish.

"We're not giving in," Wooley said.

"I'm not sayin' we should, Dad," said Charlie. "Let's just listen to what he has to say. You've seen the enemy. If we come off as reasonable, we might win the law over to our side."

The cruiser pulled up and stopped. "Evening," said the sheriff. He stepped out. "I'm Duke Clements, Sutter County sheriff." He extended his hand to Wooley, who hesitated, then took it.

"Pete Wooley."

"Ahh, I have the privilege, at last," said Duke. "My colleague up there in Jefferson County has told me much about you. I've wanted to meet you for years. You do great work."

Wooley smiled.

This guy's good, thought Charlie.

"And you must be Mr. Rainwater," Duke said, now extending his hand to Charlie. "Your reputation has also spread down this way."

Charlie took Duke's hand, content to let his reputation hang on that ambiguous hook.

"Now, gentlemen," Duke said, "here's my problem in a nutshell. You've got every right in the world to stage your demonstration. You just can't do it here, on private property. I see the news people have already documented your contact with the fish you're interested in. I suggest that you have your people turn around and move back to West Butte Road. There's more room out there, and the television people will have access to what you're doing."

Oh, that was *good,* thought Charlie. *Just the man I need to carry the message.*

"Sheriff," Charlie said, "let me talk to Chief Wooley a minute." He drew his father-in-law off to the side.

"Dad, he's right. We've made our point. Now let's move out to the road and hammer it home. If we stay here, this turns into a brawl and makes us look bad. If we go out there, we're law-abiding citizens, and you can talk to more reporters, television, the works."

Wooley nodded his approval. "Done," he said. "I'll make the announcement."

Charlie turned to the sheriff. "We agree, sheriff. We're telling our people to move back to the road. It'll take an hour or so. OK?"

"Fine," Duke said. He climbed back into his cruiser.

"Oh, sheriff, one more thing," Charlie said. He moved to the cruiser's window and bent down. "Tell this to Stilton, from me, OK?" Charlie looked across the seat to Jim. "You too, Jim. Tell Stilton that when he gives up on gas wells and pipelines, we'll consider the suckerfish safe and be on our way. Until then, we'll be at his doorstep. So long as there are suckerfish in these ponds that are threatened with gas wells, pipelines, and all the construction that goes with them, we'll be here."

As Charlie and Wooley watched the cruiser make its way back along the column, Wooley turned to his son-in-law. "I heard that. What do gas wells and pipelines have to do with suckerfish?"

Charlie smiled. "Not a thing, Dad. It's all about ducks. Always has been."

CHAPTER 38

"**W**hat?" Armand shouted.

Duke held up his hands. "Hey, Mr. Stilton, I'm just telling you what the man said. No reason to raise your voice. Jim was there with me. He'll confirm it."

Jim nodded. "That's what he said, Armand. They'll go away when they're convinced there will be no gas wells or pipelines. I took it to mean that if you go out there and make that promise to the reporters, the demonstrators will leave. We could have peace and quiet within hours."

Duke nodded. "That's how I make it."

Armand began to pace, glaring at the two of them. *They're all in with Green,* he thought. He needed to find his own way through this mess. He stopped at the window. "Who are those men?" he said, pointing at two disheveled individuals in coveralls leaning against a beat-up truck. "You said all the demonstrators were moving off my property."

"Uh, Armand," said Jim, "those aren't demonstrators. That's Junior Grimes and his partner, Lonnie. They're local boys who do odd jobs. I use them around the place. They came in a little while ago looking for work. They were pretty liquored up, so Duke told them not to drive away. I was going to tell them to sleep it off down by the boat dock. They can help me put the rest of the boats back in the water tomorrow morning."

Armand resumed his pacing. He stopped in front of his father's portrait. The commodore's eyes bore down on him, the steely image of a man whose vision never faltered—a man who maintained a firm grip on the helm.

Armand studied the portrait, seeking strength from its message. This was the man who took a fledgling copper mine and turned it into an international force. This was the man who, when confronted with strikes that threatened to choke his business, went around the strikers with his army of strike-breakers and surprised them from behind, smashing their meddling ways as he smashed their skulls. *Yes,* Armand thought, *the commodore would know how to deal with these troublemaking Indians. I'll let him show me.* Five minutes later Armand stopped pacing.

"Sheriff, thank you for your efforts. I know what I must do and I'll do it. You and your men can go on home."

Duke raised his eyebrows. "You sure about this?"

"Yes, sheriff, I'm sure. You've told me their demands, and I know what needs to be done. You are no longer needed."

"Fine by me," Duke said. He turned and left.

Armand and Jim stood by the window and watched the three police cruisers pull away.

"Well, Armand," said Jim, "I guess you're going out to talk to those Indians now. Want me to go with you? If not, I'll just take old Junior and his pal down to the boat dock and get them settled."

Armand shook his head. "No, I'm not, and no, you won't," he said. "We've got work to do. You, me, and them." He nodded toward Junior and Lonnie.

"What work, Armand?"

"Suckerfish. You did say that the Indians will stay as long as there are suckerfish here, didn't you? Well, come tomorrow, this club will be free of all such trash. That I promise. You and your two helpers out there are going fishing."

Jim shook his head and looked down. "Armand, that's impossible. You can't catch suckerfish. They're scavengers. They live on the bottom and suck mud."

Armand smiled, pleased to at last demonstrate true executive ingenuity to his unimaginative subordinate. "Who said anything about catching, Jim? You're using nets. Get out those tennis nets. We'll rig them up between my Hummer and your pickup and drag them across the ponds. By God, we'll scoop up every last one of those goddamned things. Now, get those two derelicts moving. They're your crew."

Armand loved the look he saw in Jim's eyes. True wonder.

Drake pulled a bottle of chilled Chardonnay from the refrigerator, took down two glasses from the shelf, and slid open the door to the deck.

"Are we having a party?" Claire said.

"Nope, just watching the evening show," he said. He removed the canvas cover from the telescope.

"One way or the other, this should get interesting. I can't believe Charlie Rainwater and hundreds of happy Indians are going to bed down within a half mile of Armand Three without fireworks of some kind. We've got a good view from here. It'll beat anything on TV."

"Drake, the sheriff's there. Nothing will happen."

Drake settled into one of the folding director's chairs that served as his outdoor furniture. "Duke just pulled out. I doubt he'll be back. He has a way of letting trouble unwind itself. I'm beginning to think he's on to something. You spend too much time fretting over something, you make it worse. You ignore it, natural forces take over. Problems are like water. They seek their own level."

Claire began to open the wine. "Drake Green, philosopher, saver of lives, killer of ducks…"

She filled both glasses and raised hers. Their glasses touched.

"…and, a great lover," she finished.

He smiled. "You left something out."

"What's that?" she said.

"House builder."

She nodded. "And house builder."

Drake sat forward and picked up his binoculars. "Aha. Action. Look through the scope."

"I see headlights," she said. "What's happening?"

"It's the Indians," Drake said. "Looks like they're headed off the property."

They watched as the convoy snaked back toward West Butte Road. "So," she said, "it looks like you were wrong. They're leaving."

Drake set down the binoculars. "We've plenty of wine," he said. "And the evening's young. Charlie's not a quitter." He reached for the bottle. "Neither is Three."

Armand watched Junior and Lonnie stumble as they sought to untangle the mystery of the nets. "Are those men drunk?"

"No more than usual, Armand," Jim said. "In fact, for them, they're pretty sober. They work better with a little heat on. Stone sober, they're worthless. Now, tell me exactly what you want us to do."

Armand straightened, the model of command. His voice took on a modulated intensity, and his eyes flared with the excitement of conquest to come. For a moment he was a general, explaining and simplifying a complex military operation to the men who would carry it out.

"We'll tie the nets together, forming one long net. Then we'll attach ropes to the ends, ropes long enough to reach across the ponds. We'll take the nets out to the ponds, you on one levee and me across from you on the other. Your helpers will come out in a boat and connect the ropes from your truck to mine. Then you and I will slowly drive forward, parallel with each other, dragging the net through each pond. At the end of each pass, the helpers will empty the scooped up fish from the net into your truck."

Jim didn't move a muscle. He was afraid to. Armand's eyes were glazed and wide, the mind behind them taking a stroll on Mars. *Best to just go along until he tires out and collapses from exhaustion,* Jim thought. Armand had been up since five. It was now almost nine, a record for Armand, who usually napped the whole afternoon. If Jim resisted and explained the myriad reasons Armand's screwball scheme would never work, he'd simply be touching a match to his boss's already short fuse.

"Uh, Junior, that's good enough for now," Jim called out. *Hell,* he thought, *we're never going to get that far anyway.* "Load them into the back of my truck."

"Right," Junior said. He and Lonnie hoisted the tangled mess of netting into Jim's truck.

"And now, Armand?" Jim said.

"And now, we go to the dock. Those two take a boat and meet us at Pond One. They can track us from the headlights of our trucks on the levee."

"You heard the man," Jim said. "Bring your truck and follow me."

"Oh, something's happening," Claire said. "What do you make of it?"

"Well, the rig in front is Three's Hummer. The next one is Jim's pickup. From the tilt of the third one, I'd say it's Junior's truck. Looks like they're headed for the dock."

Jim started the outboard. Then he helped Junior and Lonnie tie on lifejackets. "Just in case," he said. He handed Junior a long, powerful flashlight and a handheld radio. "The radio's on and all set. Now, just follow the water channels that take you toward our headlights. Then pull up to the bank my truck is on. Hopefully, he'll come to his senses or drift off. Then and we can fold this mess and all get some sleep." He walked back up to Armand's Hummer.

"All set?" Armand said.

"Set as they'll ever be," Jim said. "How about you?" He looked into Armand's eyes, and saw only frenzied exhaustion. *Anytime now,* thought Jim.

"Let's go, then," Armand said. "Follow me. When we get to the junction at Pond One, you go east, I'll go west. You link up with them, tie off on your end, then have them row across to me and tie off on the Hummer."

Armand pulled a huge cigar from his jacket pocket, bit off the end, and clamped it between his teeth. "Charge!"

The Hummer surged ahead.

"Now what?" Claire asked.

"Looks like a boat leaving the dock. Three's taken off toward the levee road. Jim's behind him. Jesus, they're really moving!"

When they reached the junction, Armand veered west and started along the south edge of the pond. Jim slowed and headed east, stopping where the road curved north. He climbed out with a flashlight. Junior and Lonnie entered the pond from the main channel and motored over to him.

"Jim, are we really goin' through with this?" Junior called from the boat. He held up an open jug of wine.

Jim shook his head. "Afraid so, just to humor him," he said. "I expect he'll either tire out or give up when he sees how stupid this is. Pass me the ropes."

Lonnie crawled up the bank with the rope ends. Jim pulled up slack, coiling what he calculated to be enough rope on the road. He tied off the ends to cleats on the bed of his truck. *What the hell,* he thought, just play along. *That's all I can do. The damn fool will find out soon enough.*

He watched as Junior and Lonnie pulled away and headed across the pond toward Three's Hummer on the opposite bank.

"I'd've given Jim credit for more brains," Drake said, now standing and watching through the binoculars. "They're out messing around in the ponds. I lost track of the boat, but the Hummer's on one road and Jim's truck is across from it. I told you there'd be a show. When those Indians figure out Three is messing with their sacred fish, all hell's going to break loose."

He settled back into his chair. "This is more fun than when the pigs ate baby sister."

Claire stared at him.

"Just something I heard in town," he said. "More wine?"

Armand watched Junior and Lonnie motor across the pond and realized he'd driven too far. The curve of the pond and deceptive lay of the terrain at night had fooled him. "Damn it," he muttered, "I'll have to back up."

He walked back along the road and waited until Junior nosed the boat into the bank, across the pond from Jim's truck.

"I need to back up," he called down. "Get up here and direct me. I can't do it in the dark."

Junior shrugged and took a long pull from the jug. Then he picked up the flashlight and climbed from the boat to the levee.

"Whassat?" he asked Armand. He pointed the flashlight toward a maze of pipes and lights off to one side.

"Gas well," said Armand. He set off down the road toward the idling Hummer. "The reason we're here, you drunken idiot."

He crawled back into the Hummer, took off his jacket, and folded it into a pile on top of the donut seat pad. He shoved the cigar back into his mouth and leaned out the window, craning to see Junior's guiding signal. He put the Hummer in reverse and began to back up.

"Goddamn fool, stand still," he said, as Junior's light wavered and then moved, first a few feet to the left, then a few feet to the right.

"Hey!" he shouted. "Stand still!"

The light began to move in a circle, and Armand tromped on the brake, or so he thought. Too late, he realized he'd slammed his foot onto the accelerator. The Hummer shot backward at a crazy angle, and he spun the wheel in a desperate attempt to straighten it.

He heard a grating crunch and the careening vehicle came to an abrupt stop. "Shit, not again," he said.

He crawled out and surveyed the wreckage. He'd plowed deep into the gas well's Christmas tree, its pipes and valves now a twisted mangle.

He looked around to berate Junior for his lousy guiding. A beam pointed toward the sky from the base of the levee bank.

"Down here," Junior moaned. "I fell."

"No shit, asshole," said Armand. "Get on that radio and call over to Quesenberry. Tell him to shag ass over here with his truck and help me get my truck untangled so we can finish this."

Armand walked back to the Hummer. He leaned against it, adjusted the cigar in his mouth, and pulled out his engraved Gable Farms lighter.

The column of flame brought Drake and Claire to their feet.

"Christ!" Drake said. "One of his wells exploded. It has to be."

"My God!" said Claire.

"Oh, shit," Drake said. "Three's Hummer. It's…it's…" He waited, unwilling to believe what he was seeing through the binoculars. "Gone," he said, at last.

He ran inside to phone for help.

The explosion drove Jim to the ground. He clasped his arms over his head and wriggled for cover under his truck, unsure of what to expect next. He stayed under for a full thirty seconds, his eyes clamped shut. When he opened them, he peered out into the flickering night, lit by the steeple of fire erupting from across the pond.

A cloak of utter silence had fallen over Gable Farms. The usual chatter of mud hens and resting waterfowl had shut down as if all life had been sucked away in a giant, all-consuming vacuum.

From West Butte Road, where the partying demonstrators had raised a constant din, all was quiet. The entire Butte Sink seemed to have simply stopped.

Jim crawled out. He shielded his eyes from the glare reflecting off the pond and called out.

"Armand?"

Nothing.

"Hey, Armand!"

He strained to hear something, anything. Finally he did, faint and distant.

"Jim?" It was Junior, somewhere on the opposite edge of the pond.

"Junior! What's happened?"

"I don't know. Mr. Stilton, he was backing up. I got a little dizzy and fell down. He ran into the gas. He hollered for me to call you. Next thing, boom!"

Jim fished out his sunglasses and stared into the base of the flames. He could just make out the shape of the Hummer, its windows and doors filled with white-hot fire.

"I'll be goddamned."

CHAPTER 39

"**O**ne hell of a night, Drake. One hell of a night." Duke patted the door of the coroner's van, and it pulled away. Claire, Charlie, and Wooley stood at the edge of the light from the clubhouse deck.

"Yeah," Drake said. "I had my issues with the man, but he didn't deserve to die, at least not like that."

"Well," Duke said, "it sure seems the cards were stacked against him. It was just a matter of time, and tonight his time ran out."

He turned to Jim. "I got enough from Junior Grimes that I don't need any more from you on this. I guess it closes the books on my other investigations as well. This man was just too dumb to live. Seems like he was almost trying to do himself in. Damned shame, with all that money, pretty wife, and everything."

"Uh, Duke," Jim said, "I just remembered. No one's called her. I'd better go inside and do that."

"I don't envy you, son," Duke said. "It's the worst part of my job."

Jim turned and headed for the clubhouse.

Charlie approached Drake and Duke. "Drake, got a minute?"

"Sure, Charlie. You've met the sheriff?"

Charlie nodded. "My father-in-law and I have decided to call off the demonstration, at least for now. Somehow, it just don't seem right. We're tellin' our people to pull out at dawn. Maybe we'll pick this up again, come spring, after this all settles down."

Duke nodded. "Seems like the right thing to do, Mr. Rainwater. Appreciate your cooperation."

Charlie tipped his hat and turned to leave. Then he stopped and turned back. "You know," he said, "it happens my shotgun's in my truck. Usually is. I could send the boys and their grandfather back home with Cousin Arnold. This is the last weekend of the season, isn't it?"

"That it is, Charlie. You're welcome to stay. Duke's going to join us tomorrow night for rib eyes. Right, Duke?"

"Wouldn't miss it, Drake. With the demonstration folding, I guess we'll have a day's hunt together after all."

Charlie waved and turned to leave.

"Charlie?" Drake called. "First thing tomorrow, you go into Colusa and buy a California license. You need the works, duck stamps and all. That's the downside of sharing a duck blind with the law."

Charlie kept on walking.

Jim looked at the clock as he dialed the Stilton home in Ross. 12:30 a.m. He started to hang up, but then decided to see it through. She had to know. Better sooner than later.

The telephone rang four times, then Donna's voice began to play on an answering machine. Just as it reached the end, the recording was interrupted by a sleepy "Hello?"

"Uh, Mrs. Stilton. This is Jim. Jim, at the duck club."

There was a long pause.

"Yes, Jim at the duck club. I recognize your voice." This time she sounded very much awake. "You must have something very important to tell me, calling at this hour."

"Uh, Mrs. Stilton. It's your husband. I'm afraid there's been a terrible accident."

Another long pause.

"Is he...dead?"

"Yes, Mrs. Stilton. I'm afraid so."

"I see," she said. "Is there anything else I need to know?"

"Well, I could tell you the details, how he died and all. Do you want me to?"

"No, Jim, those will keep. I'll call you tomorrow. You can tell me then. Good night. Oh, and Jim?"

"Yes?"

"Thanks. That *was* a grand slam."

At one in the morning, Louis DuBois reached across his wife to answer the telephone. He listened to Donna Stilton for a full ten minutes. When he hung up, his wife asked him who it was. "A very important client," he said. "I'll have to cancel that duck hunting thing I was supposed to leave for today."

"That's too bad, dear," she said.

"Yes, isn't it?" he said in the dark, smiling.

At eight thirty the next morning, DuBois phoned the hotel where Braxton "Dink" Deerlink and his associates were staying. After a hurried consultation Dink, Clive, and Homer decided that Armand Stilton's sudden demise was not a sufficient reason to cancel their hunting trip. Dink had no trouble convincing his partners that Armand "would have wanted us to go."

Their chartered jet touched down at the Colusa airport at three thirty Thursday afternoon. The hired limousine Jim had arranged picked them up and drove them out to Gable Farms.

After a full weekend of drinking, eating, smoking cigars, dominoes, poker, and killing ducks, Dink told Nick Pappas that they'd like to buy in, even without Armand's presence. "And Nick," he said, "there ain't no way we're gonna mess up this place with gas wells. First thing we do is tear out those three wells old Ar-mand sunk. Same for the place next door. Keepin' both properties like they are keeps the huntin' great. Jist like our good buddy Mr. Green says."

Nick happily relayed the message to Jim, who happily passed it along to Donna Stilton. She responded by telling him that DuBois was sending him a 10 year Gable Farms General Manager contract by Express Mail. As for her, she'd taken a suite at the Four Seasons, Hualalai, where she thought she'd be for at least the next four months.

Jackson Crackers returned to San Rafael, $12,000 richer from his earnings at the Gable Farms poker table. The Texans and the rest of the members had voted him an on-the-spot honorary nonshooting membership. All he had to do was show up twice each duck season and tell lawyer jokes. Also, at their insistence, he agreed to abandon all hostile legal activity against their neighbor, Drake Green.

Claire and Drake's wedding took place on the third Friday of June. Chief Wooley not only proudly gave the smiling bride away, he officiated, wearing a feathered headress that almost touched the floor of the freshly framed Waterloo Lodge. When he stood to toast the happy couple, Co-Best Man Charlie Rainwater complained about missing a weekend of trout season and they all laughed. On behalf of the Gable Farms membership the other Best Man, Jim, presented Claire and Drake with an ornate, antique duck press. Engraved on its sterling silver base was a remarkable likeness of Moe the sturgeon.

Margaret Bromeley, as past president of the Audubon Society, sent a card thanking Drake for his generous act in deeding Waterloo to the society as a gas-well free waterfowl refuge, subject to a life estate for him and Claire. The deed specified that cows were to always remain on the property.

Groundbreaking on the new Cedar Hills Rehabilitation Center and Convalescent Home took place on July 1. Donna Stilton attended, accompanied by her fiancé, Braxton "Dink" Deerlink, who had by then made it his crusade to ban gas wells in the entire Butte Sink. "It will help keep the price up," he told Jim.

The Gable Farms membership voted unanimously to ban Roto Ducks on the property and in favor of the suckerfish. They stayed.

• • •

www.ingramcontent.com/pod-product-compliance
Lightning Source LLC
Chambersburg PA
CBHW060545260626
47161CB00003B/1057